Sca

&

Silver Linings

a novel by

Kelsey Kingsley

copyright

To the Good Samaritan NICU nurses—

I once said that I'd dedicate a book to you,

And here it is.

I can never thank you all enough for your kindness, friendship, support, and ability to make sure that Baby Jude came home to us.

They say that not all superheroes wear capes,

And you will always be ours.

Every single one of you.

We love you.

Thank you.

A Note from the Author

Dear Reader,

At this moment, I'm gnawing on a Twizzler and wondering how to begin this note, but I don't know what words to string together that would feel worthy of the story you're about to read.

Because you see, this story is mine.

Well, okay, let's be real for a second. There's also a super swoony bartender in here that has absolutely nothing to do with my story, along with a bad guy you'll all grow to despise. But everything else? It's mine, it's personal, and the thought of publishing it for all to read is making me feel incredibly vulnerable and naked.

But I have to do it.

So, I am.

Kelsey

Chapter One

Two little, pink lines are supposed to be a joyous thing. They're coveted by many and impossible for too many. Yet, staring at my own two bright, pink lines, felt so unnatural, as the bottom of my stomach dropped out and my heart raced rapidly toward nausea.

I knew they were supposed to be a joyous, wonderful, and celebrated thing, but instead, these lines had now put me on a bar stool in the middle of New York City, staring blankly into my untouched glass of water and wishing it was something stronger.

Just two days ago, I'd gone from those two pink lines, to a phone call with a doctor I didn't know, to book today's blood test. It seemed perfectly reasonable that a stick I had peed on could be telling me lies, and blood seemed much more likely to tell the truth. So, I had found myself sitting in a doctor's exam room, nervously waiting on my results and hoping that the pregnancy test had been wrong. And it wasn't that I was necessarily against having a baby. I really wasn't. But when I thought about it, *really* thought about it, I couldn't decide that a baby would really fit into my life.

I had rented a one-bedroom apartment only one year ago.

I had only recently begun to make reliable money, in my temperamental career as an independent romance author.

I had just spent two nights straight wondering if I really wanted to be with Brendan.

And I continuously thought about all of those very crucial details, as I sat on the exam room table, swinging my legs and biting my nails, failing to find a suitable place for a baby to slip into.

But, let's not get ahead of yourself, Kenny, I thought, nodding with solid determination. *You don't feel pregnant. You can't even pinpoint the exact moment when you would've gotten pregnant in the first place. You could be worrying yourself to death for absolutely nothing, so chill. Just. Chill.*

Except it hadn't been nothing, as Dr. Ferdinand so enthusiastically declared, as he burst back into the room wearing a proud grin.

"Kendall," he'd said, "you should probably make an appointment with your OB/GYN."

"Why?" I asked, unsure whether the cluelessness I was feigning and holding onto had been convincing. "Am I due for a pap smear?"

The man who I had only just met chuckled. "You're a funny one, you know that?"

"That's news to me."

He chuckled again, leaning forward in his rolling stool and patting my knee playfully. "You're silly," he declared, continuing to laugh. "*And* you're having a baby!"

You're having a baby.

I shuddered now over my water glass. Those four words still felt so damning, like a life sentence to a prison cell full of diapers and bottles and burping cloths.

At the time, the room had swayed and my face blanched, as Dr. Ferdinand led me through my options: keep the baby, get rid of it, or give it up.

I'd nearly laughed in his face at that word, *options*.

None of them felt like options at all.

None of them felt right.

None of *this* felt right.

All I really wanted to do was go back to whenever it had happened and take it all back. I wanted to tell Brendan to be more careful. I wanted to tell him not to have sex with me that night at all, whatever night it was. But unless the doctor had a time machine he could lend me, going back wasn't one of my options, and I was so mad about that.

I hadn't asked for this. Especially not now. And although I knew the part I'd played in the conception of this baby, I wasn't the one who had done something differently. I wasn't the one with the essence to make it happen. I—

"You look like you could use something a lot stronger than what you're drinking."

The booming voice sliced through the damning thoughts and recollections cycling around my worried mind. I lifted my head, taking my gaze from the untouched water to the eyes of a Viking. He was

4

enormous, but not in the way you'd find intimidating. A gentle giant, with a soft look in his eyes and an enviable head of reddish-blond hair. Shaggy and purposely messy without looking unkempt. And I knew I shouldn't have found him so attractive. I knew he shouldn't have immediately caused my heart to skip a few beats. Especially not when I had only just found out I was carrying my boyfriend's baby. But I couldn't help that he was, in fact, attractive, or the sudden, erratic pause of my beating heart.

"That would be lovely," I replied sardonically, hoping he couldn't sense the jittering in my chest. "Except I just found out I'm knocked up, *so* … I can't."

"I take it congratulations aren't in order." His eyes swept over my slumped posture and ensemble of yoga pants and my most comfortable sweatshirt.

"Let's just say it wasn't planned," I replied, my tone dry.

He hummed thoughtfully as he nodded and tapped beefy fingers against the bar, buffed to a brilliant shine. "Well, I can't do much about that. But, what I *can* do is, get you a virgin cocktail that'll make you forget how badly you want the booze. How does that sound?"

"Sounds like bullshit, but I'll take it," I said, finding a hint of a smile beneath the nerves, stress, and fear.

He grinned the way a dog smiles when you come home after a long day at work. The type of smile that seems to make the bad stuff not seem so bad at all. And I couldn't help it, I smiled back, nearly forgetting about the little bean nestled deep in my belly.

5

"So," he said, pulling a big, fishbowl glass from the overhanging rack, "if you don't mind me asking, what's got you so upset?"

It was none of his business, and I had no obligation to answer. But what is it about bartenders that makes them so easy to talk to? Somewhere inside, I could distinctly feel the cork on my bottled-up emotions jiggle loose, and I didn't even try to stop them from pouring out.

"I only found out that I'm pregnant two days ago," I began, as he poured a variety of juices and ice into a blender. "I went to the doctor to confirm it today, and lo and behold, I am indeed with child," I muttered in a mocking tone, gesturing toward my stomach with grandeur.

"So, is it that you don't want a baby?"

I pushed my fingers into my sloppy, ponytailed hair, hoping I didn't look too much like a hot mess, and planted my elbows firmly on the bar. "It's not that," I huffed over the whirring blender. "I guess I just never expected to actually have one. I've always been so goal oriented and focused on my own thing. I like my alone time. I like my life."

"So, you're not sure a baby fits into everything you have going on," he accurately assessed, pouring the frozen concoction into the glass.

I pursed my lips and nodded. "Bingo."

Flashing me a smile that crinkled the corners of his blue eyes, he said, "Let's just say, I've been there."

"You've also been knocked up by your on and off again boyfriend of three years?"

6

He laughed boisterously, the type of laugh you throw your whole body into. I could never make Brendan laugh like that. Hell, I couldn't remember the last time I had made him laugh at all, and how strange it was that I hadn't thought about it until this very moment.

"No, I can't say that I have," he conceded, adding a few diced strawberries to the top of the bright pink drink. An eerily similar color to the two pink lines that had brought me in here in the first place. "*But*, I did knock up my wife of two years while I was in the middle of a bender. And I definitely knew a kid would never fit into *that* lifestyle."

Immediately intrigued, I sat up taller on my stool and asked, "You're a dad?"

"I am," he said, nodding as he slid the drink across the bar to me. "I didn't want to be at first. The night my wife told me, I drank myself into a coma. But then, the next morning, she woke me up with a swift kick in the ass and a threat that, if I didn't get my act together, I'd never see my son or daughter. And when she put it like that, I realized that I did want to be in that kid's life. So, I checked myself into rehab, turned my life around, and here I am."

I swirled the straw around and nodded slowly. "So, you're telling me you got wasted, and then had this amazing, life-changing epiphany. And now, I'm wondering why you didn't throw some booze in here ..."

Laughing again, he folded his arms on the bar and crouched down to meet my eyes. "What saying is, you've just gotten some huge, life-changing news. Nothing says you have to kick up your heels and jump for joy the second you find out you're having a baby, but nothing says you need to make any other huge, life-changing decisions right now, either. Maybe buy yourself something nice tonight. Eat whatever the hell you want. Forget about this shit for now and just sleep on it. You might be surprised by how you feel in the morning."

Exhaling deeply, I nodded slowly, and before I could think twice about it, I said, "Well, I'm glad you turned your life around."

"Thanks," he replied, his grin softening. "So am I."

I dropped my gaze to the drink and took a deep breath. And then, I nodded, before taking a sip. The burst of sweet, strawberry, bubble-gummy goodness excited my taste buds enough to force my lips to smile around the straw.

"Oh, my God, this is amazing," I exclaimed, before diving in for more.

"Told you," he said. "It's good for you, too. Lots of vitamin C."

I grinned as I watched him turn to help another mid-day customer. Two scary, little, pink lines had led me to stumble into this bar. Now, for the first time since I'd seen them appear, I felt lucky. So much so, I hardly worried about how I was going to tell Brendan the happy—or not so happy—news.

***

Looking around now, I acknowledged just how small the apartment really was, but it was mine and it had once made me so proud.

I could still remember the moment when I had looked at my bank account and realized that my book sales had finally tipped me into a place of financial stability where I could afford to venture out on my own. It had been such a colossal victory and I had felt so much triumph as I was handed the keys to the little one-bedroom apartment. I had then immediately rushed out to buy my own teapot and microwave, feeling so excited and confident.

But now, I wished it was bigger. Better.

I wished there were two bedrooms instead of one. I wished that my kitchen table could accommodate a highchair and that my living room could fit one of those unreasonably huge baby swings. I wished that it was all so much closer to my parents on Long Island.

And what about baby proofing? If I made the decision to keep the baby, how could I make an old, dusty apartment above a pizza place safe for a baby?

I slumped onto the couch and stared blankly ahead at the TV. It was amazing to me just how much those two little, pink lines could change everything. Including the pride I had once felt for this apartment.

My cat, Mrs. Potter, waddled into the room, looking like she had just woken from her hundredth nap of the day. She plonked her round butt down beside the coffee table and, starting with her paw, began her cleaning ritual. I watched her, mesmerized by the systematic motions as she repeatedly took her furry, white paw from her mouth to the top of her head. She had been a great friend for over five years now, but watching her now, I remembered what I'd once been told about pregnant women and dirty litter boxes.

"I can't even clean your litter box anymore," I muttered, planting my elbow against the arm of the couch and resting my chin in my palm. She placed her paw back on the floor and lazily turned her gaze on me. "What the hell are we gonna do?"

Mrs. Potter's only reply was a long-winded meow, telling me that it was dinnertime. I sighed and nodded, pulling myself up to walk toward the small galley kitchen. The space between the two rows of appliances and countertops was barely wide enough to open the oven door, but I had managed happily for the last year. But now, what? I grabbed the container of cat food from off the counter and imagined myself seven, eight, nine months pregnant. How big would I be? Would I be able to even turn around in this space with a giant baby belly?

I bent over to fill Mrs. Potter's little black plastic dish, and it hit me harder than it should have that, not too long from now, bending over would be a thing of the past, at least for a while. And in the stupidest display of hormonal instability, I sank to the floor beside my cat, bursting into tears as she chewed.

***

After sitting on the kitchen floor for longer than I'd care to admit, I wiped my eyes on my sweatshirt sleeve, as a growl rumbled noisily in my stomach, reminding me that I hadn't eaten all day. My nerves hadn't allowed it. But the insistent pangs in my gut told me I needed something immediately, and I climbed to my feet to raid the fridge of the pizza and Chinese I'd eaten the last two nights in a row.

I took my feast to the table, along with my phone, and sat down to dig in while doing a little calculating with the app I used to track my period.

I had known it'd been late, hence the reason for the pregnancy test. But just how late, I hadn't taken much note of. Looking at the app though, it seemed as though it was just a week overdue.

"So, five weeks," I muttered, chomping into an egg roll.

My gut turned sour as I thought back on the past couple of weeks. Hadn't I noticed that something had felt a little off? My boobs had been a little more sensitive than usual and my body had ached with periodic waves of cramps, but I'd brushed it all off. I'd assumed all those typical premenstrual symptoms, that I usually felt, were just amplified for one reason or another. But there had been a little voice of intuition, deep down, telling me something was up. For some reason though, pregnancy still hadn't seemed very probable. Possible, sure, but far from definite.

How the hell could I not have realized it was more of a possibility than any of the other ailments I had diagnosed myself with via Doctor Google?

I felt stupid. I felt like a stranger to my own, rebellious body and the little bean in my belly.

Groaning, I thrust my fingers into my hair and tugged at the roots. "Calm down," I scolded myself, closing my eyes. "Just calm down and relax."

But how?

In times of anxious worrying, I usually found solace in watching a movie or spending money on something absurdly frivolous. But right now, the usual suspects didn't seem good enough, not nearly immersive enough. So, I thought harder, I thought dirtier, and with a forceful shove, my mind moved past the pregnancy and to things I probably should have left alone. Thoughts about burley bartenders with reddish-blond hair started to crowd my mind, as I stood from the table with my empty plate.

I knew I shouldn't have felt the twinge of lust, as I washed the dishes and remembered his laugh. That deep, bubbling chuckle that had made me feel so much better than I had in two, long days. I knew I shouldn't have recalled the warmth in his eyes and the kindness in his voice, as I changed out of my clothes and into pajamas. And I knew I definitely shouldn't have allowed my hand to slide beneath the waistband of my sweatpants at the memory of his broad, contagious smile. Not when I had a boyfriend, not when I still needed to call him and tell him the news. But I needed a distraction from the hormonal turmoil in my head and the changes in my body, and I didn't have the energy to tell myself that this distraction wasn't right.

Chapter Two

"Hey, Kendo," Brendan answered when I called the following afternoon. "It's been forever since I've heard from you."

"Yeah, I know, I'm sorry," I replied, not entirely sure why I was apologizing. "I've been a little distracted. But, you know, *you* could've called or texted *me*."

"Oh, yeah, I know. But I don't like bothering you, you know that. I never know when you're writing or whatever."

This had been a topic of contention for as long as we'd been together. Brendan had issues with initiation. He hadn't asked me out or kissed me first, and he would never be the first to reach out. I could never wrap my head around it, even after three years of being together.

"If I'm working, I'll just get back to you when I'm finished." I knew there wasn't much point to continuing the conversation, but I always slipped that in there. Just in case one day he'd decide to text me out of the blue and miraculously prove to be better at communicating.

"So, what are you up to?" he asked, dodging the comment swiftly.

I sat up in bed atop a nest of six fluffy throw blankets and five pillows. There was no such thing as too much comfort, and right now I was particularly grateful for it. This was definitely not a topic I wanted to discuss on a bed barren of furry, leopard print throws.

"Um, well, I wanted to talk to you about something."

"Uh-oh," Brendan laughed forcefully. "Am I in trouble?"

I glanced at Mrs. Potter, balled up in the center of a pillow. I caught her eye and resisted the urge to chuckle, as I thought, *well, I guess that depends on your definition of trouble.*

"Well, not really, but ..." I ran a hand over my face, rethinking my decision to have this discussion over the phone. I thought it would have been much easier to snap a picture of the pregnancy test and send it away in a text or drop the bomb when there was distance and air between us. But now, my mouth froze around the words, unable to release them in the wild.

"But?"

The last thing I cared to do right now was see people, including my boyfriend. I wanted time to think things over, alone. I wanted to come to my own conclusions before allowing outside sources the privilege of throwing in their two cents, even if those two cents were from Brendan. But reason told me that this was his baby, too, and he should at the very least be given an opportunity to voice his opinion.

"What are you doing later? Do you want to grab dinner?"

"Uh, do we have to?"

I sighed, clapping a hand over my eyes. "Brendan, please. Are you able to go out? It doesn't have to be for long."

"I don't know, Kendo," he muttered with a sigh, like this conversation was suddenly the most boring event of his life. "I gotta run some errands, and—"

"Please, just tell me if you can go out or not."

"Fine," he grunted. "Yeah, okay, I can go out for a little while."

"Okay," I replied, "then I guess I'll see you later."

"You got it. Text me where you wanna go."

I sighed disappointedly but agreed. Brendan had never once in our relationship picked a place for us to eat and I couldn't expect that he would start now.

Then, he said goodbye and hung up. I got out of bed to use the bathroom and promptly experienced morning sickness for the first time. And as I threw up, I hoped it wasn't a sign.

***

"Hey, Kendo." Brendan greeted me outside the restaurant with a sweet kiss to the cheek. He slipped an arm around my waist and pulled me against him, unaware of the life inside my belly.

"Hey." I turned my head, catching his lips with mine. "I haven't seen you in so long."

"*You're* on a deadline," he reminded me, smirking obnoxiously.

"Oh, that's right!" I exclaimed in gest. "I knew I forgot something."

15

He let out a mocking laugh. "Oh, you're funny."

We walked together into the restaurant with my arm hooked around his. I remembered the early days of our relationship and how I had really loved that he was an equal opportunist and never seized control. If anything, I had always called the shots. But, three years later, I now caught myself occasionally wishing that he'd lead instead of keep the same pace. Because while a woman doesn't always want to be treated like a possession, every now and then she wants to feel possessed by the man who calls her his.

We were seated in a quiet corner. The hostess even gave us a knowing, cheeky sort of look, like she thought she was doing us a favor by putting us so far from the other diners. But the seclusion only served to build my anxiety, and I prayed I wouldn't throw up again.

"What are you gonna drink?" Brendan asked, grabbing for the cocktail and wine menu.

I shrugged and found a focal point in a smudge on the Tiffany-style lamp hanging over the table. "I don't know," I answered, not yet ready to look at him. "Probably just water."

"*Water*?" he exclaimed incredulously. "Who are you and what have you done with my Kendo?"

It must've been the hormones, but his repeated use of that nickname was picking at my nerves like an old, crusty scab. He'd given it to me years ago, after we'd first met. He hadn't liked my preferred nickname, saying that it made me sound like a boy. So, Kendo it was. It had never felt right, but I'd tolerated it and learned to live with it. I'd even found it endearing at times. Tonight, though, my tolerance was having a difficult time putting up with anything I didn't care for.

"It's not like I drink all the time," I replied defensively.

"Yeah, but you always get a drink every time we go out."

"Well, I'm trying to cut back on calories," I lied, remembering the two slices of pizza and pint of fried rice I ate the night before.

Brendan eyed me with suspicion. He didn't buy what I was saying, but he didn't push it further, and I thought the conversation had been laid to rest. That was until the waitress came around and asked for our drink order.

"I'll just get a rum and Coke, and she'll get a Manhattan."

I was so taken aback by his brazen move that it took a few seconds for me to find my tongue. When I had said I wanted him to take control every now and then, putting words into my mouth and making decisions for me wasn't what I'd meant.

"No, I only want a water, thank you," I said, smiling at the waitress, before turning a scowl on my boyfriend.

"Oh, come on, Kendall. Lighten up a little."

Brendan always meant business when he used my full name. But I meant business, too, and I sent the waitress away with a forced smile.

"Why can't you get one drink?" The man's eyes were infuriatingly stern.

"What is your obsession right now with getting me to drink?" I countered, matching his steely glare with my own.

"Because, you know ... I was hoping ..." His glare softened to a coy smile and a lift of his brows, as his hand slid across the table to envelope mine. "I was hoping we could maybe go back to my place ..."

"Brendan, since when do you need me to get drunk in order to sleep with you?"

He pulled his hand back and sat up stick straight. "Well, it's just been a while."

"I've been trying to meet my deadline."

"But it's been a month!"

It had actually been five weeks, but he was close enough.

Brendan and I weren't strangers to this song and dance. For three years now, we'd spend a few months together until one of us got busy, bored, or both, and we'd split up. Our breakups never lasted for long, only a few weeks or so, but this had never seemed to faze us. It was a routine that was neither healthy nor uncomfortable. It had given me a breather from his flakiness, while giving him the freedom to live his life as he wanted without the weight of a relationship weighing him down, and it had been fine. But now, I felt a flop of panic manifesting in my gut. Because now I was pregnant with this man's baby and there wasn't anything okay about us breaking up at a time like this.

"I'm sorry," I said, meaning it. "Things have been kinda crazy lately."

"I know," he muttered with a sigh, returning his hand to mine. "I didn't mean to guilt you. That was shitty of me."

"No, it's okay," I replied, suddenly proud of us for this moment. "Maybe I'll just say fuck the book tonight and go home with you."

"Ooh, you're gonna play hooky? What about your editor's schedule?"

I waved my hand dismissively. "She can hold off a few more days. And I really don't have that much more to go."

Brendan squeezed my hand and waggled his brows. "I think that maybe we should just get dinner to go."

My lips curled into a suggestive smile as I leaned forward against the table, acutely aware of the pain in my boobs. "I'd be down for—"

I clamped my mouth shut at the sudden wave of nausea that rolled over me, making my mouth water and my forehead bead with sweat. Brendan was immediately concerned as I wiped a palm over my face and squeezed my eyes shut while shaking my head.

"Are you okay?"

I swallowed at the saliva flooding my mouth. "N-No. I just ... I just need some air, I think. Or maybe s-some water."

He called the waitress over for the drink he'd tried to talk me out of, and when I had the cool, tall glass in front of me, I slowly took a sip. I prayed it would work, and after a few minutes, it did. My stomach settled and I took a deep, ragged breath, wiping the last few beads of sweat from my brow.

"Sorry," I said, continuing to focus on my breathing.

"You're sure you're okay?"

I nodded. "Yeah, I think I just need to eat something."

I diverted my attention to my utensils, rolled in a cloth napkin. I busied myself by unrolling and laying the napkin across my lap, smoothing it out over my thighs, before brushing the wrinkles out of my top. It was then that I raised my eyes to Brendan and found him watching me with skepticism.

"What?" I asked, flashing him a light-hearted smile.

"What's going on with you?"

My smile faltered as my hands returned to the napkin and smoothed it out again. "What do you mean?"

"You're not acting right."

This was not how I wanted this to go. This was a scenario I could picture happening in one of my novels, and as the author, I knew exactly how I would have written it. I had planned to tell him after he'd had his drink, or maybe during dinner. I wanted to approach the topic gently, with a whimsical question about the future, maybe about his plans for us and a potential family. But now I was being reminded, with another nauseating roll of my stomach, that life isn't meticulously planned out by an author and then perfected by an editor. Life is unscripted and I had to resign myself to rolling with it.

"I have to tell you something," I said, sitting at the edge of my seat.

"Okay," he drawled. "What's up?"

"Actually, um, maybe I should show you something first."

I didn't wait for his reply before digging into my purse and pulling out the pregnancy test. I had never removed it after the doctor's appointment and now I thought—*hoped*—it would affect Brendan's reaction in a positive way.

Without another thought, I slid the pink stick across the table and watched his face.

His blank, stone-like face.

"What the hell is this?" he finally asked, looking back at me with a furrowed brow and an angry downturn of his lips.

"It's a p-pregnan—"

"You're fuckin' kidding me, right?"

My nostrils burned with the threat of tears. "No. I-I realized my period was—"

"Is it mine?"

My jaw dropped at the insinuation. "*Excuse* me?"

Brendan clapped a hand over his eyes and shook his head. "Fuck. I'm sorry. I shouldn't have asked that. But," he dropped his hand, revealing his confused and apologetic eyes, "are you really serious right now? You're ... you're *pregnant*?"

I nodded. "I had it confirmed by the doctor yesterday."

"Jee-sus," he drawled, leaning against his seat. "I mean, shit, how did this even happen?"

I shrugged, feeling oddly relaxed. "I don't know. But it did."

"Are you going to keep it?"

After sleeping on it the night before, it was the question I'd been asking myself all day. The options were clear and clean cut, either keep it or not. And if I had to do it all over again, I knew I'd tell my past self to not get pregnant at all. But I couldn't go back, this was the reality I was facing, and I knew there was no way I could terminate. I just couldn't stomach the thought of it.

So, after a few moments went by, I barely nodded and said, "I want to, yeah."

Brendan exhibited his displeasure with a scoff and a shake of his head. "And was I ever going to get a say in this?"

"You can have a say," I told him, keeping my tone calm while beginning to internally panic. "But ultimately, this is my body we're talking about here, and I don't want to go through an abortion. I've thought about it and I just can't do it."

"Yeah, it's *your* body," he retorted hotly, "but it's *both* of our lives."

"So, are you saying you don't want kids?"

Pulling in a deep breath, he shrugged, keeping his eyes on the table. "I don't know what I want. Honestly, I never saw myself being a father, so ..." He hesitated, lifting his shoulders in another shrug. "No, I guess I don't particularly want kids."

That morning, as I had showered, I'd gone through every possible way this conversation could have gone. While I had considered that he might tell me he didn't want kids at all, I had just as quickly pushed that idea from my head. Because while Brendan wasn't always the best boyfriend, or friend even, I knew he was always great with children. I'd seen him with his brother's two boys and with my cousin's kids, and he was a saint with all of them. So, I guess I had just thought he'd be happy, knowing he was now going to be a father himself.

"I don't know what to say," I whispered.

"Well, I guess I can't talk you into aborting, so ..." He shrugged, diverting his eyes and staring toward the waitress.

"What if," I took a deep, cleansing breath, "what if you slept on it for a day or two? Think about it before you make any rash decisions."

"I don't need to think—"

"Please?"

He watched me with an odd blend of resentment and sympathy. He pulled in a heavy breath, then nodded. "Fine. Sure."

And with that, we decided we weren't all that hungry and went our separate ways.

Chapter Three

When I suggested he sleep on it, just like it had been suggested to me by the friendly bartender. I'd also said to take a day or two to think things over. And I guess I thought he'd call me up the next day to admit he was scared and anxious, but still willing to try. Clearly, somewhere in my hope for a miracle, I'd forgotten that Brendan never called and never texted. So, why had I thought this would be any different?

"Because it's his baby, too," I answered aloud, startling Mrs. Potter from her afternoon nap on the windowsill.

I was carrying his child. No, it wasn't planned. No, it wasn't intentional. But that didn't change the fact that it had happened. And not speaking to me for five days wasn't going to make any of it disappear.

I wondered if I should call him and ask how he was doing. I had never let this much time pass without reaching out, but this was so different for us. I understood giving him some space and time, but how much was appropriate? How much was too much?

And if I never called him, would I ever hear from him again?

My fingertips tapped lightly against the keys, light enough to not leave any imprints on the screen, while I wished my brain would stop thinking about Brendan. I also wished my stomach would stop churning in the most annoying, uncomfortable way, both with nerves and a sickness that wasn't limited to just the morning. My thirteenth novel needed to be finished and sent to my editor, Jenn, by the end of the month, but with everything going on, I had barely gotten any words down in the past week. My characters weren't talking, the flow of inspiration had stopped, and I was spending more time Googling ways to tell people you're pregnant, than I spent in the word processor. I had found that it's actually really hard to write romance and happily ever afters when you're in a doomed relationship.

"I need to eat something," I announced to my cat, even though I didn't want to. I felt so awful, eating was the last thing my body wanted to do, but not having anything in my stomach somehow made it worse. So, I stood from my chair and moved slowly into the kitchen to find my box of Saltines.

Pulling out a sleeve and opening the package, I dove in with a sigh. My morning sickness had existed for all of five days so far and I was already tired of it.

"And I'm supposed to do this for months?" I muttered to Mrs. Potter, who sighed in reply, before going back to sleep.

My phone rang in my pocket and thinking it might have been Brendan, I dropped a half-eaten cracker and fumbled until I had the phone in my hand. I was disappointed to see that it was only my mother, and I wilted against the counter as I answered the call.

"Hey, Mom," I answered in a dull tone that reflected every bit of the disappointment I felt.

"Wow, don't sound too happy to hear from me," she laughed melodically.

"Sorry, I just thought you were Brendan."

Mom had never liked Brendan, but she was also one of my best friends. She didn't like to blatantly come out and say she despised my boyfriend, so instead, she showed her disapproval in other, slightly less obvious ways.

"Hm," she grunted.

I laughed. "I know. Your favorite person in the world."

"I never said I didn't like him."

"No. You've just come up with a thousand different ways to grunt every time I mention his name."

"I don't grunt!"

"Oh, no?" I made a mocking noise that sounded very much like a grunt. "What do you call that?"

"I didn't *grunt*," she insisted, while not offering another explanation for the sound I'd grown to expect.

"Whatever you say," I replied, laughing again. "So, why are you calling me on this fine day?"

"Oh, you know, just making sure you're alive, for one."

Mom and I had talked on the phone nearly every single day since I moved out of my parents' house a year ago. Even on days that I should've been focused entirely on my work, I made sure to check in. This past week, though, I'd been neglecting my daughterly duties. I couldn't remember if I'd even sent her a text.

"Sorry," I muttered. "I've been kinda busy."

"Too busy for *me*?"

I wasn't too busy. The truth was, I had been hiding from my mom. I wasn't ready to tell her about the little bean, and I definitely wasn't ready to tell her it was Brendan's. Truthfully, I wasn't even sure how to start the conversation, so I'd been avoiding it altogether.

"You know I have this deadline."

My career had become my crutch and I wasn't proud of it. But I couldn't deny that the timing had been pretty convenient. Never mind the fact that I hadn't actually done anything to meet said deadline.

"I know, I know. I just miss you, I guess."

"Oh, now you're just being ridiculous," I snorted, even though I had missed her, too. Probably more than she missed me.

"Can you take a break this weekend?"

"Well, this weekend is pretty tied up, but maybe next weekend. What are you offering?"

"Well, I thought we could head out East and go pumpkin picking. Maybe hit up the apple orchard, too. I'm in the mood to bake a pie."

Recent events in my life had been such a distraction I'd almost forgotten what time of year it was. Mid-September and the official start of Autumn for my family. Over the next month or so, weekends would be filled with apple picking, baking, bonfires, and cider. There would be the tradition of hunting for new

Halloween decorations and at the end of October, my mom would throw her annual Halloween party. I wanted so badly to be more excited than I was.

"Yeah," I uttered on my exhale. "I'll come out next Saturday and stay overnight."

"You gonna bring Brendan?"

I swallowed at the bubbling nausea and shook my head. "Probably not."

"It's been a while since he stayed with us," she commented, edging closer to gentle interrogation.

"Yeah, I know, Mom."

"Are you guys okay?" she asked, going in for the kill.

"I don't know," I answered honestly, sinking a little further into my disappointment and distress.

"Do you want to talk about it?"

Part of me wondered if my mother genuinely cared when Brendan and I were in the middle of one of our *things*, or if she just hoped this would be the time we finally called it quits for good.

"Not yet," I said. "I'll talk to you this weekend. I just want to give it a little time."

"Well, you know I'm here."

The sentiment stung more than it should have, and tears welled in my eyes. I wanted to let go and tell her everything, spilling all of my emotions onto the floor and welcoming her advice. But it wasn't the right time, and I couldn't believe how much it hurt to feel so alone.

"I gotta get going, Mom," I said in a hurry, choking on the words.

"Kenny, are you okay?"

"Yeah," I rushed, wiping at a tear as it fell. "I'm just overly stressed, I think. But I need to get this book done, so I'll talk to you later, okay? And I'll see you next weekend."

"Okay," she replied hesitantly. "But let me know if you need anything."

"I will."

"You know I'll get on the next train if you just say the word."

"I know, Mom. I love you."

"Love you, too, baby."

We hung up and I stuffed another cracker into my mouth before throwing on some clean clothes and grabbing my keys. Mrs. Potter stared at my hurry to get my shoes on and my hair up and out of my face.

"We both know I'm not getting any writing done right now," I told her, securing my sloppy bun with a hair tie and a few bobby pins. "So, I'm going for a walk. I'll feed you when I get back."

She blinked at me through her judgment and doubt, but I wasn't going back on my plans. Because the apartment that was once perfect felt way too small, and I felt way too alone.

Chapter Four

My feet moved with a mind of their own, carrying me through the streets and avenues of bustling shops, street vendors, and hurrying pedestrians. I wondered what had made me want to live here in the first place. It was so crowded that the air I craved seemed impossible to find and the smell of boiling hot dogs wasn't helping my nausea at all.

I tried to remember exactly what had convinced me to move here. If I was honest, the list of reasons still lingered in my mind, and mostly, it had been Brendan. Him and the hope that living closer together would be enough to strengthen our relationship. But it was also the potential inspiration that might have come from being somewhere else, away from my little hometown on Long Island. It was the appeal of adventure, and the excitement of living in the big city. But right now, in my current frame of mind and predicament, I seriously questioned what had made me sign the lease and put myself so far away from my support system. Now, all I wanted was to be home, close to my parents and family, where my baby could grow up surrounded by the people who loved me.

My baby.

My. Baby.

Reality struck hard with those two little words. I was having a baby, one that I had hardly wanted initially, and one whose father didn't seem to want at all.

I felt awful.

I felt awful about *everything*.

It was then that I looked up to see the bar I'd wandered into days ago, The Thirsty Goose. It was true that I had thought about that guy and the mocktail he had made several times throughout the vitriol this past week, but I had never intended on coming back. Or so I'd thought.

I'd written about things like this. I made my money doing it. The desperate heroine always seemed to find herself at the very place she needed to be, in order to catch just a glimpse of the man she couldn't stop thinking about. It was predictable, but it was romance.

This, however, wasn't.

This was my life. And although nauseous, I was also thirsty and hungry, so, I headed inside without a second thought.

"Sweet Home Alabama" played loudly on the jukebox. A couple of day-drinking young girls swayed their hips and worked their arms to the beat. They were tourists, made obvious by the matching, midriff-exposing "I Heart NY" t-shirts they wore. I walked past them, successfully keeping my eyes from rolling out of my head as they hollered and whooped, and I approached the bar with a sudden craving for wings.

"I swear to God, if I have to hear this song one more time," the burley bartender muttered to himself, as he worked a dishtowel around a pint glass.

"Not a fan of Lynyrd Skynyrd?" I asked, as I folded my arms over the bar.

He turned in my direction and at the sight of me, his bright blue eyes seemed to get just a little bit brighter. "Hey, girlfriend, nice to see you in here again. Another virgin cocktail, or something harder?" He raised an inquisitive brow with the question.

"Virgin," I answered, reluctantly smiling as I lowered my eyes to the bar.

"So, are congratulations in order this time?" he asked cautiously.

I nodded reluctantly. "Yeah, I guess so. I ..." I pulled in a deep breath, then continued, "I decided I'm keeping the baby."

"Well, then. Congratulations."

"Thank you."

I lifted my eyes to watch him grab a large, wide glass. He began pulling together the ingredients for the drink he'd made for me last time. In the midst of his creation, his eyes met mine with a smile.

"And I *am* a fan of Lynyrd Skynyrd," he told me. "But I hate this song."

"You have something against Alabama?"

"Never been, so I couldn't say," he said, dumping the fruit and ice into the blender.

"So, what's your deal with the song, then?"

"Well, let's just say I'd like it a lot more if it wasn't played to death on that damn thing," he groaned, as he opened the bottle of orange juice and poured.

And as if he had planned it, the girls groaned disappointedly as the song ended, before promptly bouncing off to the jukebox to play it again.

"Wow," I said, glancing over my shoulder as the bare-bellied girls cheered. "I see your point."

"Mm-hmm," he groaned, and turned the blender on to buzz the fruit, juice, and ice down to a frosty liquid.

A minute later, I had a gorgeous, bubblegum pink drink sitting in front of me, and the bartender walked away with just the right amount of swagger, to grab a basket of wings from the kitchen. I sipped the drink and listened to my second dose of Lynyrd, just as the door chimed open behind me.

Glancing over my shoulder, I saw a tall, leggy blonde approaching the exact spot in which I sat. She was carrying a Louis Vuitton purse and wore Louboutin shoes that left an expensive click-click-click sound along the dark, wooden floor. I wasn't much for envy, especially when it comes to frivolous things like bags and shoes, but as she settled against the strip of bar beside me, I took a moment to admire the professionally-made waves in her hair and her immaculately applied makeup. For just a moment, without even knowing who she was, I wished I was her. Because right now, I was foolishly convinced that it was better to be anybody but me.

"Hey, babe."

Like an idiot, I looked up at the sound of the bartender's commanding voice. Why I thought that he would be referring to me as babe, I have no idea, but I looked up and smiled as if he were. That's when I realized he was referring to the bombshell beside me, and that's when I really did wish I was her.

Brendan never liked pet names, but I had always wished that he did.

The bartender placed the basket of wings on the counter in front of me before giving her his full attention.

"What are you doing here?" he asked, grinning like she was life itself and folding his arms on the bar.

"I thought I'd stop by before I headed over to the studio," she replied, as she made sliding onto a barstool look elegant.

I took note of the precarious way she sat, with her back straight and her smooth, long legs crossed. She made the act of stool-sitting seem like an art form, while I, in my frumpy sweatshirt and leggings, resembled a fat toad on a mossy log in the swamps of Louisiana.

"The studio," the bartender repeated, smiling broadly around the words. "It's still crazy to think about. I dunno if I'll ever get used to that."

She returned the smile. "I know, right? I was just telling Andrea today that I'm more nervous about reading a studio audience than I think I've ever been during a live show."

I was eavesdropping. It was wrong and I shouldn't have been, but I couldn't help it when they were right there next to me, as I silently dove into the best wings I'd ever eaten in my entire life. I groaned involuntarily to show my appreciation, and both bartender and leggy blonde turned to look at me.

"Sorry," I said, mouth full and embarrassed.

The blonde's expression was quick to change, as her smile faded, and her eyes reflected something like recollection. Like she had just found something she had lost. But the look was fleeting as she pulled another grin and gave me her full attention.

"They're great, right?"

With fingers covered in barbecue sauce, I nodded as I plucked another wing from the basket. "They seriously are. I could literally drink this sauce right now. Which is saying a lot 'cause my family is pretty big into barbecue sauce."

"That's just the baby talking," the bartender chimed in with a wink, and just like that, it hit me all over again. As if I'd only just now, in that moment, found out.

I was having a baby.

What the hell was I doing, having a *baby*?

The blonde looked between me and the bartender, surely wondering how the hell it was that her gorgeous bottle-slinging boyfriend knew about me and my recent discovery, and he said, "She came in here the other day after just finding out."

"Ah," she replied, nodding. Then, she turned to me and smiled. "Well, congratulations, then!"

"Thanks," I said, trying to force a happiness I didn't quite feel.

"Anyway," she said, returning her attention to the bartender, "I gotta get going. I'll see you later?"

He lifted his hands in a questioning gesture. "Who else would you be seeing?"

She smiled easily at his playful attitude. They were cute together, and they would make gorgeous babies. It made me feel sorry for my own baby, that he or she had been given to a couple that was neither cute together nor drop dead gorgeous.

The blonde leaned forward on the stool and puckered her lips for a kiss. Jealousy warred with maturity and reason as I turned my full attention to my drink, sucking it down to drown out the intimacy going on right beside me. I bet they'd sleep together that night, too, when he saw her after whatever she was doing at the previously mentioned studio. And that ridiculous, intrusive thought was rewarded with another surge of envy. Because where was my boyfriend and why wasn't he here, kissing his pregnant girlfriend and promising to call me as soon as he was on his way?

"Oh, and Goose?" she asked, sliding from her barstool.

"Yeah?"

The blonde turned to me and smiled knowingly. "Get her another round of wings." She laid a friendly hand on my arm, squeezing gently with her fingers, before settling her eyes on mine for a second. There was a message there, I felt it, but before I could focus and try to listen, she was click-click-clicking her way out of the bar.

The bartender brought me another basket of wings and blended another drink. As he slid the glass in front of me, another round of "Sweet Home Alabama" traveled through the speakers. While I laughed and forgot about my life, he hung his head and groaned with aggravation.

"So," I said, pinching the straw in my fingers, "your name is Goose?"

He lifted his eyes to mine and smiled. "Guilty. And since you know mine now, I think it's only fair that you tell me yours."

"It's Kenny."

"A girl named Kenny walks into a bar and meets a guy named Goose," he mused. "Sounds like the premise of one of those chick flicks or something."

"Well, you know," I said, as I brought my lips down to take a sip, "I *am* an author."

"No kiddin'?" I shook my head in reply as I drank. "Well, I expect you to write that story, then."

I swallowed and felt the residual envy fade away as the familiar yet somehow foreign feeling of newfound friendship settled in and made itself at home.

"I just might do that."

Chapter Five

It embarrassed me that, when I'd called my OB/GYN's office, I couldn't remember when I'd last had an appointment. The receptionist stalled and stumbled as she checked the file my old doctor had sent over and told me that my last Pap smear had been done over six years ago. Then, I replied with an awkward joke saying, "Well, I guess I'm about due, then, huh?"

Now, I sat awkwardly in the waiting room, quietly observing the other patients around me. They were mostly expecting women, all at different stages of pregnancy, and I marveled at the size of their bellies. I found it impossible to believe that, one day, in the not so distant future, I would be in their shoes. Bracing myself to sit down, finding it difficult to stand up, and forgetting entirely about bending over. The thought of my body changing so drastically, so quickly, filled me with enough anxiety to trigger my overly sensitive stomach which sent me rushing to the bathroom, where I threw up my entire breakfast of Saltines and frozen waffles. My cheeks flushed with humiliation as I returned to my seat, but the only looks I received were ones of sympathy.

Perks of being pregnant, I guess.

"Kendall Wright?"

I lifted my head from my phone to see a short, red-headed nurse with her arms around a tablet, standing in the doorway of the waiting room. I smiled as I grabbed my purse and headed toward her.

"Okay, so first, I'm just going to have you pee in a cup ..." She led me to a bathroom and handed me a plastic cup with a grin.

"Oh, great, that's exactly how I had hoped to start my day," I quipped sardonically.

The nurse smiled, not knowing if I was joking and not knowing how to respond appropriately.

My favorite people are fluent in sarcasm, but clearly she wasn't.

"We only need a little bit," she said, gesturing into the bathroom.

Stepping inside and raising the cup to her, I replied, "Well, I'll see what I can do."

***

"Okie dokie, here we are," the ultrasound technician said, leading me into a dark room.

I approached the exam table and began to climb up. "So, how do I do this? Do I just lift my shirt and—"

"Oh, um, I need you to please remove your pants and underwear first."

I looked at her, startled. "Oh. Right."

She gestured toward a curtain and a stool situated in the corner of the room, then instructed me to loosely wrap the sheet around my lower half. I did as I was told, while wondering what was happening. This wasn't what I'd seen on countless TV shows or movies, and I uncomfortably emerged from behind the curtain with the sheet held to my waist, wondering what was about to happen to me.

"Just hop up here and we'll take a look at your baby."

Your baby.

My baby.

The breath in my lungs hitched as I climbed onto the table and laid back. The tech situated my feet in the stirrups, and then, just as she was about to lift the sheet and do whatever it was she was about to do, she stopped.

"Oh! Do you have someone in the waiting room? Do you want them in here with you?"

I hadn't thought about it before, not as I'd entered the office or peed in the cup, but of course I thought about it now.

This was my first appointment with the obstetrician, my first sonogram, and I was alone.

Tears stung my eyes as I shook my head. "No, I'm here by myself," I told her. She didn't say anything in reply, but I thought I saw a flicker of sympathy pass her eyes as she nodded and lifted the sheet.

"So, how do we do this--" I was cut off abruptly by the smooth glide of something being inserted and moved around, reaching parts of my body often left untouched and reminding me of how long it had been since I'd gotten laid. And just as I was about to wonder if this was supposed to feel good, she smiled and pointed to the screen beside my head.

"And there's your baby."

My heart jittered as I turned to look, and there, in black and white, was a little blob resembling a gummi bear. The tears were quick to spring to my eyes before streaming down my face as the little nubs on the gummi bear's body fluttered.

"It's waving at you," she said. More flutters on the screen and she laughed. "See? It's saying, 'Hi, Mom!'"

Mom.

I laughed around another sputtered burst of tears, grinning from ear to ear, as I whispered, "Hi, little bean."

***

Instead of looking out the window on the train that evening, I stared at the picture of my baby, while the afternoon replayed in my mind.

After the sonogram, my OB/GYN, Doctor Albrecht, had given me a thorough and long overdue examination. Then, she had sat down and told me in great detail how I was at an advanced maternal age.

"So, you're calling me old," I had said.

She winced and replied, "We don't like to use words like geriatric or old, but ..."

"But you're calling me old."

"I'm calling you ... *mature*," she said with a pained smile.

Mature is really just a nicer way of saying old, but I decided not to push the argument further. Because I knew I was old. Sure, I wasn't close to knocking on Heaven's door, and maybe I still looked and felt pretty good for thirty-five, but my biological clock was ticking slower these days and I knew it. I'd been acutely aware of it for a while and had been almost fine with settling on never having kids at all. But now that I was pregnant, and hearing a doctor slap me with a high-risk warning, simply due to my age, I felt downright archaic.

Doctor Albrecht had explained all of the risks and things to look out for, while insisting everything looked perfect so far. Then, she asked if I'd like to run genetic testing on the fetus, to screen for potential illnesses or disabilities and decide what to do with it. I already knew that I liked her, and I knew she was only asking out of obligation, but I had still wrapped my arms around my stomach in response, to protect the little bean inside of me. I told her that whatever was meant to happen would happen and I wouldn't have any part in that decision.

After all, I hadn't decided to get pregnant in the first place, but here I was.

As the train pulled into the station, I could feel myself building with determination to make it through the pregnancy without a hitch and prove that my body and I were perfectly capable of carrying this kid. I could do this, and I was sure of it.

What I wasn't so sure of was, if it really came down to it, whether I could do it all alone.

***

Most kids go through a phase in their lives where they hate their parents. They're embarrassed by them and can't wait to move as far away as humanly possible. That was the case for every kid I knew growing up, and each one did move away as soon as they were able to. However, that had never been the case for me. I loved my parents and always had. Even as a hormonal teenager, I loved hanging out with them in our house on Long Island, whether we were watching a movie or playing a board game.

Truthfully, if it hadn't been for having a boyfriend in the city, I'm not sure I ever would've moved away.

So, that was the reason why, after seeing the doctor, I had decided that I couldn't wait an entire week to see my parents. I needed to go straight home, I needed to tell them, and I had to do it now. As I stepped out onto the platform and saw my mom waiting in her car, I wished I'd never left home at all. If I still lived with my parents, I'd have all the support I would need to get through this pregnancy and adjust to having a baby.

"What's wrong?" Mom asked, as I opened the back door and threw my backpack inside.

"Huh?"

I closed the door and got in through the front. Mom eyed me with prying speculation making me laugh uneasily, as the sonogram picture burned a hole through my sweatshirt pocket.

"Something is wrong," she declared, and I hated how well she could read me.

This wasn't the plan. I didn't want them suspecting anything right away. I had wanted to tell them after pumpkin picking and in a way that didn't make it seem like my entire world was ending. But I felt too guilty lying to either of my parents, and so, I replied, "I have something to tell you and Dad, but I don't want to tell you without him."

"Kenny."

I rolled my head against the headrest to face her, wearing a grin that felt too painful to be real. "Mom."

"What's wrong?"

I sighed. "Go home and we'll talk."

***

The picture of my little gummi bear was in front of my father and a frosty mug of beer was in his hand. The condensation on the glass reminded me of my new favorite drink and as badly as I had wished to be home, I now wished I was back in the city, sitting on a stool in Goose's bar.

"So, how are you feeling about all of this?" he finally asked, before taking a sip and setting his mug on the table. He clasped his hands and finally looked at me, making me breathe out a sigh of relief. I had started to wonder if he'd ever be able to look at me again.

"I don't know," I answered honestly. "It's … weird, but … I'm okay, I guess."

"Weird," Dad grunted with a nod. "It sure is."

"How does Brendan feel?" Mom asked.

"I wouldn't know," I replied with a defeated shrug.

Dad's brow furrowed with a flash of fury. "What do you mean, you wouldn't know?"

Shrugging, I eyed his half-empty glass of beer, wishing I could have just a drop to take the edge off of this night. "I told him about the baby a week ago, and I haven't heard from him since."

My father's eyes immediately darkened with a protective anger, while Mom leaned back in her chair and crossed her arms.

"Oh, really?" she said, in a tone that meant she was two seconds away from calling and giving him a hefty piece of her mind.

"Guys, it's fine," I insisted, but a vein in Dad's forehead began to throb as Mom looked beyond me and toward the kitchen wall "This came out of left field for both of us," I went on, not entirely sure why I was defending my coward of a boyfriend. "I mean, I wasn't even sure I wanted to keep it at first—"

"But are you sure now?" Dad asked, his voice soft despite the stone in his glare. I nodded, dropping my gaze to the table. "Okay. Then, as far as Brendan goes, it is what it is. Either he steps up to the plate or he doesn't. But whatever happens, as long as this is what *you* want, we'll figure it out."

My father was a man of very few words and believed that less was always more. So, after his brief but heartfelt declaration, he stood from the table, and with his copy of the sonogram, retreated down the hall and to his bedroom, leaving the half-empty mug of beer behind.

That glass was looking more tempting by the second.

My mom, however, loved to talk. So, while she left the topic to rest for the night, the next day, as we searched for a perfect, round pumpkin to adorn their front porch, she casually returned to the topic of Brendan.

"So, I gotta ask. Are you going to break up with him?"

Squatting over a nicely shaped contender, I looked up at her. "What?"

"You know what I'm talking about."

"Oh, I do." I rolled the pumpkin to its side and revealed a nasty patch of rot. "I just wasn't sure this was where you wanted to have this conversation."

"It's good to have hard conversations while doing something fun."

"Why? To kill the mood?" I retorted, before heading over to a more oblong specimen.

"No, wiseass," she replied with a healthy dose of attitude. "To balance the good with the bad. And that pumpkin isn't round enough."

"But all the round ones we've found look like crap. And I don't know what I'm going to do about Brendan."

Mom crossed her arms and turned her eyes toward an autumnal orange sky. "It's none of my business what you do with your life, Kenny, and I know you're not asking for my two cents—"

"Oh, like that's ever stopped you before," I laughed, lifting the oval pumpkin and turning it around in my hands.

"It's just that your dad and I know that you deserve a man who's not going to abandon you when you need him the most, and you *need* him right now."

"He's entitled to feel the way he's feeling," I muttered, once again defending the man who knocked me up and walked away.

"Yes," she agreed, nodding firmly. "He's entitled to feel whatever the hell he wants to feel. But he's not entitled to just walk away from the woman carrying his child. I mean, even if he has decided that he doesn't want to be with you anymore, he can at least support you and offer some help when you need it. That's what a good man would do."

"Well, I guess this is just what he feels he needs to do right now," I replied, my heart sore and my eyes stinging.

"Well, I guess he's not a good man, then," she fired back, full of anger and spite.

Deep down, I knew her feelings came from a place of love for me and I knew she was disgusted and disappointed. Hell, so was I. But the emotional turmoil siphoning through my brain could've done without the attack on my deadbeat boyfriend, the father of my unborn baby. Regardless of how right I knew she was.

As she witnessed the welling of tears in my eyes, Mom hurried to me with opened arms. "Honey, no, I'm sorry. Don't be upset."

Still holding the heavy pumpkin in my hands, I pressed my eyes to her shoulder. "I just don't want to deal with this right now, okay? I can't wrap my head around everything."

"I know," she soothed, rubbing her hand against my back. "I shouldn't have brought it up."

"I just don't know what I'd do without him."

It was a weak statement and I felt weak for saying it. I had never before felt like I relied on Brendan for happiness and security, or any man for that matter. It was how I'd so easily broken up with him countless times before, all without a flinch or a moment of hesitation. But now, with the brand-new life we had created together, growing by the second in my belly, I suddenly felt a strong reliance. It was like it had always been there, just waiting to rear its ugly head.

"It's hard to let go of something that's been there for so long," Mom said gently, stroking her fingers through my hair. "But I think it's supposed to be, so it feels *that* much better when you're finally free. Or when you find something better."

"It's not like I've been his prisoner, Mom."

"Maybe not, but you've both been stuck on this freakin' hamster wheel for years. And I know it's because you're both comfortable and going back to each other is easier than finding someone new. But maybe it's time you break out of your comfort zone," she said, cupping the back of my head. "You might be surprised by what happens if you do."

I wasn't sure I believed what she was saying, but as we left the pumpkin patch with a nicely shaped, albeit different than the norm, oblong pumpkin, I was sure of one thing.

My little gummi bear might have been cursed with a deadbeat father, but he or she was lucky, *so* lucky, to have a couple of incredible grandparents.

Chapter Six

Telling my parents about the pregnancy, left me feeling a lot lighter, as if I'd unknowingly been carrying the weight of a thousand bricks on my shoulders.

Over dinner Saturday night, the three of us had discussed baby names, and on Sunday, Mom and I threw around tentative baby shower ideas. What had recently felt like a dismal future now felt brighter and a little more hopeful, and by the time Monday morning rolled around, I was ready to face the daunting task of finishing my upcoming novel.

I had begun the year with a solid plan to release four books over the course of twelve months. I wrote full-time, I had no other obligations, and since I published everything myself, it was completely conceivable that I could pull it off. But that was so many months ago, back in January, and well before I suddenly found myself pregnant, just as I began working on book number four.

But the only way to pull off the working mom thing, was for me to actually do the work. And since I was finished wallowing in a neck-deep hole of self-pity, I had devised a plan to write diligently over the next seven days, ensuring I could send this year's fourth book to my editor at the beginning of the following week. I realized though, that in order to do that, I needed to remove myself from the usual distractions. No cat and no four walls of an apartment that no longer felt perfect. And that was how I found myself walking into The Thirsty Goose, with my messenger bag looped over my shoulder.

"Well, if it isn't a girl named Kenny."

I ignored the wiser decision of occupying a quiet table in a corner and instead approached the bar with a smile.

"Can I ask you a question?" I said, lifting onto a stool and wondering how much longer I'd be able to do it.

"Maybe," he answered with a smirk, already collecting the ingredients for the drink that was beginning to feel like mine. "Depends on the question."

"Well, that isn't suspicious at all," I laughed, as I laid my bag on the dark, gleaming surface. "You hiding something?"

"We're all hiding something from someone," he quipped, waggling his brows.

The statement warranted pause and I froze, while sliding my laptop from the bag, permitting his words to seep in. I immediately knew that I'd use them myself one day. The amount of truth between each letter was insurmountable and I loved using my stories as a way to tell the truths no one likes to speak.

"That sounds suspicious," I teased, breaking the silence after his words had become a part of me. "So, what are *you* hiding, then?"

"I'm not gonna say."

"So, you're a serial killer."

His laugh was a light slicing through the moody darkness. "What does it say about me that you automatically assumed that?"

"I'm not saying I really believe it," I assured him, pulling my computer out of the bag. "But when you say something so vague and shady like that, you have to know that people are automatically going to jump to the worst-case scenario. People are paranoid, man; they can't help it."

He chuckled, bobbing his head as he dropped fruit and ice into the blender. "Ask your question."

I returned the laugh, almost forgetting how this conversation had started. "Oh, right. I just wanted to ask, what is your real name?"

His eyes lifted to mine. "You know, you're the first person to actually ask me that."

"Get out of here," I muttered incredulously, opening the laptop. "Do you have an outlet I can use?"

He opened his hand, silently asking for the AC adapter's wire, and I handed it over. Then, as he bent to plug my computer in, he said, "You'd be surprised how many people just assume my parents were cruel enough to name me after a bird."

Typing in my password, I asked, "What parent would name their kid Goose?"

"Not mine, thank Christ," he laughed. "And it's Eric, by the way."

The moment his name was dropped into the air, it seemed so clear. Like my mind already knew but had somehow forgotten along the way.

"Eric," I repeated quietly.

"Yep. Eric Nevard, at your service."

I hummed contemplatively, nodding. "I've always liked that name."

"Well, if the baby's a boy, you have my permission to use it."

"How did you know that's why I asked?"

"You're forgetting I have a kid," he said, winking and sliding my drink over. "Now, I'm asking *you* a question. What's with the computer?"

Opening up my manuscript, I said, "I'm working."

"Working?" He grabbed a rag and began wiping away droplets of condensation from the bar.

"I told you, remember? I'm an author."

Draping the rag over his shoulder, he looked to me with intrigue and I laughed uneasily, knowing I had his full attention. He folded his arms on the counter beside me and studied me with too much interest. Eyes as interested as his could get a girl in trouble, and that observation probably should've been more of a red flag to me than it was.

"You know, I've never known an author before," he said. "What kind of books do you write?"

"Romance."

His contagious grin broadened. "Wow. So, you write the dirty stuff, huh?"

"*Well*," I wobbled my head from side to side, "I guess some of my sex scenes get a little raunchy. But I really focus more on the characters and story than on the sex."

Goose nodded thoughtfully. "So, if it was a story about a sex addict ..."

My eyes flicked quickly toward his. "Then, it would be dirty as hell," I laughed, before looking back at the computer screen. "But if I write a very character-driven story that sex doesn't fit into, then it is what it is. I mostly just listen to the characters and what they need to come alive."

"You gonna put me into a book?"

I sniffed a quiet laugh. "Maybe."

"And you'll call it A Girl Named Kenny Walks into a Bar and Meets a Guy Named Goose, right?"

"Oh, yeah," I laughed. "That has bestseller written all over it."

"Hey, you never know," he shot back, pointing a finger at me, as he turned to tend to another customer.

"I guess not," I muttered quietly, and smiled as I got to work.

***

If I was being honest with myself, I had thought that working in Goose's bar could have been a terrible idea. It was possible that I'd regret my decision and need to head back to my equally distracting apartment. But once my headphones were on, I easily slipped into the comfort of creativity and my imagination took the lead. Much to my surprise, I had hardly noticed Goose was there at all, even as he left baskets of wings and glasses of water beside my hand.

It was the best writing sprint I'd experienced in weeks, and if I could keep this up, I'd definitely have the manuscript to my editor on time.

"So, can I ask something totally out of line?" Goose asked as I collected my things and got ready to leave.

"Maybe."

"How are things with your boyfriend?"

He was right. It was completely out of line and not any of his business. He didn't really know me, and he didn't know Brendan at all. But, I figured, it wouldn't hurt to air out my dirty laundry in the presence of someone so unattached to the situation. So, poking my tongue in my cheek, I sighed and said, "I wouldn't know. He hasn't spoken to me since I told him about the baby."

He looked up abruptly and narrowed his eyes. "He hasn't talked to you at all?"

I shook my head, hoisting my bag over my shoulder. "Nope."

"You're not gonna call him, right?"

I shrugged noncommittally. "I don't know. I haven't decided yet."

Leaning against the bar, he looked down onto its reflective surface and said, "Look, I know it's really none of my business, but I'd like to think we're pals now and pals give each other advice, right?"

I swallowed at the trepidation in my throat. "Sure."

"You shouldn't call him."

I barked a bitter laugh. "You sound like my parents."

"Yeah, well, they're right. This guy should be crawling back to you, not the other way around. And if he never does, whatever."

"Whatever?" I scoffed, crossing my arms over my chest. "The guy is the father of my baby."

"Right," Goose said with a firm nod. "And if he can so easily walk out of your life, maybe he doesn't deserve to be in it at all."

It felt wrong, but I knew he was right. So, before I left, I promised my new pal I would hold firm and wait for Brendan to come back to me before giving in to him.

Chapter Seven

"That's a lot of blood," I commented, staring wide-eyed at the twelve vials of blood.

My blood.

I wasn't one to be squeamish over a little bit of drawn blood, but that wasn't a little bit. It was a lot, and from where I was sitting, it almost looked like it was enough to make me pass out.

I put a hand to my forehead.

"Whoa," I said, as my eyelids fluttered and a weight made itself at home against my shoulders.

The lab technician glanced at me. "Do you always get woozy from having blood taken?"

"Nope, but I guess there's a first time for everything, right?" Nausea shoved against my gut and I slammed my eyes shut. "Oh, God, I think I might puke."

She grabbed a bucket and handed it to me, where I didn't, in fact, puke. I just gripped the plastic, feeling it rapidly warming from the heat of my sweating palms, and muttered an endless mantra of, "oh, God, oh, God, oh, God," as if the Almighty didn't have anything better to do than rid me of the urge to puke.

A few moments later, somewhere between my sixth and seventh "oh God," a section of gauze was pressed to my arm and a piece of surgical tape was placed over it. Lastly, a little pad reeking of rubbing alcohol was held under my nose.

"This sometimes helps," the tech said, and she was right. After a few deep breaths, the dizziness and nausea faded to something a little more manageable and I sat up, wiping at my sweaty brow.

"Sorry," I felt the need to say.

She smiled, deepening the creases on her face. "You wouldn't have been the first pregnant lady to pass out or throw up in my chair."

"Well, thank you very much for draining me of my blood."

Nodding, she turned away to collect the vials. "And thank *you* for not giving me a mess to clean up."

I left the lab with a pack of cookies and a little bottle of orange juice, then stepped out onto the sidewalk, ready to head home and take a nap.

New York autumn was in full swing, with a freshness in the air and passersby bundled in cozy sweaters and leggings. They hurried along, caught up in the business of their own lives and carrying coffee cups and cell phones. I took a moment to stand beneath a strip of scaffolding, to listen to a guy playing his guitar and singing about a girl he once knew, but never found it in his heart to get over her. I smiled, listening to the music and honking cars as they slowly drove by, and I remembered that, although I moved here to be closer to Brendan, this was one thing I loved so much about the city. That beneath the rush and brash demeanor, there was heart and life, a warmth that kept us all from becoming too cold.

My phone disrupted the moment and I pulled it from my pocket to see Brendan's name on the screen. For maybe the first time ever, he had taken the initiative, and that had to say something.

"Hello?" I shouted into the speaker, plugging my other ear with a finger.

"Hey, Kendo."

The sound of his voice should have filled my ears with relief, and yet, all I could feel was a heated annoyance that he hadn't called sooner. That he could so easily just say my nickname, like all of this time hadn't passed between us, while I was busy being pregnant with his child.

"Hi."

I walked briskly from the guitarist and further down the street, past hot dog vendors and shouting cab drivers.

"You working?"

My eyes narrowed, incredulous. "What? No. I just got done having blood taken."

"Oh." He paused. "Is everything okay?"

Throwing my head back and nearly bumping into a guy and his Chihuahua, I gawked at the open sky, bordered by a frame of skyscrapers.

"Yeah, Brendan, everything's great. I'm just throwing up a minimum of six times a day and having my body drained of its life source. No big deal."

"Kendo—"

"And you know what's really awesome?" I continued, now hot with anger. "That my boyfriend, who knocked me up, hasn't spoken to me in almost *two* weeks. I mean, being abandoned to handle all of this on my own has seriously been a dream come true."

He was silent as I pulled my key from my purse and opened the door to my apartment, situated two floors up from Famiglia Bella, a hole-in-the-wall pizza place with the best pepperoni pie I'd ever eaten. It was just too bad the building didn't have an elevator. I could manage the stairs now, but I wasn't sure I'd be happy with them once I was nine months pregnant or toting an infant around.

I liked to consider myself a level-headed woman, someone who is understanding and forgiving and who only argues when it was absolutely necessary. But with Brendan's silence, I had quickly found grown more infuriated by the second. By the time I'd reached my door, the blood I had left in my veins was bubbling with rage. He'd already had a week and a half to be quiet, and I was done waiting for him to speak.

"You know what, Brendan? I'm done. I can't do this anymore." I hadn't expected the words to hit me so violently as I said them, as if we hadn't broken up countless times before. But with the keys still hanging from my limp hand, I slumped against the dingy wall beside my door and released a ragged sob. "I-I just can't do this. I can't deal with you and your, your flakey bullshit. I just can't. I can't do that to myself, and I won't do that to this baby, I … I *can't*."

"Kendall, please ..."

"No. You don't get to beg me. You don't get to act like this is so hard—"

"Jesus Christ! Will you just let me talk?!"

I snapped out of my emotional stupor at the crack of his angry tone. "You've had almost two weeks to talk!"

"I needed time! You *told* me to take some time!"

Jamming my key into the lock and finally opening the door, I shouted, "That didn't mean to abandon me for almost two—"

"Dammit, I'm sorry! Okay? I'm sorry. I was wrong for taking so much time. I was wrong for not calling you sooner. You didn't deserve that."

"No, I didn't," I said coldly, using my hip to slam the door. "But why the hell should I have thought this time would be any different? You *never* call me, and I was an idiot to think—"

"I called you now, didn't I?"

"What?" I stared ahead at the tiny refrigerator in my tiny kitchen.

"I called you now. Maybe I took too long, and I'm sorry, but I *called you*."

Chewing on my bottom lip, I struggled to keep a grasp on my anger. "Yeah, well, whatever. One time in three years doesn't—"

"Kendo, I want the baby."

Laying a hand over my stomach, I lost my grip and plummeted into relieved affection. "Oh, God, seriously?"

"Seriously."

I dropped into one of the mismatched chairs at my garage sale table and thrust a hand into my hair. "What made you change your mind?"

"I just thought about what life would be like, knowing you were out there somewhere, taking care of our kid all by yourself. I don't think I'd be able to live with that. I think I'd miss you too much. I think … I think I'd hate not knowing my kid."

Brendan's thoughts sat unsettled in my heart, with an annoying tingle that said his words weren't inherently wrong, but not quite right either. There was too much thought and not enough knowing. But I didn't allow myself to linger on that. He was trying at least. That had to mean something, and so, I allowed myself to smile.

"So ... we're really doing this. Together."

"Yeah," he said with a sigh. "Let's do this."

I touched my lips and felt the width of my grin. It was a reminder that this was a good thing, a *positive* thing. Brendan had called and come back to me with a declaration of commitment. I was happy and genuinely excited, albeit nervous, for our future, but oh, that little seed of trepidation ...

It certainly has a way of growing on its own.

Chapter Eight

The days of morning sickness, tireless writing, and unbeaten exhaustion passed slowly, yet the weeks flew by, as they carried me toward the end of October and Halloween. With my manuscript now safely in the hands of my editor, I finally had the freedom to sleep as often as I wanted, in between decorating for the holiday to trump all others.

Brendan was spending more time at my place and that made me happy, especially in the early morning, when he'd feed Mrs. Potter while I threw up violently. But it made the apartment feel that much smaller, and as I unpacked a box of spooky snow globes, I sighed at his size thirteens on the coffee table.

"Can't you just find somewhere else to put them?" he asked, not looking up from his phone.

"There is nowhere else."

"Sure, there is."

"Oh, really?" I dramatically turned my head this way and that. "Where?"

He glanced across the apartment, to the dining table. "Over there."

"We eat there."

"We can eat here," he muttered, tapping the table with his socked toes.

"Oh, my God, just move your feet!"

He turned to look up at me, completely irritated and incredulous. "I *just* sat down," he said angrily. "You can't give me a few minutes before asking me to move?"

"Fine," I grumbled, huffing an angry sigh as I stuffed the snow globes back into their box.

"You can't keep that shit within a baby's reach anyway, you know," he went on, his tone condescending and snarky.

Turning to face him, I narrowed my annoyed gaze. "There isn't a baby here yet. We'll worry about that when we get there."

"Or you could get used to it now."

His comments served as irritating little pinpricks, like tiny paper cuts on my mood, but the more he spoke, the more they stung. I turned away from him, desperate for some space, and grabbed my messenger bag.

As I headed for the door, Brendan asked where I was going, and I replied, "If I can't decorate, I'm going to work."

He snickered and shook his head, so I asked, "What was that for?"

"Nothing," he said, laughing. "I mean, it's just that, you write stories, Kendo; that's not exactly *work*."

My heart and stomach lurched toward each other, colliding somewhere beneath my ribs. In all of the years we had been together, he had never once undermined my work as an author. So, now that he had, I wanted to scream and cry and break the snow globes over his head.

63

But I didn't. I didn't do a damn thing. Instead, I rushed for the door and slammed it behind me.

Communication had never been our thing, and sometimes, a slammed door speaks far louder than words.

***

"You know there are over a thousand songs on that thing, right?!"

Despite the irritation I'd carried with me from the apartment, I still laughed at the sound of Goose's voice, bellowing over the sound of the familiar guitar intro. He stood at the bar, arms crossed and head shaking, as he stared in the direction of the jukebox.

"Why don't you just get rid of it?" I asked, approaching the bar. "Get yourself one of those fancy Bose sound systems and play your own music."

He turned at the sound of my voice, and while I couldn't say for sure, his shoulders seemed to relax just a little at the knowledge of my presence.

"Because if that song isn't here, the people won't come," he replied, speaking in a low, hushed tone, as if it was a secret.

"Okay, this is just a guess, but here me out," I said, hoisting myself onto a stool. "I think they probably show up for the booze, but I mean, don't take my word for it. I could be wrong."

"Or *maybe*," he said, hunching over and bringing his face closer to mine, "this is the only bar in the entire city with a jukebox that plays *this* fuckin' song."

64

I studied his wide, serious eyes and the firm set of his jaw and mouth. His features were pieced together so perfectly, I could've believed an artist thought him up and carved him from stone. And it wasn't an observation made from attraction, although there was certainly that, too. It was simply fact, as true as the sky being blue or the grass being green, and I wondered how it was I'd describe him in a book, if I were ever to write it.

A Girl Named Kenny Walks into a Bar and Meets a Guy Named Goose.

"You know what I think?" I asked, ignoring the strings of description swirling through my mind.

"What?" he asked, his gaze softening and his jaw loosening.

"I think you secretly love this song."

He stood up, throwing his head back and barking with a resounding laugh. "And I think you're fuckin' crazy. But I think I'll keep you around anyway, 'cause you don't use me for my jukebox."

"Nah, I just use you for your mocktails," I quipped, waggling my brows and nudging my chin toward the blender.

He smiled and bent to open the fridge door. "There are worse things."

I watched him expertly concoct a frosty drink, a white one this time. When I asked what he was making, he replied, "Well, I figured you'd be tired of drinkin' the same thing, so I did a little experimenting and came up with a couple I thought you might like."

The idea of this man, one I barely knew, thinking of me when he didn't need to pushed thoughts of Brendan's attitude and disregard from my mind. Instead they were replaced by the warm comfort of being considered, and maybe it was the hormones talking, but I was overwhelmed with an urge to hug him. But I didn't. I only watched as he poured the frosty mixture into a tall glass and slid it over. Then, he watched me, as I flamboyantly made a show of sipping through the straw and smacking my lips at the burst of flavor.

"Ooh! It's so tropical! And minty!"

He smiled with satisfaction, as he dumped the pitcher into the sink. "It's basically a mint pina colada, minus the rum. I thought the mint might be good for your stomach."

I paused on my way back to the straw and swallowed at my thickening throat. Tears pricked the backs of my eyes and burned my nose, so I sat up straight, turned my gaze to the beams running parallel on the ceiling.

"Shit," I sniffed, using my hands to wave away the moisture in my eyes. "I hate crying."

His forehead crumpled with concern. "What the hell? Don't cry! If you don't like it, I—"

"No!" I shook my head, as one lone tear escaped to race down my cheek. "No, it's just that, my boyfriend and I got into a fight today, and I really needed this, I think. Either that or my hormones are going freakin' crazy."

Goose smiled and pulled a napkin out from under the bar. Passing it to me, he said with a wink, "Let's go with the hormones thing."

Our conversation dwindled and the usual sound of Lynyrd Skynyrd filled the dead air as Goose cleaned up and I pulled my laptop out, thinking of how nice this was. Over the past few weeks, we'd fallen into a comfortable friendship that never required continuous conversation.

I pulled up the document for my newest story and slipped my headphones on to open the door to my creativity. The bar and Lynyrd disappeared and all that remained was the vision of a successful woman and her first encounter with the eventual love of her life. A smile spread across my face at the familiar jitters that coursed through my arms and hands, all the way down to my fingertips. The excitement of these sweet moments and the feeling of falling in love, had all come back with the start of a new story. And as I wrote about her first gaze into his eyes, I thought, *I have the best job, Brendan, and I don't care if you think it's stupid.*

Half a chapter in and I felt a firm tap on my shoulder. Emerging from the world of my characters always left me feeling off and a little shaken, so I abruptly pulled my headphones off to peer at Goose with a strong, unintentional feeling of annoyance. He just smiled apologetically, now used to my process, and pointed at the bar beside me. I looked down to find a basket of wings.

"Just wanted to make sure you and the little guy are fed," he said, before walking back down the bar.

"Wait."

He turned back and asked, "Yeah?"

"Little *guy*, huh?"

His cheeks pinked beneath the moody lighting and his shoulders lifted. "Just a feeling I have."

I nodded contemplatively. I wouldn't say it yet, not out loud, but I had a similar feeling. I also hoped it was a boy. To be blunt, I didn't care to have a daughter. I could never see myself having one, but out of fear of being disappointed, I was trying to convince myself that it was in fact a girl. Just to keep from being surprised or disappointed.

"What does your boyfriend think?"

I shrugged, laying my headphones on the bar before digging into the wings. "I have no idea. We haven't really talked much about it."

Goose slowly nodded as he turned on the faucet to wash a pitcher. "But he's cool with having a baby now, right?"

I bit into a juicy wing and fought the urge to groan. The wings at Goose's bar were nothing short of orgasmic and I was convinced he could bottle the sauce and make a killing.

"Yeah," I told him. "I mean, we're doing fine, I guess. He's been great with me being sick."

"But that's just you being sick," he countered, scrubbing the pitcher and rinsing it off. "How is he about the baby? Is he excited?"

I had to think about the question, because really, I wasn't sure. Brendan and I never talked much about feelings in general. Hell, I couldn't remember the last time either of us had said "I love you." It never seemed important. I mean, why push a point that's already been made a thousand times? But now, I wondered how he felt about being a father. Was he looking forward to it or was he simply going along for the ride out of fear of his child not knowing him?

"I don't really know," I answered honestly. "But, I mean, I'm not super excited about some stuff either."

With a rag, he dried the pitcher as he nodded. "Yeah, I get that. There's a lot of shit that comes along with havin' a baby. I wasn't too excited either and that's why I was such a dick at first. But the more I thought about it, like how one day there would be this little person in the world who looked like me, the more excited I felt. Like, that was my chance to change and do something good, you know? That excited the hell out of me."

I smiled, propping my chin in my palm. "I forget you have a kid."

He nodded, unable to hide the affection in his grin as he reached to the back wall and took a framed picture down. "She lives with her mom, so I only get her every other weekend, unless it's a holiday."

He handed me the picture and said, "That's Hannah."

A teenaged girl with reddish-blonde hair looked up at me. Her smile contained the same contagious warmth as her father's, and when I handed the picture back, I said, "She really does look just like you."

He nodded with pride. "Everybody says that. But I see her mom in her personality and thank Christ for that."

"Your personality doesn't seem that bad."

Goose winked and said, "We're all hiding something, remember?"

"That's what you think."

"That's what I *know*."

I smirked, then asked, "Are you seeing her for Halloween?"

With a forlorn sigh, he shook his head. "She's going to Salem with her mom this year. It sucks 'cause it's the first year I don't actually have anything going on."

"You and your girlfriend aren't doing anything?"

"Nah," he muttered with a sigh, disappointment heavy in his tone. "She's been really busy with her job."

I hadn't initially planned on doing anything other than hanging out at the apartment with Brendan, watching scary movies and bingeing on junk food. But now, seeing the letdown written clearly on Goose's face, the potential for an invitation hung wide open in the air. We got along so well, and I knew we could have a lot of fun together, but the risk of making it all awkward seemed too great. And what if Brendan or Goose's girlfriend had a problem with it? Was the chance of an argument worth it?

So, I treaded lightly as I approached the question. "If it's not a problem with her, maybe we could do something. I'm sure Brendan wouldn't mind if you hung out with us."

I braced myself, worried he'd immediately shoot me down. The worry that I'd have to find somewhere else to do my writing weighed heavily against my shoulders, and I was scared to look at him. Scared that the invitation to be a third wheel would disgust him so much, I'd feel the immediate urge to leave. But when I eventually did, I found that the moody atmosphere had brightened with the help of his infectious smile.

"Yeah, that'd be cool. I'll let you know what she says."

We exchanged numbers, and like a kid whose been given an invitation to Disney World, I rushed home to ask if it was okay.

When I brought it up to Brendan and explained the situation, he didn't ask any questions or seem at all suspicious or territorial. He simply shrugged and told me it didn't matter if I had company, because he was going to be busy, anyway. Which was news to me.

"Wait, what do you mean? I thought we were going to watch movies?"

He nodded from behind his phone. "Yeah, I know. But the office is offering overtime, so I figured I'd grab it while I had the chance."

It should have hurt or been a topic of contention between us, because why wouldn't he have said something sooner? But I didn't say a word, because all it meant was, I could spend my favorite holiday with my new favorite friend.

Alone.

Chapter Nine

We met at the stone entrance of the cemetery, on what was a chilly and dreary Halloween evening. I was dressed entirely in my appropriately favorite color—black—and so was Goose. He wore an old leather jacket and black jeans, with scuffed Doc Martens on his feet, that were a perfect match to the ones I wore. He looked different without his signature button down and vest. Different but good.

So good.

He took a moment to take in my long-sleeved t-shirt, on display beneath my open cardigan, and laughed. "Very cute," he complimented, smiling brightly in the dark night.

I glanced down at the rib cage design, complete with a skeletal baby over the belly. "Thanks," I said. "I've always wanted to buy one of these, but I was never able to because, you know, I wasn't pregnant."

We headed through the iron gate and were instructed to wait for our group to be ready to leave. The sun was setting fast and the bite in the air had me dancing on the spot and wishing I'd worn something warmer. Goose turned to face me, his hands stuffed into his jacket pockets, as he watched my jig with furrowed brows.

"You're cold," he assessed.

"Nah, I always do this when I'm about to tour a cemetery."

"You're lying."

The wind blew, whipping my hair and slicing through my shirt, and my teeth chattered as I nodded. "Yes. Yes, I am definitely lying."

Without hesitation, Goose unzipped his jacket, revealing a black sweater, tight enough to emphasize the definition in his arms. "Take this," he instructed, pulling his arms from the sleeves.

"You'll freeze."

"No, I won't."

"Seriously, I don't want you to get cold on my behalf," I continued to protest, shaking my head profusely. Afraid that if I wore his jacket, I'd never want to take it off.

But despite my insistence that I was okay, I felt the weight of the heavy jacket being laid comfortably over my shoulders, and it was like stepping into the embrace of a warm kitchen on a cold winter's day. I settled in with a sigh, relishing for a moment in the mingled scents of musky cologne and leather, while I also promised that, since being pregnant, I got hot quickly and therefore wouldn't need it for long. But Goose brushed it off, telling me to keep it as long as I needed it, and I wondered how he'd feel if I needed it forever.

Sleepy Hollow Cemetery was a gorgeous museum of exquisite stonework, art, and colored history. Our tour guide, an older woman named Doris, was just as funny as she was informative, and by the time we circled back to the gate, I was already thinking about when I'd be able to come back.

It was then that I was hit with the realization that, not long from now, I was going to be limited in what I could and couldn't do. Not just during pregnancy but after the baby was born, too. As much as I wanted to come back and check out the headstones of authors and killers alike, would I be able to, when I was knee-deep in diapers and baby bottles? And even after the baby was older, what if he or she didn't like this kind of thing? What if cemeteries and history was boring to my child, and I was stuck in a purgatory of animated movies and play dates?

My insides twisted at the thought, and I found it funny that I had been so sure about having the baby, while also still being so uncertain of how I'd handle life as a mother.

"You okay?" Goose asked on the way to our respective cars.

"Oh, yeah, I'm swell. Just thinking about how my life is gonna end once I get this kid out of me."

He laughed, nodding. "Yeah, it kinda will for a while. And you don't get to do the same things you used to do as often. But you also get to do the really fun stuff you couldn't do before without looking like a weirdo."

I snorted. "Oh, yeah? Like what?"

"Like," he drawled, shrugging, "Sesame Place. Or those hands-on children's museums."

Humming thoughtfully, I nodded. "I do love a good hands-on museum. And I haven't been to Sesame Place since *I* was a toddler."

"See? Having a kid is the best thing that ever happened to me. She put things into perspective and really made my life better."

"Well, I hope I can someday say the same for myself," I muttered, searching for a twinge of hope as my stomach continued to twist with trepidation.

"You will," he replied, and it sounded like a promise.

We reached my little red sedan in the parking lot, and I said, "This is me."

It was meant to be the moment in which we parted with a vow that we would see each other soon, and yet, I didn't climb in and he didn't walk away. The night hung imbalanced on the uncertainty of this second, not knowing where exactly it would fall, until Goose looked up to the starry sky and shrugged his broad shoulders.

"So, you wanna grab somethin' to eat?"

"Yeah," I said with a smile and a sigh of relief. "I do."

***

Horsefeathers was an old, historic pub and restaurant with dark woodwork and cool memorabilia everywhere you looked. Just a walk to and from the women's room was an interesting journey, full of pictures and encased knickknacks, and when I returned to our booth, Goose laughed and asked if I'd gotten lost.

"Sorry," I said, sliding onto the bench seat. "I was checking out this old typewriter near the bathroom."

He nodded, never taking his eyes off me, even though the menu was open in his hands. "How long have you been writing?"

Laying a napkin over my lap, I replied, "Since I could hold a pencil."

"So, you've always known that's what you wanted to do?"

"Pretty much." Then, I rolled my eyes, as I pulled a pack of Saltines from my bag, and added, "Well, okay, I went through a rebellious phase when I was a teen and refused to write anything. But otherwise, it's all I've ever wanted to do."

His eyes lit with stifled jubilation. "Wow. Your parents must've had their hands full with you."

"Hey!" I smirked, throwing a cracker at him from across the table. "You don't get it. Since I was a little kid, I was told by everyone that I would grow up to be a writer. I felt pressured into it, and not just by everybody else, but myself, too. I felt like I *needed* to write, like it was no different than eating or breathing, and it drove me crazy that I didn't have a choice in the matter."

Once upon a time, I had explained my insatiable craving for the written word to Brendan. He had snickered and brushed it away with a pat on the knee like I was nothing more than a rambling little girl. That had been the cornerstone in his feelings toward what I do with my life, and it was also why I never spoke to him much about it. Now, I waited for a similar reaction from

Goose, bracing myself for that feeling of being small and stupid.

But he never snickered or rolled his eyes. Instead, he nodded and folded his arms on the table.

"I don't have a passion like that," he explained. "But I get it, the constant drive to do something. Like your life depends on it."

"Sometimes, if I haven't written for a while, all of that pent-up creativity in my head drives me crazy and I get really cranky."

He lifted a corner of his mouth and replied, "Well, whenever you need to let it out, there's always a spot at my bar for you."

I opened my mouth to reply, just as the waiter came around to collect our order. When he asked what we wanted to drink, I expressed how badly I'd love a beer, but ordered a Sprite instead. Goose smiled at the waiter and told him he'd also like a soda.

"Don't not drink on my behalf," I told him, as soon as the waiter walked away. "I might be knocked up, but you're not."

He shook his head. "No, it's okay. I ..." His eyes dropped to the table and his hand scratched at his temple, before he looked back at me and said, "I'm kinda an alcoholic." Then, with another quick shake of his head, he added, "Well, I *was*. I haven't had a drink in a really long time, but ... still."

My jaw dropped at his confession. "Oh, shit," I blurted, then shook my head, quickly collecting my words for a more appropriate sentiment. "I had no idea, I'm sorry."

One of his pointer fingers tapped the wooden table as he replied, "Don't be. It's just one of those things I'm hiding."

"But … you own a bar," I mentioned, narrowing my eyes suspiciously.

He chuckled softly. "Yeah, I know."

"You're an anomaly."

"I guess I can't keep you in the dark on this, huh."

I laughed incredulously. "Well, I mean, you kinda dropped a bomb on me here."

Sighing, he shifted in his seat. "Okay, so, after 9/11, I was really mad at, you know, everything, and I felt like I just needed to do something. I didn't have a whole lot going for me at the time, so I enlisted in the Army. I saw some shit, came home, and started drinking."

He was rushing his words and clearly offering the abridged version of his story. My lungs tightened, as I held in the words I was desperate to say and the questions I wanted so badly to ask. But I'd always known he was right when he said we're all hiding something, so I decided to be patient, knowing his truth would be worth the wait when he was ready.

"That was my thing," he went on, his voice rough and quiet. "I was good at it. But it wasn't so good to me. So, when my ex got pregnant, she threatened to never let me see my kid if I didn't get my crap together. And asking me to do that was like asking me to cut off my own arm, because I really needed that shit. But when I thought about it, I found I needed my kid more, so off to rehab I went."

"And so, you bought a bar, to stay close to your own demon?" I guessed.

He lifted his eyes to mine and shrugged. "Like I said, it's all I was really good at."

"Well," I sighed, "I, for one, would be lost without your drinks. And those freakin' wings, man! Oh, my God, they're *incredible*."

"I know it," he nodded. "The sauce was my mom's recipe. She was from New Orleans and worked at a restaurant down there when she met my dad."

I was convinced, as I propped my chin in the palm of my hand, that I could listen to him talk about his life forever, without ever getting sick of the sound of his voice. And I knew I would do anything I could to keep the conversation moving.

"You were born in Louisiana?"

He shook his head. "Nah. My dad brought Mom up north a week after meeting her. They were married two months later and my big brother was born seven months after that." His chuckle rumbled from somewhere deep inside, and as usual, I laughed with him.

"And they lived happily ever after," I concluded, and my soul plummeted when he shook his head.

"Mom died a while back."

My lips parted in a silent gasp. "I'm so sorry."

He offered a melancholy smile and said, "Me, too."

As I thought about how life isn't as wonderful as the love stories I wrote, the waiter came with our glasses of Sprite and a promise that our food would be out in a few minutes. After he walked away, Goose raised his soda to me and tipped his head.

"To unexpected friendship."

A prominent ache ailed my heart at the declaration of being friends. I knew I had liked him and knew there was an attraction, but I hadn't considered I'd ever be disappointed at the notion that friends was all we could ever be. But he had a girlfriend, and I had Brendan, for whatever it was worth, and nothing more than friendship would be found between Goose and me.

But it's better than nothing at all, I thought, as I raised my glass to him.

"To unexpected friendship."

Chapter Ten

The story wasn't coming to me the way I had wanted it to. My characters weren't behaving, and the words weren't flowing. A distraction was needed, so I glanced at my friend behind the bar and asked, "Why do people call you Goose?"

He lifted his gaze from the pina colada he was making for a Lynyrd Skynyrd loving sorority girl and glared at me. The way he looked at me, with put-on contention, pushed me nearly to the brink of giggling.

"You already know too much," he growled, before returning his attention to the glass in his hand.

"Okay, well, can I guess?"

Snorting, he shook his head. "Go right ahead. Doesn't mean I have to tell you."

Popping a boneless wing into my mouth and then wiping my hands on jeans that were just a little too tight, I said, "Okay. I gotta make this good. Did you grow up on a farm where your job was to clean up the goose poop?"

"Nope."

He turned from me to hand the girl her drink. She left him two dollars as a tip and he sighed, stuffing the money into his pocket. "Fuckin' song brings in the customers but they're cheap as hell."

"Maybe different music would bring in a wealthier crowd with a greater respect for the working man."

"Oh, yeah?" He dried the condensation from his fingers with a towel. "Like what?"

"Like, um ..." I tapped my fingers together, studying the smoky veins running through a glass pendant light. "Josh Groban."

He froze, with a look of horror plastered on his face. "Josh Groban?"

"Yeah," I replied, nodding. "Or maybe, hmm … Andrea Bocelli."

"Jesus, Kenny. I'm lookin' for rich, not my freakin' grandma."

Shrugging, I popped another wing in and said, "Just trying to help you out."

He grumbled his thanks and chuckled, wiping the bar down, as I checked the clock on the wall. I had a doctor's appointment that evening and still wanted to jump in the shower before heading uptown, and I was running out of time.

Sliding off the stool and grabbing my sweatshirt, I said, "When you're sick and blow your nose, you honk like a goose."

He laughed. "Nope. Thank God."

"Once upon a time, you slipped in goose shit and got it all over your clothes."

"Nope."

After I pulled my sweatshirt on, I pointed at him and said, "I'll figure this out eventually."

"How will you know if I never tell you?"

"You will."

He waved his hand toward the door. "Get the hell out of here, before you're late."

"Fine. I'll see you soon and I'll be back with more guesses."

With a laugh, he turned and waved over his shoulder. "Bye, Kenny."

"Bye, Goose. Don't miss me too much."

"Don't worry; I won't."

I headed for the door but before I could push through, I glanced over my shoulder to catch his eye. He smiled then, and I smiled back, knowing that he would, in fact, miss me. And I would miss him, too.

I always did.

***

"Do you want to come to the doctor with me?" I asked Brendan, as I got ready to take my shower.

"You know I have stuff to do at home," he muttered halfheartedly, sprawled on the bed, with his attention pinned to his phone.

His attention was *always* on his phone.

"You could go home afterward."

His eyes flicked across to shoot me an exhausted glower. "Kendo, I don't have time to sit around while the doctor does whatever to you. Just tell me what she says, okay? I mean, I'm sure it's going to be the same crap she always tells you, anyway."

I sighed to cover the sting of hurt, knowing just how uninvested he was in my part of the pregnancy. He cared about the baby, I genuinely believed that, but he never thought much of what kind of work went into growing and nourishing said baby before it was born. He never seemed to think about the toll it was taking on me and my life. I just assumed most men would be like that, and when I thought about it, as I stepped into the bathroom and closed the door, I couldn't say I blamed them.

Some women seem to live for being pregnant. They love every single moment of it and revel in the miracle of growing life. I just couldn't say I was one of them. Seeing the subtle ways my body had changed so far, made me greatly appreciate what I and other women were capable of doing, and I felt lucky to have the experience. But that didn't mean I had to enjoy it, and I wasn't.

I turned the water on and stepped under the pelting spray. Since around the eight-week mark, I had found my tolerance for heat in any degree to be minimal, and so my showers had become brief. I knew it was only a matter of time before I was bathing in freezing temperatures, but I hadn't given in yet.

Just minutes into the shower, though, I was struck with an unbearable feeling of lightheadedness and vertigo. My body swayed and I had to reach out and press my hands against the slippery, tiled wall. Nausea rolled over me in unrelenting waves and I heaved with my forehead against the wall, as my mind threatened to lose consciousness and the light began to dim around my tunnel of vision.

Knowing I would hurt myself if I passed out in the shower, I quickly, albeit carefully, turned the water off and stepped out, using the wall to keep steady. I sank to the floor with my back against cold tile and forced deep breaths in and out of my lungs.

My heart was racing and rattled wildly within its cage. I reached up to the sink, to find my watch—a step counter that also tracked my heart rate—and strapped it on. Then, when it finally registered how quickly my heart was beating, the number alone nearly made me pass out.

154.

It was too fast. Not unusually fast for a panic-inducing situation, like the first time I ever published one of my books, but much too fast for something as mundane as a shower. I knew that it was common during pregnancy for your heart to beat a little faster, even a little harder, but something wasn't right and I knew it.

"Brendan!" I called, terrified, as I sat naked on the bathroom floor. When he didn't reply, I called for him again.

"What?!" he answered, clearly agitated, and I wondered what was so damn important on his phone.

"I need you to come here!"

I listened as he groaned from the bedroom, and then, heavy footsteps plodded across the floor to the bathroom. He opened the door and stared down at me, with an infuriating amount of annoyance in his eyes.

"What the hell are you doing?"

"I almost passed out," I explained, sounding breathless to my ears and knowing I needed to calm down. "My heart rate is out of control. My … my heart is beating so hard and fast; I feel like it's going to explode. I-I don't know what to do. I'm so—"

His features softened just a little, as he leaned against the doorframe. "Kendo, you're probably just having a panic attack. Try to take a few deep breaths, and you'll be fine."

Anger was the last thing I should have been feeling when I was already in such a fragile state, but anger is exactly what I felt at the condescending tone of his voice.

"I am not having a panic attack," I insisted. "I was just showering, and all of a sudden, I thought I was going to—"

"Okay, okay," he said, crouching down to take my hand in his. "But you're going to the doctor, right? So, talk to her about it. I'm sure she can do more for you than I can, anyway."

I blinked at him, as tears pricked the backs of my eyes. I had expected more from him. I had expected him to comfort me. To help more with what he could and just be there for me, while my body ran me through trials I never would've expected. But I told him not to worry about it, that I was sure I'd be fine, and sent him out of the room. Then, as I listened to him leave the apartment, with instructions to call him whenever I got the chance, I found the strength to stand and got ready for my appointment.

***

"Well, Kendall, your baby seems just fine," Dr. Albrecht said, smiling as she pulled my shirt back over my belly. "Was there anything you wanted to talk about?"

I took that invitation to explain exactly what had happened during my shower earlier that evening. She listened intently, and when I was finished, she leaned her hip against the counter in the small exam room.

"So, your heart rate and blood pressure today were similar to what they were when you first started seeing me," she said, folding her hands over her white coat-covered stomach. "I'm inclined to think that you're fine and that this was only a fluke, but with pregnancy, you never really know. So, I'm going to give you a recommendation to see a cardiologist, where they'll run some tests to rule out any potential issues. Okay?"

That word and recommendation was immediately terrifying, as it reminded me of the heart attack that nearly killed my father fifteen years ago. My palms began to sweat, as my racing mind insisted that healthy thirty-five-year-olds don't go to cardiologists and that healthy pregnancies don't require EKGs and echocardiograms. But there I was, accepting a referral and promising to make an appointment as soon as possible.

Then, I left the office with a lump in my throat and struggled not to cry. Because I loved my little bean and the thought of being a mommy, but I really, really wasn't loving being pregnant. And I especially didn't love going through it with a boyfriend who didn't seem to care much about what was happening to me.

Chapter Eleven

"If you need me to go, I'll cancel my appointment," Mom said.

I could hear the fear in her voice, and I knew that, if I had asked, she'd tell me she was worrying herself sick over my heart. Of course, I was worried, too, and I had spent the nights since my appointment with Dr. Albrecht, panicking over what could be wrong with me. But I didn't want my mom to stress, and I didn't want her to put my health over her own. Even if she was just going for a routine exam with her family doctor.

"No, don't do that," I insisted. "It's going to be fine and if I hear anything, you know I'll let you know. But there's no reason to get freaked out over it right now. Even the gynecologist isn't worried about it. This is just a precaution."

"Are you sure?" she asked, unconvinced. "Is Brendan going with you?"

I swallowed and glanced toward the bedroom, where Brendan was taking a nap. "No, he can't. He's got—"

"I'll reschedule."

"No, no, don't do that." I tipped my head back to look up at the ceiling of my tiny apartment and sighed. "I'll be fine. Don't worry about me. Seriously."

She relented with the promise that she would always worry about me, and made me swear I'd call her right after my visit with the cardiologist. When we hung up, I glanced at my watch and felt the knots in my gut tighten.

It was nine o'clock.

There were thirteen hours until my appointment.

I had lied to my mom when I said that I was fine and not at all worried, but the truth was I was terrified of what the doctor would find after he ran his tests. I didn't want to face the news alone, good or bad, but I wasn't left with many options. My parents were busy and I didn't want to impose on their schedules, while Brendan was busy with a meeting at work.

I scrolled through my phone, looking through my list of contacts and realized how few people I actually knew, now that I needed someone to be there for me. There were names of professional people I knew in the author world. A few random friends I hadn't talked to in years and a couple relatives who lived across the country. With a sigh, I wondered why I hadn't taken more time to make friends in the year I'd been living in the city, knowing it was due to being too introverted for my own good. Now, it seemed very daunting and very much like I'd be facing another doctor's appointment by myself. But when I passed Goose's name, I hesitated.

We didn't know each other all that well, and we hadn't known each other for all that long. Yet, I wondered what he'd say if I asked. So, I called.

"Goose here."

I sniffled a soft laugh at the sound of "Sweet Home Alabama" in the background.

"Hey," I said. "It's Kenny."

"Kenny! What's happenin', girlfriend?"

"Not a whole lot. You working?"

"You know it."

"Cool."

Dammit, I felt so silly, calling this guy I barely knew, to ask him if he'd hold my hand at the doctor. Sure, we had now hung out outside of the bar, but it had just been a tour through a cemetery and a casual dinner. It wasn't a big deal, and was very much unlike a trip to the cardiologist. Anxiety jounced my legs beneath the table, as my fingers tangled up in my hair. I needed to get on with it and to let him get back to work, but the words had glued themselves to my tongue and refused to come out.

"Hey, you okay?" he asked quietly.

"Yeah, um ..." I pulled in a deep, cleansing breath, realizing it was now or never. "Okay, so this is really stupid and kinda embarrassing, but I have this doctor's appointment tomorrow. And my mom could come out, but I really don't want to make her worry for potentially no reason, so I was—"

"Yeah, I'll go with you."

My jaw flapped a couple times before I managed to say, "I-I-I haven't even told you what time it is or, or anything—"

"It's fine. Whatever you need, I'm there. It's all good."

Emotions ran rampant as the tears sprung to my eyes. "Are you sure?"

"Kenny, seriously. It's not a big deal. Just text me the time and place and I'll meet you there."

And so, with a smile on my face and a gentle warmth tickling at my heart, I did.

***

"You didn't tell me you had something going on with your *heart*," he hissed, as we found a couple of seats in the waiting room.

"Because I don't know that there is," I reminded him. "That's why I'm here, to find out."

"Jesus Christ. I can see why you wouldn't want your mom here," he muttered, wiping a hand over his beard. "And this is because you're pregnant?"

I shrugged, trying to make myself comfortable in the chair. "I guess. I mean, my doctor didn't act like it was uncommon or anything."

"Krystal didn't have to go to a freakin' cardiologist." It was the first time I had ever heard her name, and when I turned to him with a questioning glance, he confirmed, "My ex-wife."

"Well, all pregnancies are different, I guess," I replied, repeating the same thing I had read countless times on Doctor Google.

"I guess," he muttered.

Goose slouched deeper into his chair and started chewing on his thumbnail, while I stared ahead at the door and waited for a nurse to emerge and lead me to the exam room. My fingers fidgeted with the drawstring on my sweatshirt, fraying the exposed threads just a little more. When the door finally opened, both Goose and I sat up straighter, stiff as boards, and waited to hear her call my name.

"Kendall Wright?"

"Right here," I said, standing abruptly and dropping my open purse from my lap, spilling its contents all over the floor at my feet. "Goddammit," I muttered, as my face grew hot with embarrassment and anxiety at the sight of the mess I'd just made.

"I got it," Goose said quietly, bending to collect my things.

"All good?" the nurse asked, smiling as though she hadn't just seen the used tissues and candy wrappers that usually dwelled in the bottom of my bag.

"Yeah," I muttered, struggling to find my own smile.

"All righty! Just follow me," she replied, tucking her clipboard under her arm. When she saw Goose stand beside me, with my purse in his hands, she added, "Your husband can come, too."

Panic reached down my throat and grabbed my tongue as I stammered, "O-Oh, he's not, we're not married. He's just a, uh ..." I turned to look up at Goose and saw the expectant raise of his brows. I smiled nervously in a way that strained my cheeks and said, "He's just my friend."

"Well, then your *friend* can come, too," she corrected with a smile.

We followed her through the door and down a hallway, where she pushed a door open. "Okie dokie,

Kendall, you can sit on the table, while your friend takes a seat over there."

So, we did as we were told and I sat on the paper-covered exam table, while Goose made himself comfortable on a chair in the corner. He held my purse in his lap, like it was the most natural thing in the world and asked if I wanted him to hold my sweatshirt, too.

"No, it's okay," I told him, only to be interrupted by the nurse.

"Well, actually, I'm going to need you to take that off, so I can attach these leads and get your EKG done," the nurse instructed in a friendly, bubbly tone.

I was only wearing a tank top beneath my hoodie, and the thought of taking it off felt no better than getting naked in front of this guy who had only just recently become a friend. But I did as I was told, moving slowly as my cheeks rapidly heated, before handing the sweatshirt to Goose's waiting hands, not quite meeting his eye.

The nurse instructed me to lay back and apologetically asked that I also pull my top up, over my bra. With some hesitation, I began to do what she asked, when Goose told me he'd turn around, to give me some privacy, and I wondered if it was more for his or my benefit. Then the nurse stuck sticky electrodes to various parts of my body and attached the leads, before watching the monitor for a few seconds that felt more equivalent to hours.

"Okay, you're all done," she announced, quickly removing the electrodes with the leads still attached. As I righted myself, she exited the room, leaving us with the instructions to wait for the doctor.

As Goose handed me my sweatshirt, he asked, "How you doing?"

"I'm okay, I guess," I muttered in reply, pulling the shirt over my head, as I wondered how okay I really would be if he hadn't been there.

"She didn't seem too worried," he offered.

I shrugged and smoothed a hand over my messy ponytail, then said, "Yeah, but she's not the doctor."

Goose nodded while grunting an agreeable sound, and then, we waited for an anxious few minutes before the doctor finally came into the room.

"It's nice to meet you, Kendall," he said, wearing a bright smile and a very obvious hairpiece.

He then asked me a slew of questions about my situation and the incident with my heart rate. He nodded as I spoke and reiterated everything I had told my gynecologist just days before. From the corner of my eye, I watched the expression on Goose's face. His furrowed brow, the tight clench of his jaw. There was also a type of concern in his eyes that felt like something akin to territorial, and I tried not to dwell too much on how good that felt, to know that someone, anyone, wanted me to be okay. Even if that someone wasn't the man I was in a relationship with.

"So, first of all, there's a very good chance that everything is just fine. But just to be sure, here's what we're gonna do," the doctor said, brushing the floppy hair from his eyes before folding his hands in his lap. "You're going to head down the hall and go for an echocardiogram. And then, I want you to wear a Holster monitor for twenty-four hours."

"Oh, that sounds like fun," I mumbled sardonically, before worrying my bottom lip between my teeth.

"You're going to be just fine," he assured me.

Then, as he leaned forward to pat my knee, his hair slid down his forehead a little, and I was so grateful to have something to giggle about as Goose and I headed down the hallway to the dark ultrasound room.

"Please promise me that, if we know each other in like, fifty years, you won't let me do that to myself," he muttered beneath his breath.

"Deal," I giggled and shook his hand, before entering the room.

Goose waited outside, while I completely undressed the upper half of my body and laid on a padded table. The technician, a sweet lady, apologetically pressed a probe to my chest and throat, taking pictures as she went, and I assured her that I didn't mind.

"This is the most action I've gotten in months," I joked, and she laughed in a quiet way that said she didn't know if I was serious or not.

Then, when the test was concluded, we headed to another part of the building for me to have the Holster monitor attached. By the time we left the cardiology practice, it was two hours later, and I was sporting a new necklace beneath my shirt, with various wires hanging from it. We walked side by side for a few minutes, not saying anything and just allowing the events of the afternoon to absorb, when finally, he spoke.

"You okay?"

I nodded slowly. "Yeah, I'm fine. I think."

"I'm really happy you asked me to come."

Snorting, I rolled my eyes to the skyscrapers. "Oh, yeah. It was a blast." Goose grinned and sighed, looking up to a grey November sky, as I continued, "I mean, really, I can't think of a better way I'd like to spend an afternoon."

Chuckling, he shook his head. "No, I just mean, it's nice that you're comfortable enough with me to want me there. I haven't had that with a lot of people, so … it's just nice."

"Oh," I replied quietly, looking at my hands as I nodded. "Well, thank you. For coming, I mean. I would've been shitting myself if I had been alone."

"You shouldn't *have* to be alone."

I didn't respond, not wanting to open that can of worms, because I knew it would only make me upset. And I knew he was right. But I also knew there was nothing I could do about it. More than that, I didn't want him to believe that I was in a relationship with a horrible man, because while Brendan was brash and consumed by his own business, he wasn't *horrible*. I didn't want Goose to think Brendan didn't support me or this pregnancy at all, because it just wasn't true. Not entirely. And I didn't know why I cared so much about what he thought, but I did. I really did, and maybe that was more horrible than my boyfriend being too busy to attend a doctor's appointment.

"Sorry," Goose finally said, a few moments later.

"For what?"

"I don't know. I just felt like I needed to say it."

I laughed, shaking my head and sending all of those thoughts away. "Nothing to apologize for."

"Okay," he replied with a sigh. "But listen, I don't want you to hesitate to ask if you need someone there. Got it? I can always be there."

"No," I protested, shaking my head. "I don't want you to let my crap get in the middle of whatever you're doing. This was …" I shrugged, blowing out a heavy breath. "I was just really scared. But I won't make a habit of it. My parents can come, or—"

"Stop," he said gently, bumping his arm against mine. "I'm serious, Kenny. None of *my* crap is too important to keep me from being there when you need someone."

Something in the sentiment resounded with me and I tucked it away, knowing I'd use it some day in one of my stories. The man was full of one-liners like that, and what was even better, was that he was always sincere in saying them. He meant every word and I held each one of them close, letting them warm my skin and heart, while knowing that would have to be enough, but knowing it never would be.

Chapter Twelve

I loved Christmas almost as much as Halloween. So, I found myself completely heartbroken, as I realized I wouldn't be able to make it to my parents' house for Christmas Eve dinner. And there was no one to blame for it except my nauseous gut.

Nothing had gone right from the moment I woke up and found Brendan at the foot of the bed, packing his things.

"What are you doing?" I had asked, already acutely aware of the uncomfortable gurgle in my stomach.

He'd looked up, startled to find me awake. "Oh, I didn't tell you?"

"Tell me what?"

"Oh, I guess I forgot to tell you," he muttered, turning to open the closet door. "I'm going upstate to see my family."

Furrowing my brow, I sat up, as anger coalesced with the nausea to force a rolling ache through my gut. "And you didn't think to invite me?"

Heeping his back turned, he sighed. "Come on, Kendo. You and I both know you'd never wanna come see my family for Christmas. You're gonna go out to see your folks, like always, and that's fine, but don't pretend like you'd actually want to come with me."

"What ..." I thrust a hand into my hair, genuinely confused and startled by exhaustion and bitterness in his tone. "But ... you didn't even *ask*. You, you have no idea what I would've said, or, um, we could've split—"

"Kendall." He turned on his heel, exasperation and annoyance in his narrowed eyes. "Don't do this, okay? You're gonna go see your parents and I'm gonna see mine. Now, drop it."

Then, hoisting his bag over his shoulder and without waiting for my reply, he hurried through a hug and a muttered Merry Christmas, before hurrying for the door.

It had left me feeling unsettled and upset. Shouldn't he have wanted to spend the holiday with me? Why wouldn't he have invited me along? Sure, in past years, we had never taken holidays too seriously before and we rarely faced them together as a couple, but shouldn't this year have been different? We were going to be a family soon, so why wouldn't we spend the holidays as one? I tried convincing myself that it was just his way out of habit, but my mind couldn't be fooled that easily.

Shortly after Brendan left, I'd taken a quick shower before starting to pack for the trip home with Mrs. Potter. I had successfully gotten my clothes and Mrs. Potter's things together, but it was when I started to stuff the gifts for my parents into a bag, that the sick feeling in my stomach was kicked into high gear.

The now familiar sensation of lightheadedness came on so strong out of nowhere. My heart rate quickly escalated and nausea continued to gnaw away at my gut.

I begged my body to behave itself, to let me see my parents and not get in the way of Christmas, but no amount of pleading would make it listen.

With sweat dotting my brow, I rushed to the bathroom and violently emptied my stomach in the sink. I stared at my ghostly pale reflection in the mirror and was startled by how terrible I suddenly looked. I had looked fine just after my shower, healthy, with pink cheeks and bright eyes, but now, I appeared sallow and sickly. I remembered the Chinese takeout Brendan and I had for dinner the night before and wondered if that could've been the culprit. It seemed likely, and after deciding that must be what was going on, I trudged my way to bed and flopped onto the mattress. I called my parents and told them I wouldn't be able to make it. Of course, they were disappointed and offered to pick me up. But I reluctantly declined, because as much as I hated to admit it, my bed seemed far more appealing at the moment than spending a night with family and friends. So, they reluctantly made me promise I'd take care of myself and call if anything got worse. Then, with a Merry Christmas and an I love you, I hung up before crying myself to sleep.

***

The next day, Christmas afternoon, I woke up feeling a little better. Even after so many hours of sleep, the vertigo remained but the nausea had thankfully subsided, so I got up to get some water and crackers with Mrs. Potter following at my heels, in search of the breakfast I hadn't yet given her. But when I passed the couch and saw the presents for my parents, the good feeling I had washed away to be replaced by a deep, lonely sadness.

This was my first Christmas away from them, and it felt wrong. I wanted to be home. I wanted to be sitting around the tree with them, opening gifts and eating candy from our stockings. I wasn't supposed to be here, alone, in this apartment that was way too small.

And then, I was angry again.

I was mad at my situation. Mad at how sick I felt, mad at Brendan for abandoning me, at my parents, too. for being so far away, and at myself for ever thinking that leaving home was a good idea. But most of all, I was mad at the little bean in my belly for existing and doing this to me, and then, with that horrible thought, I was mad for being mad.

Mrs. Potter meowed at my feet and nuzzled her face against my ankle.

"At least I have you," I said to her, wallowing in my pity party.

I got up and slogged into the kitchen to pour her some food and get my breakfast of water and crackers. And just as Mrs. Potter was crunching away and I was taking a bottle of water from the fridge, my phone rang.

I had assumed it would be my parents, calling to see how I was doing, but it wasn't and with that now familiar warmth in my chest, I answered.

"Merry Christmas, Kenny."

I found my smile with the sound of his voice. "Merry Christmas, Goose."

"Whatcha doin'?"

"Just, you know," I swallowed at the emotion building in my throat, "hanging out at home."

"What? I thought you were going to your parents' place?"

And with his question, I spilled my guts. Through a torrential downpour of tears, I told him what had happened and why I was now home alone. After a few minutes of chatty blubbering, I stopped and realized that, *oh God*, it was Christmas Day and I was bogarting this guy's time away from his own family. Who the hell was I to ruin his day, just because mine had turned out horribly?

So, I wiped my face with my palm and put on a smile he couldn't see as I told him, "But I'm okay, now. It's just the hormones and ... you know, everything. But I'm fine."

"Kenny ..." I hated the hesitation in his tone and that I had put it there.

I shook my head, wishing I hadn't said anything at all. "Stop. You should get back to your family. I'm sorry."

"Don't be sorry. What's your address?"

"What?"

"You know. Your address. Where you live."

"No," I laughed. "Why do you want to know?"

"I wanna send you something."

I tried to argue, but my attempts were all thwarted by his insistence to have something delivered to the apartment. So, reluctantly, I gave him the address before hanging up the phone and going back to bed with my water and crackers.

***

I was awoken a couple hours later by a knock on my door. Begrudgingly, I pulled myself out of bed, not wanting to deal with strenuous activities like opening the door or talking to people face to face. My robe was never a suitable replacement for my blanket, but as the knocking persisted, I had to throw it on and headed for the door, scowling all the way.

I peered through the peephole and froze, clasping at the worn lapels of my robe with both hands.

Goose was on the other side. Carrying two foil-covered dishes and a pitcher.

It took a moment to talk myself into opening the door. I really didn't want to. Not in an old, dirty, leopard print robe and pajamas with cats wearing Santa hats all over them. And not when my hair or teeth hadn't seen a brush in over twenty-four hours. But what else was I going to do? I couldn't just turn him away or pretend that I hadn't heard the door. He'd come all this way from wherever he came from, and on Christmas, of all days.

So, I unlocked the deadbolt and slowly opened the door a crack.

"Hey," I said quietly, peering through the sliver of space between door and jamb.

"Hey." Goose smiled and lifted both hands bearing gifts. "I brought dinner."

"You didn't have to do that."

"Friendship isn't about doing the things you have to do. Plus, you gotta be starving."

103

It was true; I was. But I still hadn't showered or acquainted myself with my deodorant in some time. And really, when was the last time my floor had seen a vacuum?

"No, no, I'm good," I insisted, putting on a close-lipped smile. "I had crackers, so I'm okay."

Goose laughed, filling the hallway with warmth. "Kenny. I don't care what your apartment looks like, or the fact that you're dressed like you probably own sixty cats. I just walked over here in the snow to bring you dinner, and I *really* have to piss. I promise I won't say anything or stay long. I just wanna use the bathroom and make sure you eat something."

There was no way I could turn him away after that. So, after only another moment of hesitation, I nodded and opened the door to invite him in. He stepped inside and seemed to make himself at home right away, walking past me and into the kitchen. I followed and watched as he placed the dishes and pitcher on the counter.

He turned to face me and asked, "Where's your bathroom?"

I pointed to the closed door adjacent to the living room and said, "Close the door when you're done. My cat likes to drink out of the toilet."

His lips spread in an amused grin. "How the hell did I know you have a cat?"

Rolling my eyes, I muttered, "You said sixty."

"One, sixty," he shrugged, still wearing a grin, "still a cat lady."

Watching him walk through the living room to the bathroom door, I silently marveled at the size of him. My shoebox apartment was dwarfed to the size of a matchbox in a nearly comical way and it hit harder than ever before how badly I needed a bigger space. Babies might not take up a lot of room themselves, but their things certainly do.

He returned to the kitchen moments later, sighing with relief. "You have no idea how badly I needed to pee," he groused, shaking his head as he peeled the foil off the plates and revealed two identical dishes of food.

I couldn't help but gawk. Ham, mashed potatoes, green beans, asparagus, and sweet potatoes had been loaded high and topped with a big, flaky biscuit. My mouth watered at the sight, making me quickly realize how hungry I truly was. Goose popped the dishes into the microwave, and proceeded to pour my favorite pink drink into glasses he found in one of my cabinets.

It took a lot to impress me and make me swoon. I was never easily excited, and I didn't quickly fall for gestures, grand or otherwise. But this meal and the fact that he had walked in the cold to bring it to me, made my heart lunge for my tongue, leaving me speechless and hoping this wasn't intended as anything more than a friend caring for a friend.

Goose brought the plates, then the glasses, to the table, before gesturing toward a chair. "Sit," he commanded gently, and I complied.

"This looks great."

"Thanks," he said, then laughed. "I didn't make it."

Laughing, I dug into the mountain of mashed potatoes. "Oh, no?"

He shook his head, biting into the biscuit. "My dad cooks for the holidays."

The weightlessness of my heart fell. "You were at your *dad's*?"

"Yeah," he replied, nodding as if he hadn't just ruined his day with family for me. "With my brother and his family."

Guilt filled my stomach cavity as I slowed my chewing. "You didn't have to leave for me. Seriously. I would've been okay."

He shook his head. "Are you kidding me? You saved me from the inevitable fight between my dad and brother."

Frowning, I muttered, "Well, I know I'd love to be home with my family right now."

"Don't get me wrong," he said, poking at his food with his fork, "I love them to death. But I don't love listening to arguments over politics or listening to my sister-in-law yell at their kids because they fight all the time."

"What about your girlfriend?"

Pursing his lips, Goose hesitated before answering, "She's working today."

"On Christmas?"

He sighed and shifted his gaze to the lamp hanging above the table. "She's been working on this TV show, which is great for her, but our relationship has kinda been put on the back burner because of it."

"What kind of TV show?" I asked, vaguely remembering that time I'd first seen her at the bar and her mention of a producer.

"Um, well," he hesitated for a moment, then said, "she's a psychic medium. So, she passes along messages from the dead to their loved ones and can read little bits and pieces of the future."

My jaw dropped. "Wow," I uttered. "Brendan doesn't do anything cool like that. He works for a law firm on the upper East side, doing a bunch of boring crap I know nothing about. So, he never talks about it, and I never ask."

Goose chuckled. "Tracey doesn't tell me much about what she does either," he replied, shrugging. "A job is a job, I guess."

Then, I asked, "Do you guys live together?"

He shook his head as he popped a piece of ham into his mouth. "We haven't been together for that long, and just as things started to get somewhere, where maybe we would've talked about moving in together, she landed this deal with a network." He shrugged as he swallowed. "And the rest is history."

Then, he asked, "What about you? What's the deal with you and Baby Daddy?"

Laughing, I shook my head and leaned back in my chair. "I don't even know. One day, things are great and he's really supportive and I start to think there's hope for our future. But then, the next, he's making plans to see his family for Christmas without mentioning anything to me. So ... take that for what it is, I guess."

Squeezing his eyes shut, he dropped his fork and said, "Whoa, hold up a second." He opened his eyes and leveled me with a serious glare. "You told me he was busy and couldn't be with you. You didn't tell me he was celebrating Christmas without you."

"Well, I mean, he *is* busy," I reasoned loosely.

"Kenny." He slowly shook his head, never releasing the hold he had on my eyes. "How can you be okay with this shit? You're *here*, sick and not able to see your own family, because you're carrying *his* baby. And he's not here. There's nothing even remotely okay about that."

I knew he was right. I couldn't deny that everything happening in my life, regarding my relationship, was wrong, and I hated that. I hated feeling like there was nothing I could do about it, given the predicament I was in, and how alone I was in that. But I refused to talk about it or let myself villainize the father of my unborn baby, not out loud. Instead I ate the rest of my delicious dinner in silence, while sipping on my favorite drink, and so did Goose.

When we were both finished, I took our plates and glasses and carried them to the kitchen, while Goose flopped onto the couch and patted the seat beside him.

"I need to wash—"

"They can wait. Right now, what you need, is to just relax. So, we're gonna sit down and watch a movie."

So, without dispute, I sat beside him and gave him the remote. He found *Home Alone*, a movie I hadn't seen since I was a kid, and we watched it, laughing together and enjoying the company of someone who wasn't too busy for us. After a while, I found that he had been right.

It was exactly what I needed.

Or maybe, I silently considered, *all I really needed, was him.*

Chapter Thirteen

The New Year came and went, as did the first trimester, and I found that Doctor Google had lied. Every article I had read about pregnancy assured me that the second would be so much better, so much easier, but I was still waiting for that to finally happen.

Given how horrible I continued to feel, I wasn't sure it ever would.

Brendan never apologized for leaving me at Christmas, but I also never brought it up again. Just the thought of arguing with him, while feeling so run down and ill, was exhausting. Plus, after he'd come back after a few days away, things between us immediately went back to being our type of normal. So, I had tucked it away, to that part of my brain where things go to be forgotten but rarely forgiven.

"What do you wanna have for dinner tonight?" he asked, just minutes after walking through the door after work.

I shrugged from the couch. "I don't really know."

"Kendo," he drawled in a playful tone that reminded me of why I had moved to the city in the first place. That hopeful girl still wanted to hear that voice and tone more often. "You know you're craving *something.* You always are."

I rolled my eyes, just as playfully, and huffed. "And you know exactly what it is I'm craving, so why even ask?"

"Okay, so lots and lots of boneless wings, then. You got it."

In the past couple of weeks, my desire for the wings at Goose's bar had gone from being a general liking, to an insatiable need. I found that, while any wings usually sufficed, it was really his that I craved, and so, we found ourselves regularly putting in orders.

"Want me to pick them up?"

I pressed my lips firmly together, imagining what it would be like for Brendan to finally meet Goose. It wasn't as if I'd hidden my friendship from him, and it wasn't as if Brendan had ever shown any inclination of having a problem with it. But I did wonder how that would change if he knew that Goose wasn't a four-foot-tall ogre but really an unreasonably handsome Viking of a man.

"Nah," I said, shaking my head. "I could use a walk."

He studied me and I studied him back. He wasn't unattractive, not at all, and he could wear a suit well. In the years we had been together, he'd aged a little bit. The lines around his eyes were a little deeper now and the hair at his temples was a little greyer. But he wore the age well, especially now, standing there in his crisp, white shirt and loosened tie. The scruff on his face was just a tiny bit longer than it was this morning, and I couldn't help but imagine how good it would feel on the inside of my thighs.

"Why are you looking at me like that?" he asked, teasing me with his tone, trying to pull the words, the requests and demands, out of me.

"No reason," I replied, now thinking of what it'd be like to not see my boyfriend there but a tall, reddish-blond Viking instead. How he would look all dressed up with a tie, so precariously undone and begging to be tugged off.

I turned away and gave my head a little shake. Sending the images away and wishing they'd never come back, while also hoping they'd invade my sleep later on, when I lacked the control to make them leave.

"Oh, no?" Brendan took the few steps to reach the couch, where he knelt at my feet. "So, if I took these pants off, I wouldn't find you soaking wet?"

I couldn't lie; he would. So, I simply said, "Why don't you find out?" in a voice so coy, I knew he wouldn't say no.

And just as I suspected, he didn't. He pulled my pants and underwear off in one swift tug, spread my legs, and violated my body in wonderful ways with his experienced tongue. I got off, more than once, and wanting to return the favor, I instructed him to sit down and take his turn.

But Brendan had other ideas, as he pulled himself out of his pants and pushed his way between my thighs. I hooked my ankles around his hips and met him thrust for thrust, certain it had never been so good before, while unable to stop wondering about how much better it might be with someone else.

When we were both finished and the guilt of thinking about another man burned my cheeks, hot and bright pink, he collapsed beside me on the couch and brushed the hair from my eyes.

"You should move in with me."

The command came out of nowhere and I faltered in my reaction. What I had with Brendan was fickle and I never seemed to know exactly where it was headed. But I could handle that, just so long as I knew he was ultimately there for the baby and me. But now, this invitation seemed to be handed to me out of nowhere, and I wasn't quite sure of what to do with it.

"What?" I pulled my pants on. "You want me to move in with you?"

He laughed. "Isn't that what I said?"

"But ..." I dropped my hands to my lap. "Why?"

It was the wrong thing to say. I knew that the second that little word was out of my mouth. But I couldn't help that it was unexpected, or that I wanted to know why he suddenly wanted to take this enormous step, when just two weeks ago, he didn't even want to spend Christmas with me.

Brendan reeled back and gawked at me. "*Why?*" he repeated, incredulous.

"Well, I mean, it's just that, I was never really sure where we were headed, and—"

"Where we were *headed?* Kendall, we're having a fucking baby, for Christ's sake!"

The way he said it—*fucking baby*—made me wince, as if he'd just slapped me across the face. "I know that, but I just ..." I sighed, thrusting my fingers into my hair. "I don't know. I don't know how to put it into words."

It was a lie, but I couldn't say what I truly felt, or what I was truly wondering. Not without losing him entirely and putting my child's future at risk. I couldn't be sure what he'd do, or what sort of custody battle he'd put me through. And why it had never occurred to me before that I was scared of him, I have no idea, but I was. I was actually scared, and I knew how terrible that was, while also not knowing how to fix it.

Brendan huffed an agitated sigh. "Then, we'll just say you're hormonal and don't know what you're saying."

Swallowing at the instantaneous desire to wrap my hands around his neck, I forced a smile and wondered how he could be so handsome and sexy one second and such a chauvinistic asshole the next.

"Just think about it, okay?" He leaned forward and kissed my cheek. "You know, if you can handle it, with all those hormones in your head going crazy."

***

I took my time walking to Goose's bar. It was chilly and the wind bit angrily at my nose and ears, but the cold didn't bother me.

It was the decision I now needed to make, whether I should leave my apartment or not. Did I really think I could live with Brendan? It felt right for the baby, to have both of his or her parents living under the same

114

roof. But how healthy of a living arrangement would that really be? Our hot-and-cold dynamic certainly wasn't healthy, and despite our efforts, it didn't seem to be getting any better, even for the sake of the baby. I considered that maybe things would improve if we were together full-time, but what if they didn't?

When I reached The Thirsty Goose, I noticed the tall Viking right away as he was slinging drinks behind the bar. He waved the moment he saw me and headed for the kitchen to grab my wings.

Tracey was there, too, with her laptop. She smiled at me with the eyes of someone who knew too much about everything and everyone. I wondered what she knew about me and if she could tell that I had thought about her boyfriend while having sex on the couch with mine, and with that reminder, I turned my eyes from hers.

"Hey," she greeted. "How are you feeling?"

"Awful," I laughed, instinctively laying a hand over my stomach.

"How far along are you now?"

"Nineteen weeks."

"Ah," she nodded slowly, keeping her eyes on me, "it'll get worse before it gets better. But you're going to be okay."

I began to open my mouth to reply when Goose returned with my order. He grinned and I tried to keep my cheeks from flushing and my heart from racing, but it was useless.

When I handed him the cash, he shook his head. "I don't want your money," he said, waving it away.

"It's not mine," I chided. "It's Brendan's."

"Oh, well!" He snatched the money away, grasping it tightly in his hand. "That's a different story!"

Laughing, I rolled my eyes and turned from the bar. "I'll see you later. It was nice seeing you again, Tracey."

"You, too," she said. "Oh! And Kenny?"

"Yeah?"

"You're going to say yes. To make things easier right now."

I knew she was a psychic medium. I understand that she knew things that the rest of us don't, but this was the first time I'd been on the receiving end of a reading and it left me stunned and shaking. I couldn't even reply in a coherent sentence, so I just smiled and offered a little wave before hurrying out and walking home.

Her words continued to leave me rattled, as Brendan and I ate dinner. He addressed me with irritation and a shortness in his tone, and the longer it continued, the more I was convinced that I deserved it. He was a good man. Maybe he wasn't perfect, but who was? I certainly wasn't, remembering every moment I thought about another man while I was still with him, and how could I criticize Brendan for being the way he was, when I was like this?

So, to stop his attitude, to make things easier, and to make myself feel better for my own shortcomings, I said yes.

Chapter Fourteen

"**H**ow's the sauce today?"

Goose shot an expectant look in my direction as I stuffed an entire wing in my mouth. He laughed at my expense and muttered something about all semblance of decency flying out the window.

"Shut up," I grumbled in gest. "There is nothing decent about pregnancy."

"Oh, come on. It's the miracle of life."

"Yeah," I snorted. "Leaky boobs, weak bladder, and the inability to smell cat food without gagging. What a miracle."

The side of his mouth lifted in a heart-stopping smile. "Yeah, but all of that shit is temporary—"

"My mom *still* blames me for her inability to go an hour without needing to pee!"

"Okay, so maybe some of it has some lasting effects. But what I was saying is, *most* of it is temporary. And then you get this awesome little person out of it." He shrugged, grabbing a glass and wiping it down with a rag. "It's not a bad deal. At least that's how I feel, anyway."

I sighed, laying a hand over my stomach. "Yeah, I guess maybe you're right."

Then, I stabbed another wing with my fork before raising it to my Viking friend. "And the sauce is excellent today, by the way. But you should know I'd probably say that even if it wasn't. I could live off of these fucking things."

"You kinda already do."

"Take that as a compliment," I said, before popping the wing in and groaning in a way that was undoubtedly indecent.

Turning away from me, Goose cleared his throat and asked, "So, uh, how's the move going?"

It had only been a week since I'd agreed to moving in with Brendan, and you would think I'd have been eager to get my stuff over there and out of my tiny, shoebox apartment. If only just to get it over with and have one less thing to worry about. But the reality was, I hadn't started packing. I hadn't even thought about it.

"Mm, I have so much on my mind," I explained weakly. "And there's a lot I really can't do at this point."

"He's not helping?"

I sighed and diverted my eyes. "He's really busy. I mean, with work and—"

"Didn't *he* ask *you* to move in, though?"

"Yeah, but he can't help that he's got other stuff going on, too."

Goose pursed his lips and turned away from where I sat. His dismissiveness irritated me, so I asked what was wrong.

Shrugging, he said, "It's none of my business."

"No," I replied sternly. "Come on. What were you going to say?"

He huffed a heavy breath and turned to face me, crossing his arms over his chest. "I'm just confused."

"About what?"

Shrugging and tightening his arms, he replied, "You say you're in a relationship with this guy, but every time you say you're taking a tiny step forward with him, it seems like there's really nothing to back it up. He wants to be with you, but he's never there. He wants to be a dad, but he's hardly there for you, when *you're* the one who's pregnant with his baby. He wants you to move in with him, but there's no attempt to make it happen. From either of you."

Narrowing my eyes, I disputed defensively, "For something that's none of your business, you certainly have a lot to say about it."

Goose shook his head and groaned, dropping his arms at his sides. "I knew I shouldn't have said anything."

He was right. He shouldn't have. But that didn't take back the fact that he already had, and now, every one of his words exploded one by one in my mind like strategically placed landmines. And he saw it, too. Maybe in the way my eyes widened, or the way my fingers clenched tightly around my fork. I couldn't say for sure. But whatever it was, Goose knew he had gotten to me, because he raked his fingers through his hair and groaned once again.

"Forget I said anything. Like I said, it's none of my business."

"No," I replied. "It's okay. I mean, you're not entirely wrong."

"Yeah, except I'm not really someone who should be handing out relationship advice," he laughed, busying himself behind the bar. "I haven't even seen Tracey yet this week."

"No?"

He pinched his lips and his spine went rigid. "Nope. She's been too busy with the show, I guess."

Propping my chin in my palm, I watched him fiddle with things here and there with no obvious direction or purpose. He was clearly agitated by the wedge his girlfriend's job had driven between the two of them, and I couldn't blame him. It wasn't entirely unlike my own relationship with Brendan, although I couldn't pinpoint a particular reason for his and my divide. But it still bothered me, and I was unnerved to know that my friend was also going through a hard time. It didn't seem right.

And then, an idea came to me.

"Hey."

He looked up at me from his busywork.

"So, next week, I have an anatomy scan. Brendan is coming with me and then afterward, we're going out to eat and celebrate. Why don't you guys come?"

His eyes narrowed to curious slits. "Like a double date?"

"Yeah," I said, nodding enthusiastically. "Why not?"

"Because ... I don't know ..." He shrugged, quickly flitting his eyes to various spots on the bar. "I mean, isn't that like, a personal thing?"

Smiling, I shrugged in response. "Not really. I think it's something to celebrate with family and friends, and isn't that what you are? My friend?"

Dropping his erratic eyes to the floor, he nodded slowly. "Yeah. I am. But I'm not Brendan's friend," he reminded me, cautiously lifting his eyes to mine.

"But," I said hesitantly, "maybe you could be."

Goose swallowed and shrugged. "Yeah, sure," he said gruffly. "Maybe."

"See? I want you guys there. And hopefully, we can breathe some new life into our relationships."

Chuckling, low and gruff, he nodded. "I guess it doesn't hurt to try," he replied in a voice that suggested it might, in fact, hurt quite a bit if we didn't succeed.

Chapter Fifteen

"How long do you think this is gonna take?"

Brendan practically threw his head back against the wall, before lifting his arm to dramatically check his watch for the fifth time in the past ten minutes. He sighed as if we'd been waiting a few years short of a century.

"Relax," I scolded, grabbing his hand and pulling it into my lap. "It's only been a half hour."

"Yeah, and the reservation at the restaurant is an hour from now. They're not going to hold it if we're late."

"If we have to be a few minutes late, I'm sure it's not a big deal."

He turned his head to gawk incredulously at me. "And leave these people hanging? You invited them!" he hissed.

"Oh, my God. It's just Goose and his girlfriend."

"I don't care who they are. You don't leave your guests waiting like that!"

"You're acting like we're having dinner with the Queen of England."

He shook his head, obviously disgusted. "And this is why we never do anything," he muttered under his breath.

Crumpling my brow and frowning, all while a flash of anger threatened to swallow me whole, I asked, "What?"

"Nothing. Forget it."

"No. Repeat what you just said."

He shook his head adamantly. "Stop, it's—"

"Kendall?"

We both froze, mouths open in mid-argument, as we turned to face the red-headed nurse and her iPad. She looked expectantly into the crowded waiting room and repeated my name, just as I raised my hand and stood.

"Right here," I told her, and she smiled, before instructing us to follow her.

We were led into the ultrasound room, where she had me lay on the table and pull up my shirt. After tucking a hefty amount of paper towels into the waistband band of my pants, she grabbed her petroleum jelly and smeared it around with the wand. It left my belly cool, freezing my nerves as my hands shook.

"Okay," she said, turning to the screen while moving the wand around, pressing it firmly to my lower stomach. "Do you know the sex of the baby yet?"

"No," I answered, as Brendan eagerly and sweetly laid a hand on my ankle from where he stood at the foot of the table.

"Do you *want* to know?"

Brendan nodded as I squeaked an eager albeit nervous "yes." The technician smiled and moved the wand some more, in search of my little bean, before announcing that she finally had the baby at the perfect angle. Then, in a very nonchalant tone, she let us know that we were having a boy.

Brendan's hand squeezed my ankle as I grinned, staring up at the fluttering figure of my baby. I could feel him now, just barely. Moving as faint and light as butterfly wings in the lowest part of my belly.

Him.

My heart tripled in size at the thought of being a mother to a little baby boy, and if I hadn't been in love with him already, I certainly was now.

I couldn't wait to call my parents and make plans to see them. I couldn't wait to buy clothes and furniture. And I couldn't wait to see Goose and tell him that he had been right.

***

Brendan and I didn't fight anymore that night, and we weren't late for dinner, walking into the restaurant just in time. On the way to the table, I faltered at the sight of Goose, wearing a black, long-sleeved t-shirt that fit him well. He looked good, much better than friends *should* look, but it was the logo in the center of his chest that stopped me in my tracks.

"Hey!" He grinned brightly as we approached the table, standing to extend a greeting arm toward me.

"Hey." I stood on my toes to wrap an arm around his shoulders and his wrapped loosely around my waist. "You didn't tell me you liked Counting Crows."

Chuckling into my ear, he replied, "I wasn't aware I was supposed to."

"Uh, they're only my favorite band."

He stood back as his brows lifted inquisitively. "No shit?"

I smiled, fixing my eyes on his for just a second. "No shit."

Then, not allowing myself to linger on the moment or the way his Adam's apple bobbed incessantly in his throat, I turned back toward Brendan and reached out for his hand, to pull him closer. I introduced him to Goose and Tracey, glad that the first impressions seemingly passed without any inkling of awkwardness. Drink orders were placed, menus were read, and then, while we waited for our dinners to arrive, I thought the moment felt right to drop our happy news.

"*So*," I began, grasping Brendan's knee beneath the table, "we found out that we're having a boy."

"I told you!" Goose exclaimed, his eyes sparkling with excitement. "Congratulations, guys. That's awesome."

"Thanks," Brendan replied, as his lips twitched into a proud smile.

Tracey offered her own well wishes and then asked, "Do you have any names picked out yet?"

Brendan looked at me, as his eyes dipped to my mouth. "Uh, well, we haven't really talked about it, but I really think we should name him after my dad."

His eyes lifted back to mine, and I saw in them more lust than I think he'd felt in years. I wanted to hold onto it longer and use it to keep my lips from telling him that I didn't, in fact, want to name the baby after his father. Brendan wasn't close with his dad, they never had a great relationship, and the thought of naming my child after a man I barely knew myself didn't sit right with me.

"Um, well—"

"What's your dad's name?" Goose asked, biting into a complementary breadstick.

Brendan turned to him and answered shortly, "Erik."

Goose nodded as he chewed. Then said, "That's a damn good, strong name."

Tracey laughed and explained to Brendan, "And it just so happens to be his name, too."

Brendan shot a curious look in my direction, before turning back to Goose and cocking his head, with both question and accusation in his eyes. "Huh. Then, how come you go by Goose? Middle name?"

My friend laughed heartily, as his eyes dodged quickly toward mine before looking back to my boyfriend. "Nah, my parents weren't that cruel. Goose happened somewhere along the way and it stuck."

"I've been trying to figure it out," I said to Brendan, leaning against his arm. "He won't tell me."

Tracey smiled and said, "I've been with him for years and I don't know either."

"You don't just *know*?"

Kindness filled her eyes. "I'm not really *that* kind of psychic."

Brendan folded his arms, leaning forward against the table. "I heard something about that. How does it work?"

I listened then, as Tracey explained her abilities. About how she could communicate with the dead—or

126

Spirit, as she called it—and how she also had the ability to catch glimpses of the future. She commanded the table with interesting conversation, of things I could only imagine being able to do, and Goose smiled with pride, keeping his arm wrapped around her shoulders the whole time. When the conversation steered then in the direction of my career, I wished so much that Brendan would be just as proud. But instead, he used that time to check his phone.

I resented him for that, and I was so jealous of Tracey, I could hardly stand it.

"Do you like being an author?" Tracey asked me, and I nodded halfheartedly.

"It's all I really know how to do. Like, if I couldn't write, I think I'd be completely lost."

She nodded with understanding. "I get that. I have worked in other areas before, but nothing else feels natural to me. Not like this."

"Didn't you just release a book?" Goose asked me.

I pulled in a deep breath and nodded slowly. "Yeah, sort of."

Brendan snorted then and muttered, "Either you did, or you didn't."

"I *did*," I retorted with a huff. "But the way book releases typically work is, after I put the book out into the world, I plug the hell out of it to make sales. Whether that's with some kind of PR push, ads, or both, I have to do *something* to make it more of a success. But with everything going on right now, I haven't really had the time or energy to do it. So, I'm kind of hoping word of mouth helps carry it for now, at least until I have the time to breathe some life into it."

Goose listened intently, nodding and absorbing the things I was saying, while Brendan and Tracey seemed to be on another planet entirely. Their reaction, or lack thereof, left me feeling embarrassed and small, and I shrugged the topic away.

"I'm sure it'll do better," Goose said gently, offering a lopsided smile.

"Yeah, hopefully. I mean, it's not doing bad. It's just—"

"So, what do you see in my future?" Brendan asked, putting down his phone and changing the subject.

"Um," Tracey's eyes shot across the table to mine, taken aback by the sudden interruption, "well ... I don't really—"

"No, come on, just tell me something. Any predictions?"

She was uncomfortable and Goose was annoyed, judging from the way he shifted in his seat and hardened his glare.

And I was embarrassed.

Tracey straightened her back and looked from Brendan to me, and said, "Well, the thing is, I don't know what I see for you, Brendan. But Kenny, you have an unexpectedly difficult road ahead of you. What seems to be hard right now will only get harder, and whatever seems easy won't be very soon. But I promise, you will be okay. Hold onto that."

Startled, I narrowed my eyes with skepticism. "What do you mean?"

"Wait," Brendan interjected. "Why can't you see anything about me?"

Tracey ignored him, keeping her focus intently on me. "I mean, things will get rough before they get better, but you won't be alone. And I promise, it's all gonna work out."

Closing my eyes and shaking my head, so acutely aware of a little flutter in my stomach, I said, "I don't—"

"I can't say anything else," she cut me off gently.

"Can't, or won't?"

I opened my eyes at the sound of Goose's gruff tone. He stared at his girlfriend with a steely, concerned glare, and his affection for me suddenly felt so alive and real. Brendan couldn't care less about what she was saying, and only cared that she had nothing to say about him, but Goose was alarmed, defensive, and so obviously hurt.

Tracey dropped her gaze to the table and silence fell heavy over our party. I couldn't say what was on the minds of my friends and boyfriend, but I knew I had so many questions. What did she mean? What wasn't she saying? Was the baby going to be okay? I wanted answers but I also knew I would never ask, because what would I do with the information? What *could* I do? Would it even change a damn thing to know?

We ate our dinner in a discomfort that made me wish I had never suggested the double date in the first place. Goose made feeble attempts at conversation, while Brendan kept his nose to his phone, and I wished I could go back to the rush of happiness I had felt when we learned I was carrying a boy.

When we were finished and had exited the restaurant as a group, Brendan walked off to hail a cab while Tracey rushed off to meet the producers of her show with a quick wave goodbye.

Then, it was just Goose and me.

"I guess I should go wait with—"

"I'm sorry about that in there," Goose interrupted me, keeping his voice low.

I shrugged, pretending it hadn't bothered me when it was obvious it had. "It's fine—"

"No. It's not," he interrupted gently. "She means well, but she doesn't know when to keep her mouth shut sometimes. The last thing you need is to have something else to worry about, and she should've realized that. So," he shrugged his broad shoulders, "I'm sorry."

I forced a pained smile and brushed a hand against the cold winter wind. "Don't worry about it. I mean, maybe she's wrong."

Goose looked doubtful, but still, he nodded. "Maybe. But hey, even if she's not wrong, and you have some shit coming your way, I just want you to know I'm not going anywhere, okay?"

As he spoke, his gaze wasn't on me, but directed over my shoulder, toward something—*someone*—else, and when I turned my head to take a look, I found him glaring at Brendan. My skin prickled beneath my sweatshirt, as I watched my boyfriend grow more and more angry with the task of getting us a taxi, and I wondered if Goose knew something I didn't.

Or maybe it was that I refused to acknowledge what was right in front of my face.

Chapter Sixteen

I had never been more exhausted in my life.

Every article I had read on Doctor Google told me that, during the second trimester, I would experience a burst of energy. That I could expect an inability to sleep and the desire to constantly move, move, move. But not me. There wasn't enough sleep in the world that could satisfy my insatiable craving, and my work was suffering for it.

I sat in front of my laptop, staring at the blinking cursor on the screen. I had paused mid-sentence fifteen minutes ago and hadn't written a single word since. And I was frustrated.

After the release of my last book, I felt I didn't have the luxury of waiting before writing the next. I didn't have time to mull it over or focus on myself and the pregnancy. I needed to write and plan the next release, to ensure I kept my regular flow of royalties coming in. However, the mental barriers I was now faced with were worse than any writers' block I'd ever dealt with in my life.

I groaned and pushed my fingers into my hair. "This is stupid," I muttered, quickly running through the last few lines I'd written.

That wasn't just my inner critic talking, either. It really was stupid. I was trying too hard and forcing a storyline that just wasn't working. It was too cliché, too predictable, and that wasn't me. So, I sighed and deleted the little bit of writing that I'd accomplished that day.

Realizing I wasn't going to get any work done while in my current mindset, I decided to take a shower instead. It was a quick one—I still couldn't handle the heat for long—but it was refreshing, and by the time I finished, I felt just a little lighter.

Brendan came in carrying a bag of Chinese for lunch. I stood up from my chair to offer him a kiss, only to be turned down with a gentle hand to my shoulder, holding me back.

"Gotta get the plates," he told me, before hurrying toward the kitchen cabinet.

I stood there, stupefied and confused. Brendan and I weren't the best or most affectionate couple, but he had never before refused my kisses. Now, standing back and twiddling my thumbs over my growing belly, I turned toward him and asked what was wrong.

"Nothing," he grumbled and carried the plates to the table.

"You're clearly annoyed."

"Not annoyed."

"Oh, well, now I'm convinced."

He rolled his eyes, sighed, and dropped the plates unceremoniously on the table. They made impact with a cringe-worthy clatter and I gritted my teeth at the sound.

"Kendo," he muttered on a sigh, and I was at least grateful for he used the nickname I never liked. "We gotta talk."

Those three daunting, little words landed one by one in my stomach like drops of acid rain. How many times had I written them myself, to lead my characters into that inevitable black moment, where the reader questions whether or not they will make it? Except in my books, you always know that they will and that the discomfort and sadness is fleeting. But real life doesn't always work out like a romance novel, and I couldn't be sure that this moment of sickening trepidation was temporary.

"Okay," I replied in a whispered voice.

"Sit down."

I did as I was told, keeping my hands over my belly and silently promising my baby boy that, no matter what, we would be okay. Even if Brendan and I weren't.

Brendan took a seat beside me and dropped another bomb.

"Last night really bothered me."

"What?"

"I don't like him."

"Who?"

He shook his head, rolled his eyes to the ceiling, and filled the air with a condescending little chuckle. "God, I knew you were going to do this …"

"Do what?"

"Defend him."

The discomfort and sadness I had begun to feel was replaced by a hot rush of defensive anger. "What are you even talking about?"

"Jesus Christ, Kendall. Your buddy!"

Furrowing my brow, I asked, "Goose?"

"Yes! Did we go out with someone else I wasn't aware of? Holy shit …" He shook his head again.

"Why are you shaking your head?"

"Because you're not stupid! You knew exactly who I was talking about. Don't play fuckin' dumb with me."

I had played dumb, it was true. I just couldn't accept that he'd be talking about Goose in such a horrible way, or in such a horrible tone.

"What don't you like about him?"

Brendan flattened his hands against the table and leaned back in his chair, keeping his eyes away from mine. "I don't like the way he *looks* at you. I don't like the way he *talks* to you. I don't like the way he," his lips twisted and his nose wrinkled, like he had just gotten a taste of the most sour lemon in the world, "*treats* you."

I couldn't help but bark a condescending laugh. "*Treats* me? And how does he treat me?"

Then his eyes met mine and they were full of disgust. "Like you're *his* girlfriend."

My heart hammered wildly in my chest as I shook my head. "No, he doesn't."

"Oh, no? And you think it's totally normal for him to completely ignore his own girlfriend while he stares at you and fucks you with his—"

"Knock it off," I pushed through gritted teeth, shaking my head.

He sneered, shaking his head once again. "What, you don't want me to say it?"

"No!"

"Why? Because you know it's the truth?"

Pushing away from the table, I stood up quickly, ignoring the spinning and swooping of my brain and guts. "Because it's bullshit!"

His lips curled into a sneer. "Is it, though?"

Shaking my head and crossing my arms, I stared at him, unable to believe this was really happening, while wondering if I should've seen it coming.

"Brendan," I said, flat and controlled. "You sound like a really jealous boyfriend right now, and I don't like it."

"I sound like a jealous boyfriend because I watched you look at a guy last night in a way you've *never* looked at me!"

With my back to him, my eyes widened and I wondered, was that true? Had my gaze revealed something I should have kept locked away? It was then that it occurred to me that maybe I hadn't been keeping this thing with Goose as innocent as I thought I had. Maybe maintaining a friendship with a man, I was undoubtedly physically attracted to, was a poisonous thing destined to kill every other good thing around me. Maybe it was time to end it before things got worse. Brendan was the father of my baby after all, and really, what was Goose other than the nice guy who made my favorite wings?

I was about to tell Brendan that I wouldn't see Goose anymore, because making him uncomfortable wasn't my intention. But then, I remembered that I didn't really have anybody else in the city, apart from my boyfriend. It had taken my introverted self too long to make a friend, and while I did find him attractive, I was also faithful to Brendan. Nothing would happen between Goose and me, if I had anything to do with it, and I wasn't going to give up my friend for the sake of my jealous boyfriend's feelings.

"You have female friends," I pointed out.

"Yeah, so?"

"You don't see me having an issue with them."

Brendan turned around, with his head cocked and his arms crossed. "You've never met them. So, why would you have a problem with them?"

Mimicking his stance, I replied, "Shouldn't that make me even more jealous or suspicious?"

"What the hell are you talking about?"

"I'm saying, I invited you on a double date with my friend and his girlfriend, while you always go out after work with your lady friends and I've still never met them. Shouldn't that bother me more than this is bothering you?"

"You're deflecting," he replied, cold and harsh. "I don't like it."

"You don't have to like it," I shot back. "But I'm not gonna stop going to the bar just because you said so, when I have never made any kind of demands of you."

Brendan's nostrils flared and a muscle beneath his jaw ticked. He held his mouth firm and his eyes stern for a moment, before exhaling heavily and looking away, as he wiped a hand over his mouth.

"God, I'm sorry," he said, his voice rough and quiet.

I dropped my gaze and shrugged. "Whatever, it's fine."

Then, he laid his hand over my belly and kissed my cheek. The conversation was dropped, lunch was eaten, and afterward, he left to go back to work. But I couldn't shake the discomfort I'd felt over his burst of anger and confrontation, or how suddenly it just seemed to fade away, as though it had never happened. I had never seen him quite like that before and it irked me.

I wondered what Tracey had thought about our night. I wondered if she and Goose had gotten into a fight or if they were eager to go out with us again. I considered that maybe Brendan was just a jealous, territorial ass and that there really was nothing to be angry about.

So, I texted Goose, to ask if Tracey had a good time, and although I waited and waited, I never got an answer.

"That's weird," I said to Mrs. Potter, who replied with a slow blink of the eyes and a flip of the tail.

Assuming he was just busy, I carried on with my day. I trudged through a brief cleaning of the apartment, managed my social media accounts, and then, when I was about to curl up on the couch with the latest Dean Koontz novel, my phone rang.

Reaching for it on the coffee table, I saw it was Mom. But I wished it had been Goose.

"Hey, Mom," I answered, curling up on the couch with my book and cat at my side. "How are you on this fine evening?"

"Good. I just wanted to check up on my favorite daughter and my grandson."

"Didn't you *just* check up on us this morning?" I laughed.

"Hey, if I want to call you twenty times throughout the day, I'm allowed. I'm your mother."

I smiled, laying a hand over my belly and rubbing over where I knew he was. "Well, we appreciate the thought."

"Are you spending time with Brendan?"

My hand stilled, as I inhaled sharply at the mention of my boyfriend's name. Knowing my mother's feelings toward him and how she relished collecting things to hold against him, I hesitated to mention that he wasn't, in fact, with me. But my annoyance toward Brendan was greater than my stubborn resolve to defend him and his shortcomings, so I replied, "No, not tonight."

"You weren't with him the last time I called, either."

"We don't spend every second together, Mom."

"Do you *ever* spend time with him?"

I sighed, rubbing at a headache starting to pierce my temple. "We just had lunch together earlier today."

"Oh. Well, that's nice."

"Yeah, it was okay."

"Just okay?"

With a groan, I flopped my head against the back of the couch beside Mrs. Potter, who stirred irritably and jumped down to find her bed.

"Can you just pretend to like him?" I asked. "He's gonna be in all our lives forever, so you might as well learn to deal with him."

139

"Is that what *you're* doing?"

"Mom," I groaned, laying a hand over my eyes. "Seriously, come on."

"I'm sorry, I'm sorry. I promise to look for the good in Brendan," she said, laying her begrudging tone on thick.

"Thank—"

"—if *you* promise to sound happier when you talk about him. Okay?"

I laughed beside myself and shook my head. "I know, I know … We just … didn't have a great day." With that segue, I knew I had opened the floodgates that I'd intended to keep closed.

"What happened?" she asked, and I briefly told her about our dinner with friends the night before, and the argument where Brendan's jealous paranoia and ugly envy had gotten the better of him. When I was finished, I said, "I'm sure it's nothing, though. We've just been going through a lot, you know? A lot of changes, and a lot of—"

"Yeah, but have you maybe considered it might not be nothing?"

I scoffed, trying to ignore the way my cheeks instantly burned. "No, trust me; it's nothing."

"But you said you do like this friend—what's his name?"

"Goose."

"Goose," she repeated, snickering with jest. "Where did that name come from?"

"His parents have a real appreciation for waterfowl. His brother's name is Crane."

140

"Kenny, are you pulling my leg right now? Because you know how I—"

"Oh, my God, yes, I'm pulling your leg," I grumbled, rolling my eyes and laughing. "I have no idea where he got the nickname from. He won't tell me. *Anyway*, yeah, I mean, I like him, but it's nothing like that. He's a good-looking guy, sure, but he's got a girlfriend and—"

"Is it serious?"

"Jesus, Mom …"

"What? I'm just saying, relationships don't always last forever."

"Well, even if he and Tracey didn't work out, I'm with Brendan—"

"Like I said, relationships don't always—"

"I'm not breaking up with him over a stupid, little crush!" I exclaimed, laughing at my use of a word I hadn't even thought of since I was a teenager.

"Oh, so, you admit it's a *crush*," Mom jabbed teasingly, triumph in her voice.

The fluttering in my belly encouraged a bout of guilt that left my eyes stinging with tears. I shouldn't be talking about another guy like this, regardless of who he was to me. Without my stubborn resolve to be right getting in the way, I was able to consider that maybe Brendan was right. Maybe it really wasn't healthy. Hell, if I was honest, hadn't I repeatedly let my feelings for Goose go too far since the day I met him? And it wasn't helping now, to have my mother encouraging me to consider my crush as something closer to a possibility, rather than a total fantasy.

"Kenny, you know I'm just giving you a hard time to be an ass," Mom said gently. "I don't mean to upset you, you know that."

"I'm just not in a good place to talk about this," I muttered uneasily, wrapping an arm tight around my middle.

"Okay, so let's change the subject," she said, her voice bright and determined. "The real reason I called was to ask what you wanted to do for your birthday."

I groaned at the mention. I wasn't in a good place to talk about that either. "I don't know. Surprise me," I muttered, as I wondered what Goose was doing on Saturday and if he maybe wanted to do something.

It had been a kneejerk reaction of my brain, and it immediately bothered me that I hadn't first thought of Brendan. He was my boyfriend and the father of my baby, but no matter how many times I reminded myself of that, he was never my first choice. It was possible that, after the years of back-and-forth commitment, my brain had become trained to simply not consider him. But my thoughts of Goose were consistent. And if I had finally met the guy who could put a stop to my reluctance to commit, then maybe it was him I should be with and not Brendan.

But, the flutters in my belly said, *you're still having his baby, and Goose is still in a relationship.*

And for the first time since meeting him, I wished I had never walked into his bar.

Chapter Seventeen

"I love what you've done with the place," Goose said, walking past me and into the apartment with boxes in hand. He shot a look over his shoulder and grinned. "Happy birthday, by the way. I brought everything a pregnant lady could ever want."

"And what's that?" I asked, closing the door before crossing my arms over my aching, leaking boobs.

He laid the stack of boxes out on the table and opened each one, as he said, "Cake and lots and lots of wings."

I laughed, as my heart lurched. "You really know how to make a girl feel special."

"Well, it *is* your birthday," he said, pulling his leather jacket off and draping it over a chair. "I wasn't gonna let you not celebrate."

I had planned to grab the train and head to my parents' place for dinner, cake, and presents. But I'd woken up in such a state of overbearing exhaustion and feeling as though I hadn't slept for nine hours straight that I had to regrettably called my mom to ask for a rain check. Luckily, she hadn't cooked or gone to the bakery yet, and after I thwarted her numerous offers to come out for the night, we finally agreed to get together when I was feeling better.

But it had felt wrong to do nothing, and I was sick of having to constantly cancel my plans with my parents. Brendan couldn't get out of work until much later, so I texted Goose and asked if he and Tracey wanted to do something in the meantime, and he accepted the invitation.

I just hadn't expected him to show up alone.

"Where's Tracey?" I asked, as the butterflies awoke in my stomach.

He shrugged. "Working, of course." Then, as he walked to the kitchen, he glanced in my direction, without quite meeting my eye, and asked, "Where's Brendan today?"

"Uh, working and grabbing some stuff for the baby's room."

His walk back to the table faltered as he offered a short nod. "Ah. Right. At his place."

"Yeah," I replied quietly. "Brendan's got some work thing going on over the next few weeks, but once he's done with that, we're moving my stuff. And then, I'll be there full time."

"I bet you're excited," he said, doling out the wings.

"I mean, yeah, sure." I nodded, sitting down and accepting the plate. "It'll be nice to have more space. He has a little area in his apartment that I can turn into an office, and that'll be amazing, to finally have an actual office instead of a kitchen table."

"You think that's gonna be the answer to your writer's block?" he teased, sitting across from me and grinning.

I rolled my eyes, before biting into a wing. "I think the answer to my writer's block is to get this kid out of me. I'm too distracted and exhausted with everything right now to get a single coherent thought out."

"Or maybe it's what you're writing that's the problem."

Lifting my brows, I cocked my head and said, "Oh, so you become friends with an author and now you're an expert, huh?"

He shrugged one shoulder as he chewed, then swallowed and said, "Nah, it's just that, I've sorta been there before. I don't make any progress when I'm giving all my attention to the wrong things. But when I focus on the *right* stuff," he pointed the clean bone in his fingers at me, "that's when the good shit happens."

"Okay, wise guy," I replied, folding my hands to hover over my wings. "What do you think I should be writing, then?"

Laughing, he said, "I already told you. You gotta write about a girl named Kenny who walks into a bar and meets a guy named Goose. You'd get famous off of that."

I nodded and moved my folded hands onto the table, feigning serious intent to make this happen, before asking, "Okay, so what kind of book are we talking about here? A comedy? A thriller, or—"

"I was thinkin' something closer to an autobiography, or maybe a, you know, inspired by a true story type of thing."

"Okay," I snorted, picking up another wing. "And how does it end?"

He shrugged casually and diverted his eyes, as he replied, "I dunno. I guess we'll see how this thing plays out."

His reply was sincere, with no hint of humor on his face, and the joke I was trying to carry died with the pitter-patter of my heart. I shouldn't have read into it, I shouldn't have let my mind wander, but I couldn't help it, when it was impossible to decipher what he was trying to tell me. It was just too vague, or maybe that was the point.

We dropped the topic and finished our wings with conversation about the baby and what his room would look like at Brendan's apartment. He told me about his daughter who had never been into princesses or unicorns, and instead had a room at his place decorated with sharks and pirate ships. I snorted and made a comment that she was a girl after my own heart, and he replied with candor, "You should meet her sometime."

After we finished our lunch, we cleaned up and decided to watch a movie—my pick, Goose insisted. I couldn't decide, so I offered him a choice of my three favorite movies, as I fanned out the Blu-rays on the coffee table.

"*The Crow, Breakfast at Tiffany's*, or *Shawshank Redemption*," he muttered, listing the options out loud.

Then, he brought his eyes to mine and smiled. "You have interesting taste."

Offering a smug grin, I replied, "I'd like to think I'm an interesting person."

"I'd have to agree with you there," he said, plucking *The Crow* from the assortment. "I'm goin' with this one. I haven't seen it in a long freakin' time."

"This is my favorite one of all," I said, as I popped it into the Blu-ray player. "Brendan doesn't like it, so we've never watched it together, but I love it."

He laughed, as I sat at the other end of the couch. "Not gonna lie, it's hard to understand why you guys are together in the first place."

"Yeah, I know. Everybody says that," I muttered, pressing Play.

"Tracey and I broke up."

The announcement was abrupt and took me by surprise, and I stared unblinking at the screen, not quite hearing the opening monologue. My mouth dried instantly, my heart hammered wildly, and my stomach flopped with more than just the never-ending nausea I seemed to be plagued with.

"I'm ... I'm sorry to hear that."

He nodded solemnly. "Yeah. When we were both at my apartment the other night, she, uh, told me we weren't workin' anymore."

"I always thought you guys were great together," I admitted, remembering the jealousy I felt whenever I saw them together.

He shook his head. "Here's the thing about Tracey. She's a good person, I won't ever talk shit about her, but

147

she's also a performer. She's in the public eye, so she made sure things always looked good to everybody else. But when we were together?" He pursed his lips and shrugged. "Things hadn't felt right for a while. I thought it was all in my head though, and I didn't wanna throw something away over nothing. But I guess the feeling was mutual."

A jolt of clarity struck as I recalled the argument I'd had with Brendan the day after our double date. He was bothered by my friendship with Goose, and I wondered again if Tracey had been, too. I wanted to ask, but I had a feeling I already knew what the answer would be, and I wasn't sure I was ready to hear it.

Goose didn't seem to care about that, though.

"She said she was no longer needed in my life," he said, as the movie played and neither of us paid it any attention. "She read me like I was one of her clients, which should have pissed me off, but it didn't. 'Cause for the first time in a while, I felt fuckin' free, as shitty as that sounds."

I mumbled a little contemplative sound, as the baby woke up and joined the butterflies in my stomach, throwing punches and kicks, and growing stronger with every passing week. I laid a hand right over him and smiled to myself, as Goose continued.

"I really cared about her," he went on. "But I knew I didn't love her. I feel like an asshole admitting that but," he shrugged, "she already knew, anyway. Not that it makes it better, but ..."

Then, he turned to face me and asked, "Do you love Brendan?"

I clenched my jaw and knew in an instant that he needed to leave. He was about to step over the line we'd been toeing for too long, and it wasn't okay. None of this was okay, not anymore.

So, I reached for the remote and turned off my favorite movie, then said, "I'm really tired, and I don't feel good, so—"

"Why the hell has it taken you so long to move in with him?"

I stood up and tightened my robe around my waist. "Because I had other stuff to do. But," I spread my arms, gesturing toward the stacks of boxes around us, "I'm moving in with him now, so there you go. Anyway, I'll talk to you—"

"You once told me you were only with him because of the baby," he cut me off, standing up and blocking my path to the door. "That's not a good reason to stay with someone, especially if you're unhappy."

"He's the father of my son," I spat at him defensively. "What am I going to do, break up with him and face a custody battle and child support and, and, and … whatever else?" I shook my head and walked around the coffee table to get past him. "No. I won't do that. I would never win. I would—"

I stopped my mouth the moment I realized what I was saying. The truth had spilled from my lips, and now, it was out in the open, with no way for me to take it back.

"Kenny."

I took a deep breath and wiped a palm across my forehead. "Anyway, that would never happen, because I *do* care about Brendan. And he's going to be such a good

149

father. I know he's not a great boyfriend, I know we have problems, but we're going to work on it, so … it's fine."

Pulling in another heavy breath, I headed for the door. Goose followed closely at my heels, and just as I was about to grab the doorknob and see him out, his hand wrapped firmly around my arm and spun me around. His palms found my cheeks, his lips found mine, and I loved the way his beard tickled my chin. I loved his calloused skin, contrasted by the softness of my own. I loved that I felt more in those three seconds, before I shoved him away, than I had during any of the thousands of kisses I'd shared with Brendan. And then, I hated myself for loving it.

"Oh, my God," I groaned, wiping the back of my hand over my mouth, in an attempt to wipe those seconds away.

"Kenny, I'm sorry. I just—"

"No. I don't want to hear it."

"You don't even know what I'm gonna say!"

"I don't care!" I shut him up with the lift of my palm. "You need to get out of here."

"And *you* need to leave him."

Finally, I looked at Goose, and immediately, I wished I hadn't. Because I could still feel his lips on mine, and now I wanted to know if the rest of him felt just as good. Still, I fought the urge to lunge at him by clenching my fists, wincing at the pain of my fingernails digging into my palms.

"You have no right to tell me what to do."

Groaning, he pinched his eyes shut and nodded. "I know, I know," he exclaimed exhaustedly, a hint of desperation in his voice. "But you're really gonna tell me that you don't feel what I'm feelin' right now? You're seriously just gonna stand there and tell me that I'm alone in this shit?"

I didn't want to lie to him. I didn't want him to leave my apartment, not knowing I'd spent months of my life caring more for him than my own boyfriend. But I also didn't want to fill him with the hope that this could be more than what it was. Brendan was tied to me through the baby growing in my belly, and I wasn't going to leave him and face a judge, only for the possibility of something maybe working out with Goose.

"It doesn't matter how I feel," I told him.

"Will you stop saying that shit?" he shouted.

Narrowing my eyes, I crossed my arms and asked, "What?"

"God, Kenny, it *does* fuckin' matter how you feel! You're allowed to have opinions and you're allowed to leave him! You shouldn't be afraid of the person you're with, and if that's truly the only reason why you're staying, then you—"

"Stop." I shook my head, fighting back the urge to cry Wasn't this exactly what I'd been longing for, to have the confirmation of his attraction and to finally be with him? And now that I had it and offered to me on a silver platter, I felt forced to turn it down.

"I'll see you soon, okay?" I asked, desperately wanting this conversation to have never happened and wishing I possessed the power to go back in time.

To my horror, Goose shook his head and stuffed his hands into his pockets. "No," he replied firmly. "Whether

151

you wanna admit to it or not, I know you feel the way I do. And if you wanna ignore that, then that's your decision to make. But then we shouldn't see each other anymore. 'Cause this shit is only gonna get worse, it's only gonna get harder to ignore, and I won't do it. It's not fair to myself, or you. And it's definitely not fair to the baby, so …" He shrugged, before nodding, then said, "Good luck, Kenny. I hope you leave him one day, because despite what you might think, you do deserve a lot better than what you have."

I didn't stop him as he turned and left my apartment. It had been the right thing to do, I knew that, but it still didn't stop my heart from begging me to run after him. With the feeling of his lips still lingering on mine, I fought my desperation with an iron fist, beating the urges down with the insistence that it never would have worked out. If not with Goose, then with the legal battles I'd surely have fought against Brendan.

Trying to busy myself, I set to packing up more of the apartment. But instead of focusing on my task, I had only given myself more time to think. It dawned on me how twisted it was that I would only be with Brendan out of fear. I didn't trust him, and that was the truth. I didn't trust what he'd do if I were to leave him, and Goose was right; that wasn't love. It wasn't even close.

"But then, what am I supposed to do?" I asked Mrs. Potter, who only blinked in reply. "I mean, let's be real here, if I had met Goose six months ago, before the baby ever happened, then there'd be no question right now. I'd have dumped Brendan's ass in a heartbeat. But …" I laid a hand over my fluttering belly. "Then, *he* wouldn't exist, and I wouldn't take him back for anything."

A heavy sorrow rested against my shoulders at the thought. I could so easily remember the time when I wasn't sure I even wanted the baby at all, and now, I was saddened at the possibility of him not being here. It was Goose who had done that though, not Brendan, and that wasn't lost on me either.

Chapter Eighteen

"**K**enny, look at your legs!"

Mom hurried over and instructed me to sit down on the couch. She elevated my legs by propping them on the coffee table, and rubbed my calves.

I looked down at my ballooned ankles and feet, shrugging and forcing nonchalance, then said, "I'm pregnant. Your legs are supposed to swell when you're pregnant, aren't they?"

"Yeah, that's true," she said, rubbing a little more vigorously, as if a deep tissue massage could rid me of all the excess fluids. "But this is a little more than normal for the second trimester."

"Everybody is different," I muttered, reiterating the words my doctor had said to me at my last appointment, after I'd mentioned that I still hadn't benefitted from that fabled burst of energy.

"I guess so," Mom replied, unconvinced. Then, with a pat on the knee, said, "Keep your legs up for a while and try to get some of that water retention under control. What would you like to do for dinner? You want me to go grab some of those wings you like?"

The indirect mention of Goose struck me like a fist to the gut. It had been a little more than two weeks since I'd seen him, and I missed him so much more than I missed his wings or the inspirational atmosphere of his bar.

"No," I said, shaking my head. "How about—"

"What happened?"

I shifted my gaze toward my mother and saw the look of speculation in her eyes. "What?"

"You're sad. Why are you sad?"

"I'm not sad," I insisted, while feeling a sudden urge to look away from her knowing gaze.

"Yes, you are," she pressed, reaching out to poke my cheek. "Tell your mother. What's going on?"

I hadn't told anyone about the birthday incident. Nobody else needed to know about the kiss or the things said between Goose and me. But living with that heavy weight against my heart hadn't been easy. I wasn't the biggest fan of secrets, and so, I didn't need much coaxing to tell her exactly what had happened between us.

"Well, um, Goose sorta confessed to having feelings for me when he came over for my birthday," I muttered, giving her the abridged version. "And then, he kissed me, and—"

"Whoa, wait a minute!" Mom exclaimed, raising her hands to the Heavens. "He *kissed you*?"

I nodded, instantly annoyed by my cheeks and the way they blushed at the thought of his lips pressed to mine. "Yeah. And he shouldn't—"

"How was it?"

Scowling, I shot her a steely glare. "Mom!"

Shrugging, then pulling her feet underneath her on the couch, she said, "What? I'm just curious."

"It lasted three freakin' seconds. I didn't have time to think about how it was."

"Oh, come on. That's all the time you need to know if something feels right," she groused, unamused. "So, how was it? Were there fireworks?"

"You're being ridiculous."

"Am I?"

"Yes!" I fired at her, with an incredulous burst of laughter. "And it never should've happened in the first place. Like, just because he and his girlfriend broke up doesn't mean I'm free from *my* relationship."

"Wait, he broke up with his girlfriend?"

Groaning, I nodded. "Yes. He and Tracey are done."

"Why? Because of you?"

Reluctantly, I nodded again. "He eluded to that, yeah."

"Kenny!" Mom squealed excitedly, grabbing at my arm. "This is exactly like the stuff you write about! Gorgeous guy breaks up with his girlfriend to convince the pregnant love of his life that she should—"

"Oh, my God, stop," I groaned, shaking my head and laying my hands over my eyes. "Let's remember I'm still with Brendan, okay? I'm not single, and I'm not going to just leave the father of my baby because some guy—"

"Oh, knock it off already," Mom grumbled, rolling her eyes. "I'm so sick of hearing you say this crap. Remember all those times you've told me about those annoying heroines, who perpetuate stupid situations for the sake of keeping the story going?"

"Uh-huh," I muttered, already knowing where this was going.

"Well, stop acting like one."

"Except this is real life," I reminded her. "And Brendan is having this baby with me, whether anyone likes it or not. Everybody is acting like it's such an easy thing to just break up with him, knowing very well that he would see my ass in court."

"And *if* it came down to that, we would handle it. But risking your own happiness is silly," she reasoned gently. "Especially when we both know you wouldn't be putting up with him otherwise."

"You just want me to be with someone else 'cause you hate him," I pointed out, smirking.

Mom scoffed, waving a dismissive hand through the air. "Forget about this other guy. Let's pretend for a second he isn't even in the picture. You and Brendan have never had a stable relationship. He's neglectful. He rarely takes you into consideration. I mean, you're over here, sick and exhausted, and where the hell is he? Shouldn't he be here, taking care of the mother of his child, instead of making her do it alone?"

Diverting my eyes, I pulled in a deep breath and immediately fell into a coughing fit that left me wheezing and clutching at my chest. Two weeks earlier, I had come down with a cold, and the cough and heaviness in my chest had lingered longer than I would've liked. Taking a deep breath always seemed to do me in, and I was left with an aching back, tight chest, and a raw throat, as I struggled to regain the control over my lungs. Now, Mom was here, witnessing one of these fits for the first time, and the concern in her eyes scared me.

"Kenny, you really need to get this checked out."

With a hand over my chest, I nodded. "I know. The doctor doesn't have any openings until next week, though, so—"

"What about your OB/GYN? Are they aware of this?"

"I see them next Wednesday," I told her. "A few more days isn't going to kill me."

She eyed me with skepticism, but seemed to hesitantly relent. We ate dinner—Italian, not wings—and talked more about Brendan and how crucial it was for him to step up to the plate. I knew that much was true. Whether we were romantically involved or not, the man was going to be a parent and if he struggled to be there for me now, how could I be confident that he'd be there after the baby was born? Of course, moving in together should help, but how could I be sure? Maybe me being at his apartment meant he'd just be out more.

So, after Mom reluctantly left to head back home, I called Brendan, only to be answered by his voicemail. I tried twice more, and both times I was directed to leave him a message. But I didn't. I just hung up the phone and tossed it to the other side of my bed, where Mrs. Potter glared at me irritably for waking her up.

"Sorry," I muttered, laying a hand on her back and stroking gently. "I wouldn't have to throw phones if he'd just answer me."

And the more I thought about it, the angrier I got. He knew I wasn't feeling well, and of course, he knew I was nearly six months pregnant. How was he not more alert? He was supposed to be there and I was supposed to be able to count on him. But even though he was only blocks away, I felt all alone in this big city of millions of people.

I missed Goose and his bar. I missed having someone else to talk to and rely on. I wondered if he thought about me at all, but knowing that he did, just as I thought of him. And I felt stupid, for allowing this to happen at all. I felt stupid for being with Brendan and never putting my foot down. I hated that I allowed him to be this way to me, and for what reason? Because he just so happened to knock me up and I didn't have it in me to leave him, out of fear of what he might do if I did? It was foolish and cowardly, and I couldn't stand that I'd allowed myself to become this person, so weak and unwilling to stand up to this man I once had no problem breaking up with over lesser things.

"I need to end things with him," I told Mrs. Potter. She dodged her eyes toward me, as her ears perked up at the sound of my voice. "And no, it's not because of Goose. Brendan wanted this baby, and he needs to remember that. He needs to—"

My lungs seized and I coughed uncontrollably into my fist, as Mrs. Potter scurried underneath the bed. I flattened a hand to my chest as I struggled to stifle the cough and breathe evenly. When it finally subsided, I grabbed for my inhaler on the nightstand. In those two weeks of being sick, I'd used it more than I ever had in my life, after years of suffering from weather induced asthma. It had always been a security blanket of sorts, there only for when I absolutely needed it, but now, it was critical to my health and comfort.

"Mom is right," I croaked, after taking two puffs from the inhaler. "This isn't normal."

Mrs. Potter watched me with concern, as I laid my phone beside me. I smiled weakly and reached out to stroke her head. "Don't worry," I told her. "I won't forget to call Brendan. I just can't do it now."

My lower back was screaming in agony and I struggled to find a comfortable position. After stacking the pillows up high, I laid back to a reclined seated position, closed my eyes, and hoped I felt better in the morning.

Chapter Nineteen

Over the next few days, I didn't improve at all. If anything, I felt worse. The coughing fits were becoming longer and more frequent, and the swelling in my legs was so severe, it hurt to walk. The excruciating pain in my back had blossomed, to travel through to my hips and right up to my shoulders, and I was certain I'd need a chiropractor soon.

But none of that concerned me as much as what I felt in my belly.

When Brendan came by on Monday, he asked how his little guy was doing, and I told him, "Okay, I guess. I think all of this coughing is rattling him up, though. He hasn't been moving around as much as he was."

He just smiled and laid a hand over my growing stomach. "He's just growing. He doesn't have as much room to move around."

"I don't know," I answered skeptically, diverting my eyes to the bags of food he'd brought. "What if something is—" I coughed into my elbow, as my eyes watered and my chest burned. "What if, what if something is w-wrong?"

"God, Kendo, you really need to knock that off," he chuckled lightheartedly. "And I told you earlier, nothing is wrong with the baby. Everything is fine, so stop worrying. Now, let's eat before I have to get back to work."

The urge to break up with him then was strong, at the sound of his dismissive tone and the nonchalant way he brushed off my concerns. But I was exhausted, too tired to fight, and I made the decision to end things as soon as I shook the lingering effects of this horrible cold.

Then, Monday faded into Tuesday, and the hours dragged by until it was finally Wednesday. The day of my scheduled appointment with the OB/GYN. I opened my eyes to a cloudy day and instantly felt as though I hadn't slept for ten hours the night before.

"God, I don't feel good," I croaked, through my constricted chest. Mrs. Potter looked at me with concern and I stroked her cheek, offering a reassuring smile. "It's okay, sweet girl. I'm going to the doctor today. Everything's gonna be fine."

I tried to believe it, too, even as the whispers of my intuition told me something wasn't right. I crawled out of bed, made a cup of tea, and picked at a slice of toast, before mustering the strength to get ready for a shower. But just that little bit of effort left me exhausted and weary, and I retreated back to bed, with tears stinging my eyes and nose.

"This isn't good," I complained, curling my arms around my stomach. "God, why can't I shake this freakin' cold?"

I scrolled through my social media accounts for a few minutes, trying to regain the strength I needed to finally shower, when my lungs suddenly constricted with an angry violence and the battering cough wracked through my entire body. I sputtered, cupping a hand over my mouth, as the tears flowed freely from my pinched eyes and into my pillow.

"O-Oh, my ... God," I managed to utter, as the episode finally subsided, and I was allowed a few seconds to focus on catching my breath.

I imagined it was like having an elephant sitting on my chest, as I coached my lungs to inhale and exhale. It hurt to breathe, it hurt to move, and all I could do was lay a hand over my belly and say, "God, baby, this is killing me."

What made me say those exact words, I couldn't be sure. It was just a feeling I had, to say those words out loud instead of keeping them locked away in my head. Now, with them out in the open, they felt closer to the truth than a simple worry. When I finally opened my eyes, knowing I still had to shower and get ready for my appointment, a new strike of panic crushed against my already worried mind.

"I can't see," I stated simply and breathlessly.

My heart then galloped with anxiety as I squeezed my eyes shut again, praying I was okay and that it had only been my mind playing tricks on me. But when I opened my eyes once more, I found that the vision in my left eye was in fact gone, while my right eye was too faded to be useful.

"O-Oh, my God," I said, more panicked than before. "Oh, my God, I can't see. Why, why the hell can't I *see*?"

For a moment, the need to react and the desperation to simply panic wrestled in my mind. Panic shook me to the very core of my soul, while reason whispered reassurances and instructions. Finally, reason won and I sat up to reach for my phone. Because there was nobody else here to help me, and the only person who could help my baby, was me.

So, with what little vision remained in my one eye, I managed to navigate through to my list of favorited contacts. I called Brendan, then my parents, and I got no answer from any of them. Frustration and panic chilled my veins and I bolted upright, wondering what the hell I was supposed to do now. I couldn't see well enough to navigate my way to the street to hail a cab, I wasn't sure if this situation warranted a 9-1-1 call, and I couldn't read my phone screen to find the doctor's number in my contacts. The only other person I had favorited was Goose, and after a moment of hesitation, I hit the button to call his number. Because even though we were no longer speaking, and for good reason, this was still an emergency. And I knew I could count on him to answer.

"Hey, Kenny."

The amount of relief I felt in hearing his voice couldn't be reflected in my tone as I began to cry and said, "G-Goose, I can't see. I can't fucking see, and I'm, I'm scared. I am s-so—"

"Whoa, hold up, what's goin' on?"

I took a deep breath, coughed, and then, in between sobs, tried to explain. "I-I've been sick. I've been really sick and this cough will not go away. And just before, I started coughing and coughing, and when it finally stopped, I couldn't see."

"Okay. So, you're blind, right now?"

"Yes! O-O-Oh, my God, what the hell is wrong with me?" The tears were pouring down my cheeks, as I stared unseeing into my bedroom. "I'm so fucking scared. I-I don't know what to do. I'm so scared."

"Hold on, okay? Stay right where you are. I'm coming."

"God," I cried, laying my face in the palm of my hand. "What if some-something's wrong with the baby? What if something's ha-happening to him? I can't … I can't deal with this. I can't fucking do this."

"You're gonna be okay, Kenny. I'm gonna be right there, and we'll get you to your doctor."

I nodded erratically, feeling as Mrs. Potter nudged my fingertips. "O-Okay. Please hurry."

"I'm comin' as fast as I can."

***

Goose got to my place just a few minutes later. In the freezing cold, he had run from his bar to my little apartment in record time. I heard him knocking, and using my hands to feel my way, I managed to get to the door and opened it for him. I felt the warmth of his presence, the sturdy width of his chest, and I collapsed against him in a heap of worry and tears.

"I got you, Kenny," he whispered against my hair, with his arms tight around me. "I got you. You're gonna be okay."

He found my shoes, purse, and jacket, and then, with his arm around my shoulders, he led me in my pajamas down to the street, where he called a cab. On the quick ride to the doctor, Goose found the number in my phone and gave them a call, letting them know I was on the way.

But, by the time we reached the OB/GYN's office, just two hours before my scheduled appointment, my vision had already begun to return. Now I felt like an idiot, as we took a seat in the waiting room. But Goose just took my hand and assured me there was nothing to feel stupid about.

"What if they don't find anything wrong and I came here early for nothing? I'm wasting their time now," I said. "It was probably just an anxiety attack or something."

"Then, consider yourself lucky," he replied gruffly, keeping my fingers tightly wound with his.

As we waited, I wondered if I should talk to him about what had happened between us, just to clear away any residual awkwardness that still permeated the air. I wanted to apologize, for my reaction to his kiss and for still having his number in my phone, but before I could say anything, the red-headed nurse was calling me back to an exam room.

She now recognized me from previous appointments and, while eyeing Goose skeptically, asked, "Is your boyfriend on the way?"

"No," I answered sheepishly, feeling like an idiot in my worn flannel jammies and leopard print slippers. "But, um, my friend is here, so …"

"You're okay with him being in the exam room?"

Truthfully, I wasn't so sure that I was, but all things considered, I was even less okay with being alone. So, I nodded without hesitation, and she instructed us both where to sit. She asked some questions about the incident with my eyes and the other symptoms I'd been feeling lately. She took my blood pressure and temperature, and then, told me the doctor would be in to see me shortly.

Now, in the quiet of the sterile room, and sitting on the exam table, I clenched my fingers together while my legs jittered nervously, and said, "God, what if something is really wrong?"

"Nothing is wrong," Goose assured me gently. "You're going to be fine."

"You don't know that."

"Yes, I do. You're fine."

They were empty words. There was no way he could know if I was, in fact, fine. But it felt nice just to have him there, to not be alone, and I allowed myself to relax just a little.

When Dr. Albrecht finally came into the room a few minutes later, she noted the unusual amount of swelling in my legs and told me they wanted to do a sonogram. "But first," she said, "you mentioned to the nurse that you haven't felt the baby move as much lately."

"No," I said, shaking my head. "I figured it's just because he's got less room to move around in there or something."

She nodded and instructed me to lie back, then laid her hands on my stomach and felt around, pressing and prodding. My heart pounded loudly, terrified of what she might say, until finally, in an eerily calm tone, she said, "Okay, my dear. So, before we do the sonogram, I think we should run a nonstress test. Follow me."

"What? Why?" I asked, as my heart dreaded what her next words might be.

She smiled reassuringly. "We just need to make sure everything is okay."

Without any other questions, we did as we were told and followed her down the hallway and into another room I hadn't seen before, one with two cushy recliners.

"How did you know I needed a nap?" Goose joked, and Dr. Albrecht wagged a finger at him.

"No, no, this is not for you," she said, just as the nurse entered the room. "Kendall, we're going to strap a monitor to your belly and you're just going to relax. Every time you feel the baby kick," she handed me a long, thin device with a button at the top, "you're going to press this button. Like playing a video game. Okay?"

As the nurse positioned the monitor and secured it tightly to my belly, I nodded. Then, both doctor and nurse told me to sit tight for a few minutes and to feel for the baby's kicks, and with that, they left the room.

Sitting across from me in a less comfortable chair, Goose said, "Try to relax. They're just running tests as a formality. You're going to be fine."

I tried to smile at his attempt to ease my worry. "I really hope you're right."

Click.

"You felt him move?"

I nodded. "Yeah, a little bit."

"See? That's a good thing."

Click.

"Girlfriend, you're gonna pass this shit with flying colors."

I laughed, shaking my head. "I just can't get rid of this feeling that something isn't right. It's just … I dunno, I feel like something is really wrong. I feel like the baby is—"

"Hey, so how have you been doing lately? I mean, besides all of," he waved a hand in my direction, "you know, this."

"Well, I, uh," I shrugged and clicked the button again, "I did my glucose test last week."

"Oh, shit, I remember Krystal telling me about that one and how she puked all over the place when she had to drink that crap. How did you do?"

I managed to smile, as my anxiety settled just a little to a more manageable level. "It really wasn't that bad. Everybody had horror stories for me, but I dunno. I kinda liked it."

"That's because *you're* badass. Krystal, though," he laughed, shaking his head. "There's nothin' badass about that woman. She's laid up for a week if she stubs her freakin' toe."

Click.

"You've never really talked about her before."

He shrugged, lifting the corner of his mouth in an easy smile. "Nothin' much to say. We knew each other in high school, dated for a few months before graduation, then broke up when I found out I'd be goin' to Iraq—"

"Wait, why did you go to Iraq?"

"I told you I was in the Army," he answered without hesitation.

"Oh, right, I remember you saying something about that. But you didn't tell me you went to Iraq. You were in combat?"

Click.

He nodded in reply, then said, "Like I've always told you, everybody's hidin' somethin'."

Suddenly realizing just how little I knew about this man, and just how little that seemed to matter, I nodded, not knowing what else to say.

"Anyway," he continued, clasping his hands between his knees, "after I came home, we got back together, got married, and got pregnant. A few months later, we were divorced, and I was in rehab, trying to get my shit together. Now, we're really good friends who happen to share a pretty awesome daughter."

"You don't think you'll ever get back together?"

Click.

He pursed his lips and shook his head. "Nah. Some people are just better off not being romantically involved, you know? That was me and Krystal. We were never a great—"

"Okay, Kendall, let's have a look," the nurse said, announcing her return to the room.

She headed toward the machine the monitor was attached to and quickly scanned the stream of paper that had draped itself over the table and onto the floor. I watched as her forehead crumpled and listened as she muttered a quick and unhappy, "hm," before running out the door in a hurry without another word.

My heart raced inside my tightening chest. "Oh, God," I groaned, as I clicked the button again. "Something's wrong. I told you, something is—"

"Hey, you haven't guessed why they call me Goose in a while," he cut me off, leaning closer to my feet.

"W-What? I can't—"

"Come on," he nudged my slippered foot and offered a reassuring grin, "just give another guess. Lay it on me."

I blew out a long-winded breath and stifled a cough, then said, "Um, okay … maybe, uh, maybe you secretly have webbed feet."

Goose laughed. "No. But I like that one."

"Or, um, you hoard little glass goose figurines. You probably have hundreds of them."

"Oh, God, that'd be weird."

"Maybe you—"

"So," the doctor said, entering the room unannounced and sitting down on the chair beside Goose, "you, my dear, are heading to Labor and Delivery."

"What?" My eyes volleyed between her and Goose, unsure I had heard her correctly. "Are you, are you *serious* right now?"

"Very," she said, maintaining an eerie calm. "They're already expecting you. You just go down to the hospital, head up to the sixth floor, and the on-call doctor will monitor you for a little while. Okay?"

"O-Okay," I stammered, not knowing what else to say, as the nursed hurried in and helped me to my feet, then began to unstrap the monitor from my belly. "Wha-What's going on? What's happening?"

"Well," the doctor said, "it appears that your baby is in quite a bit of distress, but we don't know why."

"Oh, my God," I said, unable to breathe, as I turned to look in Goose's direction. "I told you. I told you something was wrong. I—"

"We don't know what's wrong, Kendall," the doctor gently interjected. "It might not be anything, but just in case, we're sending you to the hospital. Because that will be the best place for you and your baby right now. Okay?"

I nodded quickly and asked, "Okay, when … when do I have to be there?"

The doctor didn't waste another second, as she replied, "Right now."

Without further instruction, Goose grabbed my hand and we hurried through the waiting room and to the elevator. We rode silently down to the street, where he waved down a cab and helped me in. Then, as we zigged and zagged through New York City traffic, he turned to me, never letting go of my hand, and looking right into my eyes, said, "You're going to be fine, Kenny. Okay? I swear to God, I'm not going to let a fucking thing happen to you or your baby."

With my hand wrapped in his and tears frozen in my eyes, I spent the rest of the ride to the hospital thanking God that, of all the bars I could've stumbled into that day in September, I happened to stumble into his.

Chapter Twenty

They had been waiting for my arrival, just like Dr. Albrecht had said. The nurse that greeted us ordered Goose to wait in a chair. But as she led me down a long hallway to a room of hospital beds, curtains, and monitors, I soon wished he hadn't been made to stay back. I didn't want to be alone, as they, without any explanation, instructed me to put all of my clothes and belongings into a bag and to change into a gown.

"Okay, Kendall, just lay down here and we'll get you set up with an IV," one of the nurses said with a reassuring smile.

"What's happening?" I asked, flitting my eyes around to look at every one of the hospital personnel crowded into the room. "Why do I need an IV?"

"Just in case we need to administer any medications," she replied, as another nurse began to ask me a myriad of questions about my health history and the medications I was currently taking.

"What is going on?" I asked again, and the nurse handling the IV finally answered, "We're just doing all of this as a precaution, just in case you need it. We don't want to have to waste any time."

In case I need it? I thought frantically, furrowing my brows. *In case I need it for what?*

The on-call doctor entered the room in a winter jacket, like she had been getting ready to leave before answering the call to come see me. She smiled at me, introducing herself as Dr. Gellar, and asked for a brief run-down of what I'd been experiencing over the past couple of weeks. I told her everything that I'd previously told my doctor, and Dr. Gellar nodded, removing her jacket and revealing her scrubs.

She's in scrubs. Why is she in scrubs? What the hell is going on here? Why won't anybody tell me what's going on?

My thoughts were running a mile a minute, as my eyes volleyed between the doctor and other medical staff, scurrying purposefully around the room. They washed their hands, tended to computers, and I felt like I was an actor on one of those hospital dramas. Nothing felt real, nothing felt right, and I wondered if, at some point, I would wake up from this nightmare and find I'd never been sick.

Finally, Dr. Gellar stopped to peer over a nurse's shoulder, at the screen she was working on, and asked, "Kendall, have you noticed any leakage?"

"Leakage?" I squeaked through the panic rising in my throat. "I … I don't know?"

"It would have been a thick, sticky discharge," she explained. "It could've happened over time, or all at once."

"I mean, I've had discharge, but I thought that was normal …"

One of the nurses abruptly announced, "BP is one-eighty over ninety."

Hurriedly, Dr. Gellar turned to a nurse and asked, "Do we have a room ready?"

"Yeah, we do."

"Okay," she answered. Then, she looked back at me, and without a smile on her face, she said, "Okay, Kendall, you're having your baby tonight."

"What?" I was too stunned to stammer, too shocked for it to register exactly what it was she had said.

"Your baby doesn't have the fluid he needs to survive in your uterus anymore, and your body is in a great amount of distress. He needs to come out as soon as possible, to give you both a fighting chance. So, we're going to be taking you to the operating room, to perform an emergency C-section, and we're doing it right now. Do you have anybody here with you?"

I'm only twenty-seven weeks pregnant. The baby is too little. He's going to die, my brain frantically reminded me, as I said, "Uh … um … my friend, he's in the waiting room, but um, I—"

"Someone go tell him what's going on, right now!" Dr. Gellar shouted into the room, then said to a nurse, "Prepare her for surgery."

Then, of all of the things I could've thought to say, of everything I could've plucked from that last ten minutes of chaos, I looked down at my wrist and said to nobody in particular, "My watch. I'm, I'm still wearing my watch."

One nurse smiled reassuringly and said, "That's okay. We'll just take that off."

"I'm-I'm sorry," I found myself saying, stunned and unable to feel my own mouth as it moved. "I didn't realize I'd have to. I just, I just thought …"

"It's fine, honey," she replied kindly, helping me to remove my watch, the device that had once alerted me to the racing of my heart. "And let's just get these earrings out, too, okay?"

Hands were on my ears, undoing my earrings and dropping them into a plastic cup. And all I could do was lay there, staring at my belly and wondering what the hell had happened. Things were going so well. The pregnancy had been relatively healthy, hadn't it? I knew I had the issues with my heart rate and sensitivity to heat, but all things considered, that wasn't too bad. So, what had happened to put me here and in this position? Could I have done anything to avoid it?

A mother is supposed to protect her children, and I had already failed mine before he was even born.

"Kenny?" Goose approached the bed hesitantly, as if he felt he shouldn't have been there. "What the hell is going on?"

The moment I saw him and the concern written plainly on his face, tears filled my eyes for the first time since entering the hospital. "They're taking the baby."

His face paled, his jaw dropped, and his eyes widened with shock and fear. "Wait, what?"

"Th-They said he n-n-needs to come out," I said, my voice shaking, as if I was freezing in this room that felt too hot.

Goose laid a hand over his mouth and I watched with a warm, terrified heart as his eyes flooded. "Oh, God, Kenny …"

"I'm fucking scared," I confessed, as the army of nurses unlocked the bed wheels and got everything ready for transport. "I don't want to do this. I don't want to fucking do this."

"Kenny. What do you need me to do?" he asked, as they began to wheel me out of the room.

"Call my parents. Call Brendan," I called to him, desperate to catch one more glimpse of his face. "Tell them what's happening!"

"Okay," he replied, his voice quivering. "I'm gonna be right here when you get out! You got this, Kenny! You got this!"

They wheeled me down a hall and into a brightly lit room. As I was instructed me to shift from the bed to the operating table, with my shivering arms and legs, I repeated those words to myself. Hoping desperately that I would believe them, as they maneuvered my body as if I were a doll, sat me up, exposed my back, and administered the stinging epidural into the base of my spine.

You got this, you got this, you got this …

Chapter Twenty-One

"I don't like this. God, I don't like the way this feels."

"You're okay, Kendall. You're doing great."

"No. Oh, God, I feel nauseous. I hate this. I fucking hate this."

"It's a boy."

"The time is 8:07."

"Oh, God, oh, God. I don't like this. I don't feel good."

"Okay, Kendall, I'll give you something to make you feel better. Do you want me to do that?"

"Yes. Oh, my God. Yes, I can't do this."

***

"Hey, Kenny. How do you feel?"

"Thirsty... hungry..."

"Here, you can have some ice chips."

"Have you seen him?"

"Not yet, honey."

"Who ... who's gonna take care of Mrs. Potter?"

"We got it covered."

"Get some rest, honey. You need to …"

***

I opened my eyes to the sun streaming through the window. A nurse was already at my arm, taking my blood and vitals for what felt like the millionth time. She smiled, acknowledging that I was awake, and I asked for some water through a dry, scratchy throat. She obliged without question or protest, putting a stop to her work to bring me a cup and a straw. As the nurse held the cup for me, I drank like I hadn't been given a sip of water in weeks, and when I was finished, I flopped back against the pillows, exhausted.

And there, snoring in the chair beside my bed, was Goose.

I squinted at his figure and tried to remember everything that happened the night before. It was all a blur, after the anesthesiologist had knocked me out. I could only recall bits and pieces of what had happened the following morning. But what stood out to me, more than anything else, was that Goose hadn't left.

"He's so sweet," the nurse whispered to me, following my gaze. "He ran out before and brought back coffee and doughnuts for the morning shift."

Looking back at her, I cocked my head with confusion. "He did?"

She nodded. "Yep. You're lucky to have him."

Then, with the promise that she'd be back later to take more blood and to bring my meds, she left, and I was alone with a man who wasn't really mine.

But God, I wished he was.

***

After falling asleep, I woke up again, unsure of how much time had passed and saw my parents entering the room. In their hands, they carried flowers and a stuffed cat that looked an awful lot like Mrs. Potter.

"Oh, she's awake," Dad whispered to Mom, before grinning and heading toward the bed. "Hey, Ken, how you feeling, honey?"

"I'm okay," I croaked, not sure yet if that was a lie.

"Has the doctor been in yet?" Mom asked, dropping everything into a chair.

I shook my head. "I don't think so."

Then, I glanced around the room and noticed Goose was gone. My heart sank with an overwhelming need for him to be there, and I asked, "Where's Goose?"

"We just saw him in the lobby on our way up," Mom said. "He told us he was going home to shower."

"Oh," I muttered, not intending to sound so disappointed.

"But he said he'd be back later, after he stops at work to let them know he'd be out."

"Oh, and he said that, if there was anything you wanted him to bring back, to send him a text," Dad chimed in, taking a seat in the chair that Goose had slept in.

Mom brought the vase of flowers she carried to the table beside the bed. "We grabbed these in the gift shop. They're kinda wilted, but," she fluffed the blossomed roses and daisies a bit, perking them up and making them prettier, "they'll have to do until we can get some nicer ones."

"They're fine, Mom," I said, barely able to bring my voice above a whisper.

"We also got you this," she said, picking up the stuffed cat and handing it to me. "I know it's not Mrs. Potter, but it kind of looks like her, so we thought you might like it."

Tears filled my eyes as I hugged the floppy stuffed animal. I missed my cat. I had left in such a hurry, I didn't have time to say goodbye or make sure she was all set for the night. I hoped she wasn't confused, and I hoped she wouldn't be angry whenever I made it back home.

"Thanks," I managed to say.

"So, we talked to the doctor last night after we first got here," she went on, folding her hands in her lap. "They're pretty sure you have severe preeclampsia, judging from the way your blood pressure spiked so suddenly. They said if you had come in even just a couple hours later, you would have had a stroke, and the baby would've already been gone."

The baby.

I laid a hand over my empty stomach at the reminder of my poor baby. How had I not thought about him, first thing after I woke up? How could I have been so selfish?

181

"Is he …" I couldn't get the last word out. *Alive.* I hugged the stuffed cat closer to my chest, unable to believe that I was actually wondering if my baby was still on this earth, when just yesterday, he was still in my belly. Kicking and still so far away from being ready to be born.

"He is," Mom answered softly. "They have him in the NICU right now. You don't remember one of the nurses coming in last night to talk to you?"

I tried to recall such conversation from the night before and came back with nothing. So, I shook my head and replied, "No. I don't remember much from last night. Just little bits and pieces of things."

Dad nodded understandingly. "You *were* pretty out of it. They must've put you to sleep during surgery."

"Yeah, they did," I said, recalling the moment the anesthesiologist told me he would give me something to make me feel better. "After they took the baby."

It was all so surreal, and no matter how many minutes passed by in that hospital room, the reality of the situation didn't seem to settle in. I kept trying to force the truth home. That I had given birth to my baby boy, and that he was here, three whole months premature and in the neonatal intensive care unit. But there was a big part of my psyche that seemed to be too detached from it all, and I just couldn't seem to accept that this was my life. No matter how hard I tried, I just couldn't believe it was real.

After I forced myself to eat some fruit and a muffin, Dr. Gellar came in to run me through what they knew about my condition. Just as my mother had said, I was

182

diagnosed with preeclampsia, a condition that causes high blood pressure in pregnant women. Coupled with that, my amniotic fluid had been almost completely depleted for reasons unbeknownst to the doctor. She ran me through the magnesium sulfate treatment I was currently undergoing, and the variety of medications I was on, to try and control my blood pressure.

"I'm so hot," I complained, rolling my head against the pillow.

"I know," she sympathized, nodding. "You're going to be warm from the mag, and you might find it harder to breathe for a while, from the fluid around your lungs. That's why we have you on the oxygen," she said, gesturing toward the canula in my nose. "You're going to be uncomfortable for a couple days, but we're watching you very closely, and you're going to be fine."

A question burned against my tongue, and I knew I needed to ask. "Was it something I did?" I asked, fearing her answer, as I clutched the stuffed cat and kept my eyes diverted from the woman in the white lab coat.

"No. God, no," she assured me, reaching out to lay a hand on my blanket-covered knee. "There was absolutely nothing you could have done differently to prevent this from happening. Unfortunately, this just happens sometimes, and it is in *no way* your fault."

I heard what she was saying, and I believed she was telling the truth. But I still couldn't accept it. I couldn't accept that my body had simply decided it no longer wanted to carry the baby. I couldn't accept that I had taken something so natural like pregnancy, and completely failed at it, for no other reason than, "it just happens sometimes."

I couldn't accept that I had almost killed myself and my baby, just by being pregnant.

"Usually," Dr. Gellar explained further, "the preeclampsia goes away right after giving birth, but in some cases, the complications linger for a while. And right now, your blood pressure is still high. Hopefully, we'll see some improvement over the next couple of days."

I nodded through the fog I was in. "Okay."

"Just take solace in the fact that you listened to your intuition and got to the doctor when you did. You listened to your body, and now, you and your baby are exactly where you need to be, because *you* did the right thing," she went on, offering a spiel I didn't feel quite up to hearing.

"Okay," I repeated, and then, added for good measure, "Thank you."

With a nod and the assurance that she'd stop back in before she left for the day, Dr. Gellar left, and I was once again alone with my parents.

The tension in the air was heavy and thick, filled with the weight of my condition and what had happened. Then, coalescing with the fear and worry, were the questions that weren't being asked. How long would I have to be here in this room? How long would the baby have to be there? Was he going to survive? Was I?

I tried to push the unknowns from my mind, and finally asked the one question I could get an answer to, "Was Brendan here last night?"

Mom looked across the bed at Dad, then shook her head and said, "No, he never came."

The magnitude of what that meant and how it felt instantly brought tears to my eyes.

"He never came?" I croaked through a clot of emotion. "Was he, was he called?"

Mom nodded stiffly. "Goose called him, and so did I."

"Did he answer?"

"Not for Goose—"

"Oh," I said, sniffling and nodding. "He probably didn't know who's number it was."

"Right," Mom replied slowly. "But he *did* answer when I called."

"Well, what did he say?"

Mom gave me a smile that was so forced I couldn't even come close to believing it. "You know, maybe we shouldn't be talking about this right now. You should get some—"

"Come on," I groaned, laying one of my bandaged hands against my forehead with a heavy sigh. "I need to know what he said and I'm not going to stop thinking about it. So, please, just tell me."

With a sigh from my mother and a gentle nod of my father's head, Mom finally replied, "Brendan said that he was wrapped up in some work stuff and couldn't get out of it. So, he said he would come by later when he had some time to spare."

My throat tightened around the persistent lump of sadness, hurt, and betrayal. "Oh. Well, that's just great.

I'm glad he can just *decide* when to spare a few minutes to deal with this."

"Kenny," Dad said, laying a hand on my thigh. "This is a lot for anybody to deal with. Don't—"

"Sure, sure," I answered, nodding profusely. "I mean, of course, this is a lot for him to cope with. I get it. It's not every day you find out your girlfriend almost died from having your baby three months early. He needs time to process and cope before he can even *think* to ask if I'm okay," I muttered sardonically.

"Well, hopefully he'll be by later," Mom said, offering an encouraging smile.

"I won't hold my breath," I muttered, while still hoping she was right and wondering when it was I'd eventually get sick of hoping.

Chapter Twenty-Two

"**W**e need to get you up and moving," Michelle, one of my nurses, said.

The anesthesia was taking its dear, sweet time wearing off and so many hours after my surgery, I was itchy and ready to crawl out of my skin. The incision just above my groin was sore, still noticeable even through the heavy-duty painkillers, and made it difficult for me to cough, let alone move.

There was no way I was going anywhere yet, but Michelle was insistent.

"Come on, just try. Don't you want to see your baby?"

My baby. My little baby boy.

The baby I had failed. The baby I feared—what he looked like, what he sounded like, what he would think of me, if he could think at all.

How the hell could I face him, when I could barely face myself? And what if, after all was said and done, he was destined to not be my baby at all? What if he died?

The barrage of questions and uncertainties formed a boulder in my throat, and I nearly choked, as I finally told her, "When I feel better. I'm, I'm still a little dizzy."

"Okay," Michelle replied reluctantly, clearly a little disappointed but didn't want to let it show. "I'll check in on you in a bit. Try to rest."

She left me alone then, keeping the door to my room open, and I laid a hand over my empty womb as I listened to a newborn baby cry. The wave of jealousy and rage came in slow but completely swept me away before I could realize what was happening, and a sob bubbled up and pushed past my lips. I squeezed my eyes shut and rolled my head toward the window, praying for sleep or death to take me away, when I heard someone enter my room.

"Hey, Mama!" a cheerful voice said, and I could only cry a little harder into the uncomfortable, crinkly pillow beneath my head. "Hey, what's wrong? Oh, honey, don't cry."

"Close the door," I cried to the stranger. "Please, just close the damn door."

"Okay, Mama. Okay, I'm closing it now."

Her voice was friendly, one I immediately could imagine myself growing attached to, if I wasn't so focused on the unrelenting pain in my heart. I heard the door click shut, and then, moments later, the bed was weighed down and a hand laid gently against my upper arm.

"Okay, look at me." I shook my head, and she pushed me a little further. "Come on, I'm not gonna bite you. Just look at me."

So, I did. I rolled over and took in the blonde sitting at the edge of my bed. Her hair was pulled back, her makeup was done well, and she was dressed nicely in a blazer and a pair of black pants. She didn't look much like the rest of the hospital staff, in their scrubs and lab coats, and I narrowed my teary eyes at her with skepticism.

"Talk to me. What's going on?"

"Um …" I was struck with an embarrassing amount of stranger danger that no thirty-five-year-old woman should feel in a hospital after just giving birth. I mean, for crying out loud, these people were regularly changing my bloody maxi pads and emptying my bag of urine, while I couldn't remember most of their names.

This woman could clearly sense my hesitation, and smiled kindly. "I'm Elle. We met last night. I'm your son's nurse in the NICU."

"Oh," I replied, nodding. "Well, you might have met me, but I definitely don't remember meeting you."

She laughed easily, nodding her head as her ponytail bobbed. "Yeah, you were pretty out of it. Those drugs are pretty good, huh?" I shrugged, not in the mood to joke around, and she continued, "Well, like I said, I'm Elle. I was there last night, to take your baby boy to the neonatal intensive care unit, right down the hall, and admitted him. He's been mine these last couple of nights, but I haven't seen you in there."

Shame heated my cheeks as I shrugged. "I haven't really wanted to get up and move around."

"Oh, believe me, I get it. My last pregnancy ended with an emergency C-section, too. You don't want to do anything at first. But let me tell you, it'll help you feel a lot better if you just try."

"I highly doubt that."

189

"Well, I mean, don't get me wrong. It's no walk in the park at first. But you won't start to heal until you make up your mind that you're going to."

I allowed her words to settle for a moment. There was truth in them, and I knew it, as I remembered my last surgery. Just a year ago, my gallbladder had been removed, and while that wasn't the most serious surgery to have done, it was still surgery and it had taken a bit of time to feel better again. But I remembered pushing myself to move as much as I could before needing to rest, and I knew that was a reason for my quick recovery—along with the help of some great painkillers.

I knew having a C-section was much more serious than a laparoscopic gallbladder removal. But I also knew that allowing myself to do nothing but lay in bed wasn't going to help at all. Even if that was all I really wanted to do.

Elle smiled and I think she knew she had gotten through to me. "I wanna see you down there in a little while," she said. "You and your baby have a long road ahead of you, and neither one of you can do it alone."

***

An hour later, my mom pushed me in a wheelchair down the long hallway of the Mother and Baby ward, to the hospital's neonatal intensive care unit. I was terrified, as I waited for the large automatic doors to open, not knowing what to expect. I didn't know what I would see once I was in there. But, as she pushed me to the NICU's door and rang the bell to be let in, I resigned myself to not backing down.

My baby was in there, and I didn't want him to be alone.

There came a click as the door was unlocked from the inside and my mother pushed it open. We entered a small room, with computer monitors, a sink, a desk, and one nurse. She smiled and pointed at the sink.

"Mama, I just need for you to wash your hands and then we'll get you checked in, okay?"

Mama. I don't think I'll ever get used to that, I thought, as Mom wheeled me over to the sink and I scrubbed my shaking hands with such a sickening, nervous excitement rushing through my veins.

The nurse at the desk then led me through another door to a larger room full of incubators and their tiny inhabitants. Nurses hurried around, tending to their patients and chatting with one another like they were hanging out with friends. Elle spotted me from where she stood at one of the incubators and smiled kindly, as she made her way over to me.

"I got this, Liz," she said to the other nurse, and then, she directed her attention to my mother and me. "You guys made it!"

I nodded, unable to look at her as I stared at the tiny babies with red-colored skin. "Yeah, I tried to walk, but I was still too dizzy."

"Oh, that's okay," she assured me, taking the wheelchair from my mom and steering me toward the back of the room. "You got down here and that's what matters. I'm proud of you."

Then, after turning a corner, she parked me at one of the incubators and said, "Mama, I'd like to introduce you to your little boy."

My breath was stolen away by the sight of the scrawny, little baby, lying on a bed of blankets and bolstered pillows. There were wires and tubes coming from nearly every part of his body. He was a dark red in color, with thick and deep hair and eyes that were hidden behind the tiniest pair of eyelids I'd ever seen. Some would have looked at him and called him a fetus, and I guess they wouldn't have been wrong. That is essentially what he was. But to me, all I saw was, my baby boy.

Mom stood beside me but didn't speak a word, as I looked up to Elle and asked, "Can I touch him?"

"Oh, of course, you can," she encouraged, nodding enthusiastically. "Babies this young are very sensitive though, so stroking his skin isn't the best idea. It might make him irritated and cranky. But you can certainly hold his hand, or gently cup his head. In fact, it's important that you do. He should know the feeling of your hands, because touch is sometimes the best medicine for these little guys."

I nodded and began to extend my hand toward him, noting the heat radiating from his incubator, then stopped. I was frozen with fear, terrified of knowing what he felt like. But Elle reassured me it was okay and that I wouldn't hurt him, and so, with trembling fingers, I closed the gap between his hand and mine.

His skin was paper thin and soft, and his fingers were so fragile and delicate. But God, he was so meticulously crafted in every way and so delicately designed. I would be lying if I said I'd seen or touched anything more perfect in my life.

Mom snapped a few pictures of our first touch, as I sat there, holding his hand and smiling, while tears pooled in my eyes, but never fell. I didn't want him to feel my sadness. I didn't want him to sense my fear or concern. But he was so small and fragile, and I couldn't help but think of the likelihood of him ever getting to see the world outside and coming home. He was hooked up to all of these beeping machines, these things I knew were keeping him alive, and I couldn't help but be reminded of just how badly I had failed him.

Releasing his hand, I turned to my mom, standing behind me, and said, "I think I need to lie down."

"Are you sure?" she asked, her face falling. "You can spend more time—"

"No, I'm really tired."

I was deflecting and I knew it. I wanted to avoid every one of the fears sitting right in front of me. I knew my mom could sense that, but she didn't argue, as she took the handles of the wheelchair and thanked Elle for everything.

Then, we left the NICU and headed back to my room, where she helped me into bed and I forced myself to sleep. Just to disconnect from the reality I didn't want to face.

***

When I awoke early the next morning, it was to Elle entering the room. She immediately apologized for waking me up, but said she needed to say something to me before leaving for the day.

"Okay," I muttered sleepily, raising the bed to face her.

"Your little boy *will* come home," she said, and immediately, my throat constricted around the fear of having to say goodbye before we'd barely said hello.

"You don't know that," I croaked, turning away to face the wall.

"Kendall—can I call you Kendall?"

"I prefer Kenny, but sure."

"Okay," she replied, laying a hand over mine. "Kenny, trust me, okay? I have been doing this for a very long time, and I have taken care of hundreds of babies. Believe me when I say he *will* go home. He just needs time. That's all. Time and love and patience."

Turning back to face her and her assuring smile, I bit my lower lip and then asked, "What if he doesn't make—"

Elle held up her hand and shook her head. "There won't be any of that talk, got it? If I *truly* felt there was something wrong with your baby, I would tell you, I swear. But I don't. He's just small, and he needs to grow. That's all."

I took a deep breath and allowed a tear to fall, as I nodded. "Is there a chance something could go wrong down the road?"

"There's always a chance," she replied honestly, and as difficult as it was to hear, with that bit of truth, I now believed every one of her words. "But I and all of the

194

other nurses are going to do everything we can to make sure that doesn't happen. Okay?"

"You swear?"

Elle nodded gently and squeezed my hand, as she replied, "I swear."

Chapter Twenty-Three

That evening, my parents left to head back to my apartment. As always, they had wanted to stay longer, and I knew they would've stayed forever, if they could. But they were both barely able to keep their eyes open, and I demanded for them to get some sleep. Before they left, they promised to be back bright and early in the morning. I told them to take their time, because as much as I loved having them with me, I could've used some space, too. I knew some time away from them and their worried glances would do me good, and finally, I had it.

The sterile room was feeling a little more comfortable to me, after being there for a little over a day. The TV glowed with the still image of a woman holding a baby and a message to contact my nurse if I wanted to set my room up for cable, which I didn't. What I did want, was wanted to read a book or maybe even take another nap, before the next round of blood and vitals. But just as I was about to settle in, a knock came at the door.

Groaning, I rolled my head against the pillow and called out, "Yeah?"

The door cracked open and there was Goose, shielding his eyes with a hand. "Hey," he said cautiously. "I didn't know if you wanted visitors or whatever, but uh, I brought you dinner." He waved a bag into the room.

A smile was slow to spread across my face, but before I knew it, there it was. "Why are you covering your eyes?" I asked.

Hesitantly, he lowered his hand and peered into the room. "I didn't know if you were doing something you didn't want me seeing."

"Like what?" I giggled for the first time in days and it felt good.

He laughed, walking into the room and closing the door behind him. "I don't know! When Hannah was a baby, Krystal always had her tits—*boobs* hanging out, so …"

"I think that's for breastfeeding moms," I replied quietly, dropping my eyes to the plain, boring blanket draped over my legs.

Goose's eyes widened, surprised and taken aback, before saying, "Right! Right. So, I guess you're not—" He cut himself off, shaking his head and squeezing his eyes shut. "Sorry. I'm sorry. That was fuckin' stupid of me to say. I'm sorry."

"It's okay," I replied, even though it wasn't. He hadn't meant anything by it, and it wasn't as though I'd ever had dreams of breastfeeding my baby the moment they entered the world. But the fact that I didn't have a choice served as another dash of stinging salt in the gaping, bloody wound.

Goose came to sit by the bed, and I was suddenly all too aware of how timidly he was behaving. He was nervous, maybe even scared, and his discomfort was only adding to my own. It wasn't all that long ago that he had kissed me. Just weeks ago, he had confessed his feelings for me, and when they weren't openly reciprocated, we had made the silent but mutual agreement to cease contact. But then, at the drop of a hat, he had rushed to my aid and then stayed with me. He had saved our lives, and now, he was behaving like a stranger.

I hated it.

Come to think of it, there wasn't much I didn't hate right now.

I hated this room. I hated this gown. I hated that I still couldn't walk without wanting to fall over. I hated the constant interruption of hospital personnel every time I tried to sleep. I hated that I couldn't take my baby home. I hated that I couldn't feed him, see his eyes, or even hold him. I hated that I couldn't take care of him.

What kind of mother can't take care of her own baby?

As Goose grabbed the hospital tray and opened the box of wings, tears filled my eyes. He turned to look at me, took in the sorrowful state of my face, and then, reacted in horror as the flood drowned my features.

"Hey." He pushed the tray away from the bed and sat beside me, taking my sodden face in his big, calloused hands. "Kenny, what's wrong?"

"Y-you're joking, r-right?" I sobbed.

"I mean, I know things are hard, but I'm asking for specifics here, okay? Help me out."

198

I pulled away from his grasp and attempted to mop up my tears with the blanket. Goose stopped me and handed over a wad of napkins he'd brought. I thanked him and shook my head, as I said, "I just want to go home. I want to take my baby and go home."

"I know," he replied, stroking my dirty, knotted hair from my face. "I know you do. But you can't. One day, you will, but not now."

A fresh batch of tears soaked my cheeks as I nodded and whispered, "I know. But I hate this, Eric. I hate this so fucking much. And I hate that I can't do a fucking thing about it."

I don't know why I used his real name. I don't know why Eric had popped out of my mouth instead of the nickname I'd grown so accustomed to, and I don't know why it felt so right to say it. But it had, and something in that moment happened to him, too, as his mouth shut and his throat bobbed, only slightly visible beneath his well-groomed beard.

Then, in a rush of determination and absolution, he took my hand and squeezed it in his, as he said, "I joined the Army after my mom died on 9/11. I had my heart broken and I was fuckin' pissed off, so I wanted to do something about it. I wanted to get my revenge. They shipped me over to Iraq, and I made some friends, *good* friends. They were the kinda guys that I would've known for the rest of my life, we were *that* close.

"Anyway, we always had each other's backs in combat, we were always lookin' out for each other. But this one day, we were out, just the group of us, patrolling this street. And this fuckin' dog comes out of nowhere. It was hot as hell, I mean, it's the desert, for fuck's sake. So, I went to give this poor mutt a drink of water from my canteen. But while I'm there, distracted by this stupid fucking dog, my buddies go on, tellin' me to catch up when I'm done fuckin' around. Then, not even fifty feet away, they get ambushed by these fuckin' guys. And it was bad. I mean, it was a fuckin' bloodbath. These pieces of shit had machetes, and they were just swingin' at whatever they could get their hands on. And by the time I got over there and pumped these motherfuckers full of bullets, it was way too fuckin' late."

The air in the room evaporated with every one of his words and by the time he had finished talking, I thought I would suffocate. Nausea swept over me as I sat there, stunned and searching his eyes with mine. I had never noticed it before, all the pain he held inside, but I saw it now in the depth and darkness surrounding that bright shade of blue. There was so much tragedy in that darkness, it was amazing it hadn't swallowed him whole.

"After I was sent home, I couldn't live with the guilt of being alive. Like, I was here, living my life, when I also should've been slaughtered in that fuckin' street, too, if it hadn't been for that goddamn dog. So, I drank. I mean, I had always liked booze and drinking, I was a big partier back then, but this wasn't about having a good time. It was … it was about numbing the pain and forgetting the sounds and all that fuckin' blood …"

He pinched his eyes shut and shook his head, then said, "Anyway, in rehab, I learned to believe that everything happens for a reason, even the really bad shit. I convinced myself that I had been spared to have my daughter, to be a good person, and to honor the brothers I lost. So, that's exactly what I've been doing all these years since then. And when I met you, I added you to that list of reasons to be alive. Because whether this is ever more than just ... this, or not, I care about you, a lot. And when I thought I was gonna lose you ..." He sniffed and pinched the bridge of his nose, before continuing, "I felt so fuckin' helpless, and so fuckin' scared, because for the first time, I couldn't do a goddamn thing about it. There was no war to fight, nobody to seek revenge from. And nothing has *ever* made me want to drink more than that."

I hardened my glare and looked up at him. "You didn't, did you?"

He shook his head slowly. "Nah. I called up this buddy of mine and talked to him instead. That's the nice thing about making friends in rehab; they always have your back, when you need it most. But what I'm saying is, I know this is hard and that it sucks. I know nothing is the way it should be and that you would change everything if you could. But you gotta be strong and you gotta fight, 'cause that little guy down there needs you. And so do I."

***

After we ate the wings he'd brought, I set my iPad up on the tray, and finally, we watched *The Crow* together. During the rare moment of peace, I told Goose that, if I were to ever get engaged, I'd want the ring that the main character, Eric, gives to his girlfriend, Shelly, and he scoffed.

"What?" I asked.

"It's not even a nice ring."

"What do you mean? I think it's beautiful," I mumbled, staring at the modest diamond and delicately scrolled, gold band.

He shrugged, keeping his arms tightly wound around his middle. "Most chicks want the bling."

"And who says I'm most chicks?" I mocked with a roll of my eyes in his direction.

"Nah, I guess you're not," he muttered, lifting his mouth in a small, gentle smile.

"You think you'll ever get married again?" I asked, settling against the pillows and fixing my eyes once again on the screen.

I listened to him sigh and say, "I dunno. I wasn't a great husband. Not sure I ever wanna screw someone over like that again."

"You were dealing with a lot of shit, though."

"You don't know what I was like back then."

"No, but does it matter if I know who you are now?"

Another sigh. "I guess not."

His hand rested on the bed just beside my thigh. I wanted to reach out and take it, but I wouldn't. My resolve to stay faithful to the missing father of my baby was frustrating to everyone, including myself, but I wouldn't allow myself to break it now. Not when I was so vulnerable, not when I knew it would be an act of impulse, despite how much I knew my feelings were true and genuine.

"Have you picked a name for the baby yet?" Goose asked, keeping his eyes on the screen as Eric Draven burst through the bad guy's apartment door.

"I really like Alexander," I said. "I have to ask Brendan what he thinks, but that's what I'm leaning toward."

"Hm," he grunted in reply, and I could sense every drop of anger in that small sound. Then, he quickly added, "It's a good name. I like it."

With all of the commotion, I hadn't had much of a chance to think about Brendan. And now that I had mentioned him, and thought of him, I was realizing that I hadn't seen him. Nobody had mentioned him. Not even one of my nurses. Nothing.

"Hey," I said, "has Brendan been around, do you know?"

"I haven't seen him," he muttered bitterly.

And just like that, I spent the rest of our movie wondering where he was, what he was doing, if I would ever see him again, and if he would ever meet the baby he had once claimed to want.

Chapter Twenty-Four

O n day four of my hospital stay, Brendan finally showed up.

He rushed past hospital security on his way to my room and ignored the nurses, demanding that he stop. I was sitting on my bed, finally without a catheter and finally in a fresh pair of clothes, when Brendan burst through the door.

Goose and I were eating lunch while my parents napped at my apartment. This was now the routine. When my parents were able to, they hung out with me, and when they needed to get some rest or take a much needed shower, Goose left the bar and sat by my side. After four days in the hospital, I was quickly becoming accustomed to it, along with the frequent trips down the hall to see my baby. So, when Brendan showed up unannounced, I was surprised to see him. And maybe even a little disappointed.

"Kendall." His tone was harsh and alarmed, coming out with a breath of anger and not one of concern. "What the *hell* is going on?"

"Well, in case you haven't noticed, I'm in the hospital," I replied sardonically, and he rolled his eyes.

"*Why*? *Why* are you in the hospital?"

"Are you serious?" I asked, incredulous. "I've been here for *four* freakin' days, Brendan. I've been trying to call you—"

"*I* called you repeatedly, the night I brought her in here," Goose chimed in, and Brendan shot him with a disgusted look, as though only realizing then that we weren't alone.

"I haven't checked my phone in a few days," he replied hesitantly.

"In *days*?" Goose fired back, with skepticism written in his furrowed brow.

"I've been a little preoccupied—"

"With what?" Goose demanded, raising his voice.

"Whatever," I interrupted hurriedly, despite wanting to know myself why exactly he hadn't checked his phone in half a week. "I had the baby four days ago," I told him when I knew I finally had his attention. "I have severe preeclampsia, and the doctors are still trying to get my blood pressure under control."

"You … *had the baby?*"

"Yes! Didn't my parents tell you this?"

"They made it sound like you just needed to be watched for a day or so. I didn't realize the baby was *already born.*"

"I highly doubt that's what they said," I muttered. "Anyway, the baby was in a serious amount of distress, so they had to rush me into an emergency C-section."

Brendan's jaw clenched and his brow set in an angry line. "What did you do to make *that* happen?"

"Excuse me? I didn't *do* anything."

"Well, you must've done *something*. That type of shit doesn't just *happen*."

"The doctors and nurses said it was nothing I did—"

"Right. That's just what they *have* to say, to make *you* feel better." He looked around the room in a hurry, then asked, "Where is he? I want to see him."

"He's down the hall," I replied, fighting the quiver of my bottom lip and the burning in my nose.

"What? He's not in here? Why not?"

"Because he's in the NICU, Brendan."

"The, what? Are you saying he's sick?"

"He's tiny," I replied in a hushed tone, picturing my tiny baby, laying in his incubator, the bed they called an isolette. Too small to come out, too small to open his eyes, too small to cry or hold.

"What do you mean, he's tiny?"

I sighed, desperate to hold onto my composure. "He was born three months early. He's only one pound, ten ounces, and—"

"I want to see him. Right now," Brendan demanded, and so, with Goose's help, I got out of bed and led Brendan down the hall to meet his son.

***

"Hey, Mama!" It was the customary greeting from the nurses in the NICU whenever I entered.

"Hi," I replied, still not at a comfortable level with these wonderful and kind women.

"Are you Dad?" one nurse, Debbie, asked Brendan, who nodded stiffly. "Oh, great! So, we're just going to sign both of you in over here …"

I walked with Brendan to the sink, where we washed our hands, and then, we were written into the log. They took his information, told him they'd have to get him a hospital bracelet to wear, and then, I led him through the room of nurses, equipment, and isolettes, to our son. He was laying beneath the bili lights, to help with his jaundice, and a thick covering of gauze covered his eyes. Brendan stood to one side of the isolette, while I took the other.

Smiling over the plastic cover, I said, "I was thinking of naming him Alexander. It's a good, strong name, and he's a strong, little guy. He's been doing great, they said, and—"

"Kendall. Why the hell does he look like this?"

Startled by his question, my jaw flapped a couple times before finally asking, "What … what do you mean?"

"He looks like, like, like," he thrust a hand toward the isolette, "like a freakin' *alien*. And what the hell are all of these machines hooked up to him?"

Tears immediately sprung to my eyes as I dropped my gaze back to my beautiful little boy and said, "He's exactly the way he should be, Brendan; he's just *small* and needs to *grow*. And all of these machines are keeping him alive right now, so—"

"Because *you* couldn't."

"What?" I shot my gaze back to him and found him backing away from the isolette, shaking his head angrily.

A few of the nurses had begun to look in our direction. Their eyes were narrowed with disgust and anger, and if I wasn't so on the verge of tears, I might have looked just as angry. Or maybe I just felt sad. Sad and so unbelievably betrayed.

"I can't do this," he said, and then, rushed past me and through the door.

I shot an apologetic smile toward the nurses and a silent promise to my little boy that I'd be back, even if his father wouldn't, and then, I hurried as quickly as my sore, battered body would allow. Catching up with Brendan was impossible, he was too fast, and so I called to him when the pain and exhaustion got to be too much.

"Will you just hold on a second?" I shouted breathlessly, leaning against the wall for support.

"Mama, do you need help?" a passing nurse asked, her face and tone full of concern, and I shook my head.

"No, I just need to rest, thank you."

She looked toward Brendan with uncertain speculation, as he stopped and turned around, then nodded, before moving on.

"Where the hell are you going?" I asked him, trying to catch my breath. I was no longer on oxygen, but this level of exertion was still too much for me to handle. I knew I'd need a breathing treatment with the nebulizer later on, and I just hoped this interaction with Brendan would be worth it.

"I can't do this, Kendall," he said, calm, clear, and just barely apologetic.

"What do you mean, *you can't do this*?"

He shook his head, his hands stuffed deep into his jacket pockets. "I *mean*, I can't do this. I've been with you for a long time, and I mean, we've had fun, but ... all of this shit, with you and the baby ..." He sighed and let his shoulders drop. "I went along with it at first, because the idea of having a kid sounded kind of nice, but *this*?" He thrust a hand toward the NICU door. "I didn't sign up for this, Kendall. A sick, dying baby? And then, you want me to believe you did nothing to make it happen? God ..." He slammed his eyes shut and shook his head again. "This isn't what I want."

"He's not dying," I replied, choking on the words, but even as I said them, I wasn't yet sure I believed them.

"Yeah. Sure. Whatever you gotta tell yourself to feel better, but Kendo, look at him. He's *sick*."

Then, he turned to head back toward the elevator, and I called to him again.

"So, you're just leaving? That's it?"

Looking over his shoulder, he nodded. "Yeah. That's it. I told you, this isn't what I want. And I don't have to stick around and waste any more of my time on it."

"And what about what *I* want?" I shouted at him, as the tears finally broke free and streamed down my face. "Do you think I *want* this? Do you think I want to look at my baby through a freakin' plastic box? Do you think I'm *happy*? God, Brendan!" I shook my head and ran a hand over my tear-streaked cheeks, as a nurse slowly walked by but didn't say anything. "I didn't ask for this either. This isn't what I *want*. But I'm fucking dealing with it, because I *have* to."

"Well, I guess that's the difference between you and me, then," he replied, so cold and distant. "*I* don't have to."

In that moment, I was glad I was angry. I was glad for the rage I felt watching my boyfriend walk away to abandon me and his newborn son. Because if I hadn't been so angry, I would've been too aware of my heart as it stopped beating and shattered. And after everything I had been through, dying over Brendan wasn't worth it.

Not when I had Alexander to live for.

My parents and Goose had been livid when they learned of Brendan's dramatic and heartless exit. They had willingly expressed their intentions to either slaughter him while he slept or completely destroy his life in every way imaginable. But as angry as I was with him myself, I didn't feel that it was a productive use of energy. Especially with everything else going on. So, I successfully talked them down from their witch-hunt, and diverted their attentions to something more important.

Like Alexander. And me.

Chapter Twenty-Five

After I had spent a week in the hospital, with a couple more blood pressure spikes and scares, the doctors finally made the decision to discharge me. They provided me with an arsenal of prescription drugs, a referral to a home nurse to check my blood pressure weekly, and strict instructions to follow up with my doctors, while assuring me that I should be completely fine.

But I wasn't fine. In fact, I couldn't stop crying. Because while being discharged meant that my health was good enough to be trusted on my own, it also meant that I had to leave my baby behind. Nothing in the world felt more unnatural and horrible to me than that.

And so, I cried.

I cried while I took a shower and got dressed. I cried while packing my stuffed cat and the few things I had with me, and then, as I shuffled my way down the hall to say goodbye to Alexander.

When I entered the NICU, I was greeted with those same cheerful voices I'd grown to expect, but as soon as they saw my tear-streaked face, those voices immediately expressed concern.

"Oh, Mama," Debbie, Alexander's nurse for the night, said. "It's okay. Leaving him the first time was always going to be hard, every mom feels like that, but you'll be okay. You're strong, and you're going to get through this."

"I know," I said, pressing a hand to the warm plastic of his isolette and trying hard to keep from becoming a blubbering mess. "It just feels wrong. Like, I'm his mom and he's just a baby. I'm not supposed to leave my baby."

"I know it feels wrong," she replied sympathetically. "But you know he is exactly where he needs to be, and you know where you need to be is at home. You won't get any better being here. You need your own bed, your own shower and clothes—"

"And my cat," I added with a tearful laugh, looking through the clear plastic and watching the rapid rise and fall of my baby's chest.

"Exactly." Debbie smiled, as she reached out and rested her hand on my arm. "Everything is going to be okay, I promise. And you know you can call us to check on him anytime you want, day or night. We are always here."

I nodded briskly, as the exhaustion from standing for too long in the heat of the NICU began to get to me. It always did, and I couldn't stand it. I also couldn't stand not spending longer with him, when I always felt like I should. I couldn't stand not being able to do more than just look at him, when I felt like I should. And I couldn't stand the idea of walking away from him and through those doors, when I knew that I didn't have a choice.

Tears filled my eyes again as I whispered to him, "I don't want to go. I don't want to leave you here. But I'll be back, okay? I'll be back tomorrow and the next day and every single day after, until you can come home, okay?" I stroked the plastic with my thumb, wishing it was his skin, and added, "I love you, my beautiful baby boy."

Then, I forced myself to turn toward the door as the tears dripped from my chin. I pushed one foot in front of the other, severing the tethers that held me to my son, and felt them stretching, snapping, and fraying as I made my way out of the NICU.

And even despite how good it felt to have the fresh air on my skin for the first time in a week, I cried all the way home.

**

"Are you sure you don't want us to stay?" Mom asked, as she and Dad packed their things.

They had plans to catch an early train the next morning. After spending a week in the city, their list of things that needed to be done was growing longer by the minute, but so was their desire to stay by my side during recovery.

"I'm gonna be fine," I told her, finding a comfortable spot on the couch beside Mrs. Potter. She purred wildly, nuzzling her cheek, chin, and nose against every part of me that she could reach.

"She's missed you," Dad commented with a gentle smile.

"The feeling is mutual," I said, taking her little head in my hands and massaging her cheeks with my thumbs.

I was so happy to be home I could've cried just from smelling something other than disinfectant. But I was also so sad to be this far away from my son, even when it wasn't that far at all, and the war of emotions was leaving me feeling heavy with exhaustion.

"I think I'm going to sleep," I announced abruptly, using the arm of the couch to get up, even though I had just sat down. "A good, long sleep in my own bed sounds really freakin' nice right now."

"Okay, honey. Sleep as long as you need to," Mom said, coming to my aid, even though I refused the help. "Do you want us to wake you up when we leave?"

I shook my head. "You guys don't need to do that," I told her. "I just wanna sleep until my body wants to wake up."

She was reluctant to agree, as her fingers worried the hem of her sweater. I knew it was killing her to leave me in such a fragile state, just as it was killing me to be so far away from Alexander. But I needed rest, they needed to work, and it was for the best. I knew this, and so did Mom, as she closed her eyes and nodded.

"Don't forget we are only an hour away. You just say the word, and I'll be on that train," she said, as though an hour wasn't far at all. But right now, thinking about the distance it felt like an eternity.

"I know, Mom."

"I'll come by a few times this week, to check up on you," she added. "So, if you need anything, give me a call. I'll start making a list."

"Okay, Mom," I groaned playfully, laughing despite the stinging across my lower abdomen.

"*And* don't forget, you have Goose, too," she reminded me with a barely noticeable but hopeful, suggestive smile. "And he's not far."

Mom loved Goose. She had made that abundantly clear throughout my weeks stay in the hospital. Every day, when he left or his back was turned, she would make a comment or gesture, indicating just how much she adored him. I tried to thwart her suggestions to pursue something romantic with him, because what kind of woman starts something new just after a breakup and right after having a baby? Didn't I have enough to deal with? But, as reluctant as I was to admit it, the temptation was growing stronger by the day.

Still, I disputed, "Mom, I can't be bothering Goose all the time. He does have a family of his own, and a job."

"Kenny," Mom sighed. "We both know you're not a bother to him."

I wasn't oblivious, and I knew I wasn't a bother. With every infuriating protest I made, the more I reminded myself of the obnoxious heroines I wrote about in my books, and the reviews readers sometimes left about how much they couldn't stand them. And as I wandered into my room, with my trusted feline anxious at my heels, I wondered if maybe it was about time I stopped being exactly what I couldn't stand and got my hero.

Chapter Twenty-Six

"Bassinet, clothes, diapers, wipes …" I stopped writing my list of essentials for the baby, to readjust the pumping flange over my nipple. I moved it half a centimeter too far to the right and winced in pain.

"Dammit," I whined, pulling it off to attempt readjusting it. Again.

Since being in the hospital, I had diligently tried pumping breast milk for the baby with very little evidence of my efforts. The breastfeeding consultant and NICU nurses all insisted it would take time to get the hang of it and build my supply. But over a week of tireless pumping and feeling like a dairy cow was beginning to take its toll on my sanity. Not to mention my nipples. But the very moment I began to wonder if I should throw in the towel, was the moment I reminded myself that a couple of weeks wasn't that long at all and that I needed to try harder.

So, when it seemed like the flange was on correctly, I went back to work writing my list.

Since Alexander had made his appearance much sooner than expected, I never got the chance to have a baby shower, and now he needed things—or he would, once he was out of the hospital. Mom insisted that we would still have one, but the truth is, I didn't really care to have a party now. There was a lot to celebrate, sure. He was alive, and so was I. But I knew as well as anyone how easy it can be to settle into a false sense of security, and I didn't want to celebrate something that still had so much room for sadness and fear.

So, instead, I wrote a list of things to buy myself, with the hope that one day I'd feel secure enough to actually purchase them.

"Bottles, pacifiers ..."

I took a peek at my watch. 5 o'clock. It was getting late and I still had to shower, pump again, and grab something to eat on my way to the hospital. I sighed and impatiently stared at my nipple as it was sucked in and out, in and out of the flange. Time management had never been my strong point but lately I could never seem to find enough hours in the day. What would I do once the baby came home and I had to get back to work? The last thing I wanted to bother with was hiring a babysitter, especially when money was already tight, but I wondered if I would need to consider bringing someone in to help. Would I need it, or would Alexander be one of those good babies who sleeps well and lets me get stuff done?

I bottled the little bit of milk I'd pumped and put it in the fridge. The shelf was full of little bottles, each one holding a little less than half an ounce of breast milk.

Glancing at Mrs. Potter, I said, "A whole lot of effort with not a whole lot to show for it, huh?"

She blinked.

"Yeah, I hope I can make more, too, 'cause this is ridiculous. What the hell am I gonna do when he starts drinking more? I won't be able to keep up."

I looked across the living room and into my bedroom, where my bed waited in all of its comfortable glory. It beckoned me with promises of soft blankets and sweet dreams, and all I wanted to do was take a nap. But I had showers to take and babies to see, so with a sigh, I headed into the bathroom and turned the water on.

***

"Hey, Mama!" Elle greeted me with a grin.

Every time I saw this woman, I wanted to wrap her in a tight hug and thank her for that night about two weeks ago. In some way, I believed she had saved me, and I wasn't sure how I could ever repay her for that.

"Hey," I replied, holding out my freezer bag of breast milk. "I brought presents."

"For me?!" She feigned girlish glee, clapping her hands and bouncing on the spot. Then, she took the bag from my hand and said, "I'll just go put these in the fridge. You want me to grab you a chair?"

"Nah, I got it."

She eyed me skeptically, knowing I'd just been through major surgery and shouldn't be lifting anything substantial. But the chairs were light, and I dragged one over with no problem.

"Well, will you look at Superwoman over here," she jabbed playfully. "I'll be right back. Then, I'll give you the rundown on your little man, okay?"

As Elle ran off to put the milk away, I situated myself at Alexander's bedside. He was sleeping; he usually was. But that didn't make me any less happy to see him, and it didn't make me any less sad. His color was coming in a little more, and I could see it in his ears more than anywhere else. He was also gaining weight at a steady pace. But he was still intubated and too unstable to hold. So, I opened one door of his isolette and held his little hand with two of my fingertips, and we sat just like that, until Elle returned.

"So, Alexander the Great is doing pretty well today! He had gained a bunch of weight overnight, but then, he had a really big poop today, that got all over his bed …" She laughed, shaking her head, and I laughed with her.

"Were you a bad boy?" I said, lightly stroking my fingertip over his impossibly small knuckles.

"So, he might've lost a couple of grams," she said, resting her hip against the base of his bed.

"Is that a big deal?"

"Oh, no," she replied, shaking her head. "It's normal for him to fluctuate. It's all a part of the process. Other than that, he's doing great. I think we might try to get him off the vent soon."

"Really?" The thought of seeing my baby's mouth without a tube shoved between his lips lit me up like a Christmas tree. "When?"

Elle shrugged, looking down into the isolette. "I'm not totally sure. I think we might give it a shot next week, but I'm not making any promises. This is all up to little Alex here."

I gently squeezed his hand, not too hard, but just hard enough for him to know I was there. I wanted him to know I was rooting for him. And even though he only had me in his corner, I hoped that would be enough.

I thought about that on the cab ride back to my apartment, about Brendan and how he told me just months ago that he'd be here for the baby and me. He told me I'd have a bigger place to live and that we'd be a family. I rarely thought about him now, I didn't have the time, but every so often, I allowed him to creep in and haunt my mind. With shame, I sometimes thought about how lucky he was, to be out there somewhere, doing God knows what, while I was stuck in this repetitive world of never quite getting enough done. Never doing enough in the apartment. Never making enough milk. Never spending enough time making money. Never spending enough time with my son—*our* son.

Dammit, he was our *son*. Didn't he care about that? How the hell could he not?

In those rare times when I did think about him, I also found that I hated him for what he did to me, what he did to us, and I hoped to God karma would find its way to his door.

Once I got to Famiglia Bella, the pizzeria below my apartment, I quickly stopped inside to grab a few slices. The cashier, a friendly man named Moe, took one look at me and insisted it was on him. I protested, pulling my wallet from my bag to show I had the money, and still, he shook his head.

"Honey, it's not about whether or not you have the cash," he said, offering a friendly smile. "Sometimes, it's just about doin' somethin' for a sweet, young lady, who looks like she hasn't had somethin' nice happen to her in a long, long time."

I worried my lower lip between my teeth, struggling to keep it from quivering, as he collected my dinner and passed the plate over the countertop. I thanked him quietly, before turning around to head outside and up the stairs to my apartment.

Once inside and not bothering to turn on a light, I passed the table to plop down on the couch with the charitable donation to my wellbeing and ate in silent darkness. Beside me, Mrs. Potter begged, by nudging my thigh with her paw every so often, and I repeatedly swatted her away, until finally, I gave her the crust from one slice, knowing very well she wouldn't eat it. Sometime during the night, I knew I'd step on it and curse at her under my breath. But right now, I couldn't care about that. I was too stressed, too frustrated, and way too disheartened, and I knew I needed to perk up before I allowed myself to succumb to the endless darkening gloom.

So, I did the only thing I knew to bring in the light.

I called Goose.

"Hey, girlfriend," he answered cheerfully, despite the distinct sound of "Sweet Home Alabama" playing loudly in the background. "What's shakin'?"

"Just got home from the hospital a little while ago."

"How's my main man doing today?"

"Um, pretty much the same as yesterday, but Elle said he might be off the ventilator soon."

"Hey, that's awesome news!"

I nodded into the dark. "It is," I replied, as the smile I needed slowly spread across my face. "He held my finger tonight. Like, usually, I hold his hand and he just lies there, sort of unresponsive to my touch. But tonight, he actually wrapped his hand around my finger, and it just ..." A sudden wave of emotion swept me up and carried me away, and I hiccuped on an unexpected sob.

"Hey, you okay?"

"Yeah," I replied, quickly collecting myself. "It was just really nice. Like, for the first time, he really knew I was there."

"Kenny, you're his mom. He *always* knows you're there."

I sniffled and nodded again, wiping a hand over my cheeks. "Yeah. I know."

"Did you eat?"

"Yeah, I grabbed some pizza from downstairs. That guy, Moe, gave it to me for free. It was freakin' embarrassing. He said I looked like I needed cheering up."

"Moe's good people. My buddy, Vinnie, has known him forever," Goose replied, before excusing himself to help a customer. Then, when he returned, he asked, "So, why did you need cheering up? What's wrong? I mean, aside from the obvious."

"Because ..." I shrugged to the room and went on, "Because I'm stressed. I have so much to do and not enough time to do it, I can't remember when I last sat down to write, I'm not making nearly enough milk for this kid ..."

"Being a single mom is rough," he said softly, understandably, and all at once, it hit me.

I was a single mom.

"God, I never thought of it like that before," I answered quietly, as if my volume could control the onslaught of tears. "I'm just so mad at Brendan for doing this to me."

"You're better off and you know it."

"I know," I said, weeping and nodding. "I know. I just never thought I'd be *here*. Our relationship was always unstable, and he was always a flaky jerk, but I never expected *this*."

"*Nobody* would expect this," he replied sympathetically, before saying, "Hey, what are you doing tomorrow for St. Patrick's Day?"

"Nothing," I replied hesitantly.

"Awesome."

"Why?" I asked, narrowing my eyes with excited curiosity.

"'Cause I'm comin' over."

Chapter Twenty-Seven

I was born a mutt with a fairly small percentage of Irish in my blood, but from the time I was born, I was raised as an Irish-American. I loved all things Ireland and had big dreams of visiting one day, when book sales did more than just pay my rent. So, every year, St. Patrick's Day was a pretty big deal in my family. We went all out with the food, decorations, and of course, Guinness and Bailey's. But this Saint Patrick's Day, the first holiday with Alexander in the world, I didn't want to do anything.

Because he wasn't home.

But I took solace in knowing Goose would be coming over to spend some time with me. I still wasn't sure if it was the right time to pursue our relationship as more than just friends, but hanging out with him was some of the best medicine I could get during my time of healing.

So, when one o'clock rolled around, I smiled at the knock on my door and ran to answer it, wearing my pajamas and fuzzy slippers. But when I saw a crowd of people standing on the other side, I blanched and struggled to muster the ability to vanish into thin air.

"Hey, girlfriend," Goose said, amidst the people he apparently brought with him, before he pushed past me into the apartment. "I brought my family. Hope you don't mind."

"Uh, well, um …"

I did mind. Especially when I hadn't gotten around to cleaning or laundry or even showering in over a week. The last thing I wanted was a gaggle of strangers crowding my tiny apartment and smelling the fumes I was polluting the air with.

But they all entered the apartment anyway, carrying an array of bags and containers, and I watched with embarrassed hesitation as they immediately made themselves at home.

"I'm Krystal," a tall woman with sleek black hair said, offering a smile and displaying a set of gorgeous, perfect teeth. "I'm Goose's ex-wife and best friend."

"You're definitely not my best friend," he quipped from the kitchen, where he dropped off a heavy-looking box that clanged and rattled as he set it down.

"Fine. Second best friend."

"Hmmm … Okay, sure, I'll accept that."

He came to stand beside me, placed his hand on my shoulder, and pointed to a young lady, who I instantly knew was his daughter.

"This is my spawn, Hannah," he said, confirming my suspicions. "She's decided she doesn't like us anymore, because she's fifteen, and only wants to look at her phone. So, don't take it personally if she just rolls her eyes and grunts a lot."

"Stop it, Dad," she muttered, crossing her arms over her chest and turning her gaze toward the ceiling.

"That's also my new name. It used to be Daddy, but now, it's Stop It, Dad. I think it has a nice ring to it." He looked at Krystal and asked, "What do you think, Krys? I'm thinking about getting it tattooed somewhere, so I don't forget."

The older man Goose had brought with him stepped forward and grumbled, "Stop tormenting your daughter, Goose," before smiling at me and saying, "I'm Mitch, Goose's father. It's a pleasure to finally meet you."

"It's nice to meet all of you, too," I said, finally able to get a word in. There were only four of them but their personalities were big enough for an army.

Goose showed me the contents of the bags and containers they had brought and it was enough to move me to tears. Corned beef and cabbage, steamed vegetables, Irish soda bread, cake, and a case of Coke, along with paper plates and plastic utensils. When I went to help get everything ready to serve, Goose shook his head and Krystal put her hands on my shoulders.

"We have this. You go take a shower and when you come out, it'll be time to eat," she said.

"W-What? No, I can't just—"

"Go," she cut me off gently, then nudged me in the direction of the bathroom.

I looked to Goose for backup, but he only shook his head and said, "Listen to the lady."

And so, I did.

***

After I had scrubbed away days' worth of filth and frustration, I emerged from the bathroom in clean clothes and feeling better than I had in weeks. But when I saw my tiny apartment, once filled with empty boxes but now straightened up and smelling of good food and a candle I hadn't burned since sometime before Christmas, my jaw dropped and my stomach clenched with nervous gratitude.

Dirty clothes were picked up off the floor, and the rug had been vacuumed. The scattered pile of work papers and reference books had been shuffled into a neat stack beside my computer, and the coffee table was now barren of dirty mugs. Goose's daughter was by the TV with a dust rag in hand, and when she spotted me staring, she pointed toward the kitchen.

"He made us do it," she muttered begrudgingly.

Knowing all too well who *he* must've been, I offered an apologetic smile and walked to the small galley kitchen, to find Goose, his ex-wife, and his father crammed between the countertops.

"You had your daughter clean my apartment?" I accused abruptly, alerting the three of them to my presence.

"We all did our part," he corrected me, lifting the corners of his mouth in a smile I couldn't help but return.

"You *really* didn't have to do that."

Krystal grinned and came to me with arms extended, like we were best friends and had known each other forever. "We wanted to," she insisted, wrapping an arm around my shoulders. "Taking a shower is the best thing ever when you're so busy with a baby, right?"

I nodded gratefully. "It seriously is." Then, I looked up into her eyes and said, "And thank you. Seriously. You don't even know me. You didn't have—"

"Stop," she scolded gently. "Goose told us all about you and what you're going through. We're more than happy to help in any way that we can."

"Food's gonna be ready in a few minutes," Goose announced, before throwing some instructions at his father to set the table and pour the soda.

Krystal took the moment to pull me into the living room and sat me down beside her daughter, who was busy making friends with my cat.

"So, I hope you don't mind, but Goose mentioned that you were having a tough time with the whole, you know, breast milk thing," Krystal said quietly.

I felt my cheeks burn with embarrassment and shame at the mention, but I shook my head. "No, it's okay."

"Listen. I tried for weeks with Hannah, and it just would not work for me. She wouldn't latch, I wasn't making enough, my boobs hurt like hell, I developed a killer case of mastitis …" She rolled her eyes and waved a hand flippantly in the air. "I felt so crappy and I spent too much time crying and making myself feel like a failure because this thing that's supposed to be so beautiful and natural just wasn't happening for me."

"It makes me feel like it's just one more thing out of my hands," I confessed, shaking my head. "Like, everything about this entire situation has been completely beyond of my control, and I hate it all so much. So, when the nurses first mentioned breastfeeding in the hospital, I thought, well, I have control over my own boobs and at least that's something I can do for my son. But as it turns out, I don't even have control over that. I feel like, like nothing about my body is good enough for my baby, and nothing feels more unnatural than that to me."

I tried so hard not to let the tears come, but I lost the battle and looked away, struggling to swallow them down and wish them away.

"I can't pretend to know what you're going through," Krystal replied gently. "But I can tell you that you are more than good enough for your baby. I mean, so what if you can't make enough? You got help when you felt something was wrong. You got him exactly where he needed to be. He doesn't need breast milk when they make formula that'll do just fine. What he really needs is you to be happy and sane, and if that means you give this up, then so be it. Sometimes, the absolute best thing you can do, is give up. And if you don't want to give up yet, then whatever you are able to do is better than nothing at all."

I allowed her words in and let them settle against my heart, as Goose told us that the food was ready to eat. I didn't have enough chairs at my table, so we instead sat around the living room, on the couch and the floor, with loaded plates and full glasses of soda. The time spent eating was filled with comfortable company, and I had the best afternoon I could remember having in a long time. I hadn't realized how much I'd missed talking and laughing with people, even if we'd only just met—except for Goose, of course, who sat close beside me, with his thigh pressed to mine.

I found that I loved the way he felt there, searing his warmth into me and penetrating the chill that had invaded my heart the day I almost died with my baby. I knew that, as the minutes went by, I was moving closer, leaning in further, and occasionally touching my head to his shoulder. I knew that he had to notice, but not once did he make a move himself. And I guess he didn't really have to, when things were just sort of happening on their own, the way it does sometimes. Where there are no boyfriends or girlfriends, no formal declaration of what we were. It just sort of came to be, through some unspoken agreement, and I think that's exactly what happened between Goose and me, on Saint Patrick's Day in my tiny apartment, where we were surrounded by the people that he loved and I had only just met.

All because he knew I needed help but would never ask.

And I couldn't have imagined us happening in a better way.

Chapter Twenty-Eight

"Hey, Mama!"

I entered the NICU a little over a month after Alexander was born. I never thought it could happen, but coming to the hospital every day was becoming more and more of a regular part of my life, almost to the point where I was beginning to wonder if I'd ever adjust to not coming here. Or if I could ever adjust to caring for a baby on my own.

"Hey, Debbie," I said, grabbing a chair and dragging it over to Alexander's isolette.

"Notice anything different about your little man?"

"Huh?"

She shot me a smug smirk from the station she was working at and said, "Take a look."

Peering into Alexander's bed, it was hard to miss. Where there was once a thick tube obscuring a lot of his face, there was now only lips, with a thin tube hanging from the center of his little mouth. A different tube was now over his nose, secured by tape on his cheeks, and a band wrapped around his little head, holding it all in place.

"No more ventilator!" I exclaimed happily, unable to control my already aching grin.

"Nope!" Debbie said, coming to stand beside me. She looked into his bed, smiling right along with me, as though she were looking in on her own child and not just another patient. "We put him on the CPAP this morning as a trial run. He's doing pretty well on it, too. We've been watching him really closely and it looks like this might be for good, but we'll see."

During our time in the NICU, I had learned that so much went on trial and error. Like anything in the medical world, sometimes you didn't know if something would work until you tried. In some cases, they found out after trying that they needed to take a few steps back, and I hoped that wouldn't be the case in Alexander's situation.

"Fingers crossed," I replied, opening the door to his isolette and taking his hand.

Surrounded by the working nurses and beeping machines, I enjoyed the simplicity of holding his hand and looking at his beautiful face, when Debbie came close to my side and asked if I'd like to hold him. It was a moment I had been waiting a long time for, but it had been so many weeks since he was born and I was beginning to foolishly believe it would never happen. But now, with the opportunity presented to me, I nodded eagerly as my bottom lip trembled.

Debbie set me up in a chair, then went through the seemingly difficult task of rearranging his tubes and wires. She instructed me to open my sweatshirt, and before I knew it, my baby was tucked into my tank top, nestled between my breasts and against my heart. I shuddered with a sob at the feel of his skin against mine, and I couldn't imagine a better way to spend an afternoon.

***

"Guess what!"

"You figured out how to make them stop playing this fucking song?" Goose asked, flashing me a pair of hopeful, blue eyes.

I shook my head sorrowfully, as I slid onto a barstool. "Only way that's gonna happen is if you get rid of it."

"And get rid of my customers?" He scoffed and rolled his eyes. "Think again, girlfriend."

"Okay, what's your next guess?"

"You're in the mood for a basket of wings and a particular pink mocktail?"

I pursed my lips and feigned deep thought, tapping a finger to my chin, before saying, "Yes. But make that a cocktail."

"Woah! What's the occasion?" he exclaimed, folding his arms over the bar across from me.

"Well, rumor has it, a certain baby is off the ventilator." I couldn't say it without grinning and tearing up.

Goose slapped a hand against the bar, drawing the attention of a few customers. "Holy shit! You just made my freakin' day."

"I was so unbelievably happy," I told him, taking out my phone to show him the few pictures I took. "Like, I can finally see his little face. Look at how adorable he is!"

He took the phone from me and grinned adoringly at the pictures of my little boy. "What a beautiful kid he is," he said, handing it back to me. "That's such fantastic news."

"And," I continued quietly, as my heart began to dance happily in my chest, "I finally got to hold him."

His eyes softened and his head cocked, as he said, "I'm so happy for you, Kenny. Seriously. That's amazing."

I nodded, swiping quickly at a tear before it could slip down my cheek. "It felt like the first really good thing to happen in weeks," I admitted. "I mean, I know he's gaining weight and getting better every day, but this was such a huge step forward, and … I don't know. I'm just so happy."

"And for that, you deserve one fancy fuckin' cocktail," Goose said gently, with a heartwarming grin.

I watched as he put together the drink, my first since before finding out I was pregnant, and I began to wonder something I hadn't thought about before.

"Hey," I said, leaning further over the counter. "Can I ask you a question?"

"Anything."

"You said you were an alcoholic."

He nodded. "Yes, ma'am."

"Then, how do you own a bar?"

"By having a whole lotta self-control."

I narrowed my eyes at his answer and shook my head. "That really doesn't sound healthy."

"So," he began, placing a big, frothy drink in front of me, "one of the most important things I learned in the Army was self-discipline. And after I left and turned to booze to numb everything, I used that discipline to make the choice to ignore what I had learned. Eventually, after a whole lot of therapy and rehab, I managed to take control again."

"No, I get that, but why a bar? You could've done anything."

He considered the question with a cock of his head, then shrugged a few seconds later. "'Cause I'm good at it, I guess. I never really had any talents, you know? I think I told you that a while ago. But I'm a people person. I like socializing and making others happy. And I've always been pretty gifted when it comes to pouring drinks. I just keep in mind that I'm doing this for other people; it's not for me, other than to pay the bills."

I hummed contemplatively as I sipped my drink. The sting of alcohol bit at my tongue and warmed my throat as I swallowed with the anticipation of heat filling my belly.

"I write for myself," I said, thinking out loud. "It's my escape from reality. I just happen to make money doing it."

"You make money by *releasing* what you write. That's what you do for other people. You make them happy by putting your work out into the world," he corrected. "But you *write* for yourself."

"Well, then couldn't you sort of say the same for yourself?"

"How do you figure?"

I pointed to him and said, "You said you like to socialize and make people happy, and that's why you decided to open up a bar."

"And because I'm amazing at mixing drinks."

"Okay. So, you mix the drinks for other people, yeah, but all of this," I spread my arms out, addressing the bar and its patrons, "is ultimately for you. This is what makes you happy."

With a rag in hand, he polished a glass and stared at me, wearing a lopsided grin and a set of hooded eyes. The look made me shift on my barstool, as something old and familiar brewed deep in my belly and heart, and I dropped my gaze to the drink in front of me.

"What?" I asked, giggling nervously and wrapping my hand around the stem of the glass.

"*You* make me happy."

My cheeks flushed and my smile grew wider. "I *am* pretty great, huh?"

"The best."

"Well, I guess that makes us even," I replied. "'Cause you're pretty great yourself, and I guess you make me happy, too."

"You only guess, huh? I'm gonna have to work on that."

The bar was then filled with another raucous round of "Sweet Home Alabama" and Goose threw his head back, groaning loudly. I could only giggle, my lips pressed to the edge of my glass.

"I really hate this fucking song," he muttered to the ceiling.

Then, in an attempt to change the subject, I asked, "Do you hate that *I* drink?"

Looking back at me, he replied, "Why would you think that?"

"Well, I just wasn't sure if it made it harder for you to hold onto your control," I said, shrugging.

He shook his head. "If it bothered me, you'd know about it."

"You're sure?"

He smiled. "Communication is one of *my* strong points," he said, and I knew immediately that it was a gentle jab at a particular person I hadn't seen in weeks. "But thank you for asking."

***

"How's my favorite grandson?"

I snorted as I headed up the stairs to my apartment. "Oh, I guess you don't care about me anymore."

Mom uttered a small, careless sound. "I've had thirty-five years to hear about how you're doing. It's Alex's turn."

"Touché," I laughed, fitting the key into the lock and opening the door. "Well, he's off the ventilator. So, that's his big news of the day."

"That *is* big news!"

"Yeah," I agreed with pride. "And I got to hold him."

"Oh, finally!" she exclaimed happily. "That's amazing, honey. I'm so thrilled."

"Right? They say he's progressing leaps and bounds above what they had expected. I mean, I've seen other babies in there, born into very similar situations, and they aren't doing nearly as well as him. Honestly, it makes me feel a little guilty to have him doing so well, when others are struggling."

"You shouldn't feel guilty, and you shouldn't be comparing," Mom replied sternly. "It's not a race. All you can hope for is that every one of those babies gets better and gets to go home, but that they take as long as they need to get there."

"No, I know."

"And remember, Elle told you that things can be very unpredictable. They can—"

"I know," I said, cutting her off abruptly. "Believe me, Mom; I'm more than aware of everything that can go wrong."

"Obviously, everyone is hoping for the best."

"I know," I replied softly, as I nodded.

"You know, I was actually talking to Mary at the drugstore. She was telling me that her grandson was born three months early, too. But now, he's a very healthy twelve-year-old. You'd never know how he started."

"Wow, that's great," I muttered, kicking off my shoes and walking into the living room to sit on the couch.

In the weeks since Alexander had been born, I had heard it all from everyone. All the success stories. All the worries and fears. And I was sick of it all. I was happy for the babies who made it, and I was sad for the ones who hadn't, but none of them were *my* baby. And nobody was more aware of what could go wrong than me.

"Anyway, let's just hope for the best," Mom said, and I gritted my teeth, knowing she meant well. "Your dad and I were thinking today ..."

"About?" I persuaded, putting her on speakerphone and taking off my shirt and bra.

The whole breast pumping thing still wasn't going quite as planned, and I knew for sure I wasn't making nearly enough milk, especially now that Alex was drinking more every feeding and they were supplementing with formula. Nothing I was doing was working, no matter how hard I tried. But after talking to Krystal, I had made a decision to pump whatever I could for him during the time he was in the hospital, with hopes that things might change once he came home. And if not, so be it. At least I could say I tried, and that had to be good enough.

"Well, we were talking about the future, and we started thinking that, maybe after Alex comes home, you could move back home for a while."

I fitted the flanges over my nipples and turned the pump on as I gawked at the phone. "Seriously?"

"I mean, your room is still there, and there's the guest room right next to it. That could be turned into a nursery, no problem."

I stared at the hypnotic motion of my nipples as I recalled the reason why I had moved into the city in the first place. It had been Brendan and my feeble attempt at turning our relationship into something it was never going to be. I had never loved living here, but now, I had Goose, and while it never sat well with me to stay here for Brendan, staying for Goose almost felt right.

But it wasn't only me I had to think about now. I had the baby, and even though his doctors and nurses were here, my parents weren't. I would need to think and decide what was truly the best for both of us, and that wasn't a decision I could make right now. Not when I was too busy playing the role of dairy cow.

"I gotta think about it, Mom," I replied honestly. "I do appreciate it, though."

"Oh, I know there's a lot to consider. But just remember the offer is there and it isn't going away. We are always here for you, honey. Whatever you need, whenever you want it, we're here."

Chapter Twenty-Nine

For days, I thought long and hard about my mother's proposition. The more I considered it, the more appealing it was, to be around the people who would help me in the middle of the night, when the baby wouldn't stop crying and I desperately needed a break. It hurt me to think about leaving the man my heart was growing fonder of by the day, but I couldn't ignore the fact that I had already stayed in the city for a man before. I was beginning to wonder how valid that reason really was, especially without any promise of commitment.

Still, I was enjoying my time with Goose, and I was enjoying the progression of our relationship even more. He had a way of making me smile on the days when I didn't want to smile at all, and I never stopped loving the way I could make him laugh.

"A girl named Kenny walks into a bar," he said, as I approached the rich mahogany I had grown so fond of over the months since we'd met. "What'll it be, girlfriend?"

I spotted Hannah, sulking at the far end, her nose glued her phone. "Well," I said, bringing my eyes back to his, "I was thinking dinner and a movie at my place, but I don't want to get in the middle of your daddy-daughter time."

He nodded, turning his gaze on his daughter. "Krystal had a date tonight, so Hannah's mine until tomorrow."

"Okay, another time—"

"Well, I was gonna say," he brought his eyes back to mine, "I'm ordering Chinese. Hannah has never seen *Donnie Darko* and I'm pretty sure that's a must for any moody teen. So, if you wanted to swing by my place, there's a spot on the couch between me and Tony, if you're interested."

"Tony?" I asked, smiling and already buzzing with nerves at the thought of spending an evening with him, his daughter, and whoever Tony was.

"My dog," he clarified, pointing behind him at a picture on the wall of a black and tan, scruffy-looking shepherd mutt. "He's got a thing for the ladies, but he's a good guy."

I laughed, slowly drowning in the warmth surrounding my heart. "So, a night with you, your daughter, and your dog, huh?"

"Don't make it sound so glamorous," he mumbled with a chuckle.

"You sure Hannah won't mind?"

Goose looked down the bar at his daughter and called, "Yo, Hannah, you mind if Kenny comes over tonight to hang for a bit?" Hannah turned and shot a disgruntled look at her dad, before mumbling, "I don't care." Then, he looked at me, shrugged, and said, "See, she doesn't care."

"Can I bring my breast pump?" I laughed.

"Only if I can watch."

"Oh, because it's so hot," I muttered sardonically.

"I'm just kidding," he replied. "But of course, you can bring it. Honestly though, I'm willing to agree to anything at this point, as long as you'll say yes and not leave me alone with Grumpelstiltskin."

I laughed harder than I had in weeks, holding a hand over where my incision was. He grinned while apologizing, telling me not to bleed out on his floor, as I leaned against the bar and caught my breath.

Then, when I looked back into his eyes, to see the hope and silent plea burning brilliantly amid the brightest blue I'd ever seen, I couldn't say yes fast enough.

***

I arrived at Goose's apartment a few minutes late, after spending some time at the hospital with Alexander. I stood there at his door, awkwardly holding a pie Elle had insisted I bring, and waited for him to answer. But he never did. Instead, the door was thrown open by Hannah, with her eyes trained on her phone.

"Hi," I greeted hesitantly, peering around her into the neat and tidy apartment.

"Dad's in the kitchen," she muttered, before walking away.

"Oh," I muttered quietly, stepping in and closing the door behind me. "Because I know exactly where that—"

"Hey," Goose said jubilantly, rushing out of a doorway with a dish towel in his hands. "Sorry I let Wednesday Addams open the door. My hands were full and—"

"It's fine," I replied, smiling, while offering the bakery box. "I brought pie."

He nodded, scrubbing his hands in the towel. "So I see. I'll just put it in the fridge, and you can join my spawn at the table. Food only just got here, so you're just in time."

He took the box and I walked down a hallway, aimlessly searching for where the table might be, when a large, tail-wagging beast ran into my legs.

"Oh!" I exclaimed, startled as the mutt lifted on his hind legs and pressed his forepaws against my shoulders. "You must be Tony," I said, petting his head while frantically avoiding his wet, slobbering tongue.

"Tony! Jesus Christ, dude," Goose groaned, hurrying over and grabbing the dog by the collar to pull him back down. "We like women, man, but we don't wanna scare them away, you got me?"

He looked back at me, smiling sheepishly, while scrubbing his hands over the grinning dog's face. "Sorry. I forgot to mention he's a big fan of hugs and kisses."

"It's okay. He's really sweet."

"I'm surprised you'd think so, considering you're such a cat lady."

"I might be a cat lady, but that doesn't mean I hate dogs," I pointed out defiantly.

"My apologies for assuming," he said with a chuckle, as he led me to the dining room.

Hannah was already eating, while still tapping away on her phone. Goose pulled a chair out for me, then sat down himself, before reaching over and patting his daughter on the shoulder.

"Hey, no phones during dinner."

"Stop it, Dad," she whined, turning away.

"Come on, I'm just asking for fifteen minutes of your precious time. Then, you can get back to chatting with all your homies, okay?"

She sighed and rolled her eyes, then surprised me when she obediently put the phone down on the table and gave her full attention to her plate and us.

"Thank you so much, daughter of mine. Now, tell me how school's going."

I remained quiet, as we ate and Hannah told her father about how her English teacher was encouraging her to submit one of her poems to the school newsletter. I found that I liked her, despite the typical teenage attitude and the ironclad attachment to her phone. I saw a lot of myself in her, from her black clothes and heavy black makeup, to her obvious affection toward writing and keeping to herself. I was surprised to find myself hoping we could be friends one day, maybe even close friends.

"Kenny's an author, you know," Goose said, looking toward me.

"Really?" Hannah asked, suddenly interested in my presence. "Like, you're published and everything?"

I nodded, smiling. "Yeah, well, I'm self-published, but—"

"Hey," Goose said. "Don't talk like that doesn't count."

"I just mean, it doesn't have the same level of prestige as being published traditionally," I said, poking at the lo mein on my plate. "I'd like to one day do both, be independent *and* traditional, but for now, this is what I'm doing."

"That's awesome," Hannah commented. "I wanna be a famous poet one day."

"Like Edgar Allan Poe?" I asked, smiling across the table.

Her expression was then one of sheer euphoria as she pressed her hands to her chest. "He's my *favorite*. How did you know?"

"Lucky guess," I replied, shoveling a heaping forkful of fried rice into my mouth. "And he's mine, too."

***

The living room was lit with only the glow from the TV, and as the end credits of *Donnie Darko* rolled, Hannah slept, curled up to her father's side. I sat on his other side, my elbow resting on Tony's hip, and during those moments of easy comfort, I thought, *I could get used to this*.

I imagined how it would be if Alexander was also here, sleeping soundlessly nearby, in a bassinet or swing. How comfortable it would be, to sit here with Goose, while the kids and dog slept. I had to remind myself repeatedly that we weren't a family, and that I didn't belong here, but it felt like, maybe one day, I could.

"I should get her to bed," he whispered, slicing through the cozy quiet with his voice.

"Okay," I replied with a nod.

"I don't want to get up, though." He turned to me, and the light from the TV danced across his face, the shadows emphasizing his features. "I'm too comfortable."

"Me, too."

His eyes dropped to my lips, and mine dropped to his, as he replied, "You should probably stay, then."

"Yeah, but … I gotta feed the cat …"

The words coming from my mouth were hushed by his lips, as he moved in and kissed me softly. I imagined every kiss I had ever written about, and wished that they had all been inspired by this one, as his arm wrapped around my shoulder and pulled me closer to his side. My hands reached up, to clench the flannel of his shirt in needy fists, and I whimpered pathetically when his lips parted to coax mine open with a hesitant touch of his tongue.

"Ew, Dad."

Goose cleared his throat, then smiled against my mouth, before saying, "Go to bed, Hannah."

"Why, so you can make out on the couch?"

"Probably," he replied lazily.

"You're so gross," she groaned, snatching her phone off the coffee table and stomping toward the hallway.

"Good night, Hannah. Love you."

I caught the faintest hint of a smile as she glanced over her shoulder before disappearing down the hall, and said, "Love you, too, Daddy."

Goose grabbed the remote to turn the movie off, and I rubbed my sweaty palms against my thighs. Brendan and I hadn't been together in well over a month, and I hadn't heard a peep from him since. There was nothing to stop me from doing whatever I wanted with Goose, and I had known for weeks exactly where this was going. Still, that acknowledgement didn't stop the newness of this situation from being scary, and Lord, I liked him so much, and somehow, that made it so much scarier.

"You okay?"

I looked to his concerned expression and smiled. "Yeah, I'm fine."

"You don't look fine," he commented. "You kinda look like you're gonna puke."

I laughed, shaking my head. "Definitely not gonna puke."

"Well, thank God for that."

Pulling in a deep breath, I said, "I think I'm just a little freaked out."

His big palm covered my knee, as he said, "Tell me why."

"Because …" I thought of every cliché I could say, knowing they were cliché for a reason. And even though I didn't want to sound like another pathetic heroine with a repertoire of practiced lines, I still said, "Because I don't want to screw this up."

"Why do you think anything's gonna be screwed up?"

"I don't know," I replied, sighing and shrugging. "Maybe because everything was screwed up with Brendan."

"Yeah, and my past two relationships were failures, too," he said. "But I only need one to work out in the end."

"And what if this doesn't?"

Goose pressed his lips together, considering the question, before replying, "I don't know for sure that it will, but I have a pretty good feeling."

"Hm," I muttered with a nod.

Then, he settled in closer beside me, wrapping his arm back around my shoulders and pulling me into him once again. I couldn't help smiling and settling in, lifting my leg and wrapping it around his thigh, while my arm hugged his waist. The fear kept whispering every little thing that could go wrong into my ear, but that alone couldn't stop this from feeling so natural and right, and so unlike anything I'd experienced before.

"How about this," he said, pressing his cheek to the top of my head. "What if you really were writing the story of a girl named Kenny and a guy named Goose? How would you want it to end?"

Taking a deep breath, I considered the question, then replied, "I think it'd have to be one of those series that just goes on forever, because I don't think I'd have the heart to end it."

He nodded, tightening his hold on my shoulder, and said, "Well, I guess it's up to us to make sure this goes on forever, then."

Swallowing at the lump growing in my throat, I held on tighter to his waist, and replied, "I guess so."

"But," he went on, squeezing my shoulder in his large, warm hand, "since this is gonna go on forever—"

"Hopefully," I interjected playfully, poking at his side.

"Right. *Hopefully*," he corrected, grinning. "We can take our time, you know? So, if you wanna ease into this, like we've been doin' this whole time, then … I'm cool with that, too."

"Really?" I asked, turning to look at him disbelievingly.

Nodding with assurance, he replied, "You said you don't wanna screw this up, and neither do I. So, if that means you wanna call it a night and get home to your cat, then I'm cool with that."

I didn't want to call it a night. What I wanted was to stay there with him, making out until the sun came up, to remind myself of what it was like to be with a man who truly wanted to be with me. But there was also the fear of rushing in too quickly, of engaging in sexual activities, even after my doctor had said it would be fine. So, with a reluctant nod, I told him I'd give him a raincheck, and with an adoring smile, he promised to use it whenever I was ready.

I hoped to be ready soon.

Chapter Thirty

"No, no, no. You are not getting up right now," Goose protested, reaching out with both hands to stop me from leaving the couch.

"As much as I would love to make out with you for hours, I really need to pump before my boobs explode," I said, swatting his hands away to make myself comfortable in my chair.

He sighed and stood up, straightening his shirt. "I guess it's fine," he muttered, feigning hurt. Then, he added, "I have to get to work, anyway. Gotta do that adult thing. But you wanna hang out tonight, or do you have work to do?"

"Well, I *do* have work to do, but I wouldn't mind hanging out, too," I replied, unclipping my bra and securing the flanges to my poor, battered boobs.

"Sounds good to me." He leaned over and kissed the top of my head. "I'll come by after closing and grab a pizza downstairs."

"Man after my own heart."

Goose ruffled the fur on Mrs. Potter's head and left with a promise to text me once he was at the bar. I sat back, letting the pump do its work, and sighed with the revelation that I was in a good, honest relationship with a man who liked to take the time to text me, just to let me know he got to work in one piece. It was so nice to have something to smile about, while the fear of my baby's uncertain future was still very much alive in my heart.

***

"Hey," Goose greeted me, kissing my cheek before hurrying into the kitchen with the pizza box. "Sorry I was late. Krystal came by and wanted to talk about a meeting with Hannah's teachers."

"Everything okay?" I asked, closing my laptop to get ready for dinner.

"Well, not really," he replied, as he carried two plates holding slices of pepperoni pizza. "She's failing science and math. And she's dangerously close to failing English, too, which doesn't make any sense whatsoever to me. The kid is obsessed with reading and writing. I mean, she's never been great at science or math, so that doesn't surprise me too much, but English?" He shook his head as he sat down beside me. "I don't get it."

"Have you talked to her about it?"

He bit into a slice and looked toward the pendant light hanging over the table. "Not yet. Krystal's gonna try tonight. I'm hoping she'll get through to her right off the bat, so we don't have to play good cop, bad cop. I really hate that shit."

Then, he looked at me and asked, "How's Alex doing today?"

I grinned. "Well, today, I walked in there and Debbie was really excited. So, I went over to his isolette to find that he's off the CPAP." My voice rose an octave, unable to contain my excitement and joy. My smile strained my cheeks, and tears stung my eyes. "I am just on freakin' cloud nine right now. He has completely surpassed every one of our expectations." Then, not wanting to be too excited, I shook my head and added, "I mean, I know the reality of the situation. I know things could turn around so quickly, but …" I shrugged, grinning wider. "Right now, it just feels so good that he's doing so well."

Goose watched me, with a grin spreading in slow motion across his face. Then, he said, "You know, when you first walked into my bar, I thought, wow, that chick is beautiful, but you also looked so … I dunno, defeated, I guess. Like, life had kicked you around a little and you were just sick of dealing with it. And I remember how unsure and scared you were about having a baby, and how weak you thought you were. But now, I can honestly say, you are the strongest woman I've ever known, and you have never looked more beautiful than when you talk about him."

The declaration was unexpected and my mouth slowed in its chewing until it had stopped altogether. Words like that were spoken in love stories, in romance novels that were so meticulously crafted to woo the reader and make them fall in love with the hero. Even though I wrote stories like that, I had always thought it was unrealistic to expect a man in the real world to ever speak like that to anyone, let alone to me. But there Goose was, proving me wrong. Again.

"What?" he asked, laughing easily, as he bit into his pizza.

"I don't know how you just *say* that stuff," I confessed.

"I say it because it's true," he replied, shrugging like it wasn't a big deal.

"But nobody has ever talked to me like that before."

"Then, I guess nobody has ever fallen in love with you before."

I wasn't sure that I had heard him through the nonchalance, so I asked him to repeat himself. He chuckled and replied, "I *said*, I guess nobody has ever fallen in love with you before."

"Are you saying ..." I swallowed and squeezed my eyes shut. "Are you saying you *love* me?"

"Yeah," he nodded, "I am."

"Wow."

It was such a stupid thing to say, and I couldn't understand why I had said it, or why I behaved so awkwardly throughout the rest of our dinner. It shouldn't have been a surprise, given the progression of our friendship, and then relationship, over the past several months. Yet, it was. A lot of things irked me about the moment, much like the time when he had first kissed me. But nothing bothered me more than the fact that I hadn't said it back.

We cleaned up in an almost comfortable silence, as I thought about the past seven and a half months of my life, and of how many things had changed and everything

I had been through. It was a lot for anyone to process and keeping up with it all had been a challenge. But even though I had been there, enjoying our relationship and where it had got to, I never once stopped to think about how his feelings—or mine—had changed with it. And although I knew the truth was that I loved him, too, and just hadn't taken a moment to realize it, it felt like a cop out. I knew Goose would understand, but that didn't stop me from feeling awful.

Later on, as he grabbed his jacket and announced he had to get back home to feed Tony, I knew I couldn't just let him leave. Not when there was so much I hadn't said or done. There was too much hanging in the air, and when I told him to wait, he did.

I approached him without speaking another word, taking his jacket and throwing it back on the couch. My hands did the talking, as they slid up the front of his plaid button-down shirt and felt the contours of his stomach underneath the soft fabric, before resting against his chest. I stood on my toes, beckoning him in for a kiss, and when he obliged me, offering his tongue and moaning into my mouth, I decided I wasn't waiting any longer to be sure about this, or him.

As if reading my mind, he picked me up and carried me to my room, like the gallant hero that he always was. I hoped he would throw me on the bed and truly exhibit his strength, backed purely by carnal intent, just like the men I wrote about. But instead, he laid me down with care and adoration. Our clothes were slowly stripped, landing on the floor in haphazard fashion, until there was nothing left but us.

For the first time, I saw every inch of his body, and he could see every inch of mine. In that moment, I felt self-conscious and ashamed, unable to keep my hands off my scar, wanting to hide it and make it disappear. And I couldn't take my eyes off of his.

"Let me see," he coaxed gently, taking my hands and prying them away from my lower belly.

It was still so new and fresh, and it still ached and twinged. One side was puffier than the other, and although my doctor had insisted it was normal and done beautifully, I hated it. I hated everything about it. How it felt, how it looked, and what it represented. It was a constant reminder that my body wasn't good enough for my baby, and that I had to be cut open for him to be put somewhere better. Somewhere *safer*. Safer than *me*.

"They did a good job," he said, as if I should take it as a compliment.

"Thanks," I replied dryly, not knowing what else to say but wanting so desperately to run away from the moment and back into my clothes.

"You hate it, though."

My bottom lip quivered as I nodded. "I really do."

He bent over to press his lips gently against it, treating it as a treasure and not as a curse, before rising again on his knees. He didn't wait for me to ask about the scar that ran the width of his abdomen, just above his belly button, as he laid a hand over it.

"That day, when my troop was ambushed, I was sliced right here," he said, tracing the thick, white, puckered line with his finger. "I was quick with the gun but this one bastard I hadn't noticed before was quicker

257

with his machete, and he got me really bad. And I dunno if it was the adrenaline or what, but I hadn't even realized what happened to me until after I had called it in and I couldn't stand on my feet anymore. I lost a shitload of blood, and honestly, it was fuckin' amazing that they could even put me back together."

My breath tripped in my throat as I whispered, "Jesus."

"Yeah, it was bad," he agreed, nodding. "I told you before, I should've died. It was plain, dumb luck that I didn't. And I hated this scar for a long fuckin' time. Every time I felt it, it was like … like a time machine, taking me back to that day. I could feel every goddamn thing, like it was still happening."

Tears sprung to my eyes and my heart raced to a gallop, as I nodded my silent agreement. Because I might not have fought a war in the traditional sense, but I was fighting a battle every single day. Except the enemy I was in combat with, was me.

"I don't …" I took a deep breath, then continued, "I don't even know how you can talk about it, after everything you went through. Because I can hardly stand thinking about my situation, and talking about it just seems like … like fucking torture."

"A lot of vets can never talk about it," he explained gently. "Hell, I rarely do, but I talk to you because I feel like I can. And maybe one day, you'll be able to talk about it, too. Or maybe not. Maybe you'll never want to, maybe you'll hate that scar for the rest of your life. But something I learned about mine is that, it isn't necessarily a reminder of how I almost died," he went on, tracing the silvery line one more time. "It's the proof that I survived, and that's the part I choose to hold onto instead of all the bad shit that came along with it. And that's what I hope for you, too."

With those final words, and in a surge of desperation and pure, primal need, I reached for him with both hands, grappling for his arms and pulling him down to me. We kissed with a divine passion, tangling fingers with hair and limbs with limbs, and as our bodies aligned and joined, my face tightened as a pained gasp passed through my lips.

"Are you okay?" he asked immediately, stroking his thumb across my cheek.

I met his concerned eyes and nodded. "Yeah. It's just … a little sore," I said, wincing before smiling apologetically. "I'm okay, though."

"You're sure? Because—"

I shook my head, pressing my hands to his cheeks. "I'd tell you if I wasn't." Goose watched me in doubtful pause, and I said, "I promise, it's fine."

It was more than fine. It was slow and delicate, an artful display of emotion and not the frenzied coupling I'd always imagined it'd be. He touched me like I could break under his hand and I thought that I might, as my body was reintroduced to sex and intimacy. But it was sweet, and it was perfect, just like him, and afterward, I clung to his body, hoping we could stay in that bed forever.

"You're okay?" he asked again, trailing his fingers through my hair.

"Yeah," I replied, nodding against his chest. "I'll be okay."

"That's kinda implying that you're *not* okay."

"No, really, I am."

He exhaled like he'd been holding his breath, then nodded. "I'll take your word for it."

We laid there for a few minutes in silence, just living inside the sanctity of our hearts beating and the bubble of happiness I knew would burst at any moment, because that's how life is. But for the moment, this was bliss and it was ours, and before I fell asleep, I whispered, "I love you, Eric."

Chapter Thirty-One

Pancakes woke me up the next morning, as the sweet scent wafted through the apartment, and I opened my eyes to see Goose carrying in a loaded plate and a glass full of orange juice.

"I have never gotten breakfast in bed before," I said, hating how often I compared him to my previous relationship, while knowing it was impossible not to. They were just too stark in contrast, and the wounds from the past were still so fresh.

"Well, don't get used to it," he laughed. "I'm not usually a morning person."

"Oh, no?"

He shook his head. "Nah. Night owl all the way."

"Me, too," I replied with a grin. Then, narrowing my eyes with curiosity and lifting the glass of juice, I asked, "So, why are you up, then?"

"Your phone was ringing earlier, and I couldn't get back to sleep, so I ..."

Before he had finished his sentence, I stopped listening and reached for my phone, to check my messages. I had trained myself to listen intently for the phone, even in sleep, just in case the NICU called, even though it happened so infrequently. It figured that, on the day I actually allowed myself a moment to relax and sleep in, I had missed their call.

"Oh, my God. I'm a terrible mother," I groaned, dialing the number and trying not to worry.

"You're not," Goose insisted, sitting beside me and running his fingers through my hair.

"Yes, I am," I disputed, as someone on the other line answered the phone.

"Neonatal intensive care unit, this is Cheryl. How can I help you?"

"Uh, yes, h-hi. I got a call from you earlier. I'm just checking to make sure everything is okay. My son is Alexander Wright."

"Okay, Mama. Just give me a second to transfer you to his nurse."

In the moments it took for the call to be transferred, I imagined every horrible explanation for why they could be calling. He relapsed, he was sick, he was dying …

Or maybe he died.

The thought weaseled itself into my psyche and I scrubbed a hand over my face, hating myself for even thinking of that word, and superstitiously believing I could think it into reality. Tears filled my eyes, and I took a deep breath, as I prayed to whoever would listen that he was anything but gone.

"Everything okay?" Goose asked, and I opened my mouth to reply, when the call was answered by another nurse.

"Hi, Mama. I'm not sure we've met, but I'm Samantha, and I have your little man today."

"Hi, y-yeah, I think we might have met."

"Oh, okay! Well, first of all, Alexander is doing just fine."

"Oh, thank God," I said, releasing a sigh of relief that left my lungs empty.

Samantha laughed. "I know, I'm sorry. It's always scary when we call. I just wanted to give you a heads up and tell you that we had to put your little guy back on the CPAP. Just so you aren't surprised when you come in."

I swallowed, reminding myself that none of the scary things had happened and that he was okay. He was safe. But the disheartening disappointment of a setback was so heavy on my heart, that my shoulders slumped a little under the weight.

"Oh," I said quietly. "Okay."

"It happens sometimes, you know? We try something for a little while and then we find that they're just not ready for it yet. He will be, though, I promise. He just needs a little more time."

"Right," I replied, nodding. "Of course."

"Don't worry, Mama. He'll get there."

"I know," I said hurriedly, ignoring Goose, watching intently by my side.

"Have a great day. We'll see you later."

"Okay. Bye."

I hung up and dropped my phone on the bed, before setting out to eat my breakfast. I didn't taste the pancakes, as I chewed and swallowed mindlessly, and after only eating for a few minutes, I realized I wasn't hungry. Without a word, I stood up in a hurry, to head into the kitchen to collect my pumping supplies. It wasn't until I had assembled the bottles and pump, that I realized I was missing one of the flanges.

"Dammit," I exclaimed, standing up in a hurry, and completely disregarding my blood pressure and how it still made me dizzy if I moved too quickly. I lost my balance and fell into the wall, banging my hip and catching myself with the arm of the chair. Gritting my teeth, I pinched my eyes shut and muttered, "Fucking hell."

"Kenny, what can I do?"

"Nothing," I replied brashly, righting myself and walking quickly into the kitchen. "I need to take my damn pills and pump. Then, I have to get some work done, because I need to have another book out in a couple of months, or else I'm not going to—"

"Kendall."

In between grabbing the pill bottles off the counter and the missing flange, I turned around to face him with exasperation. "*What?*" I shouted, just as my bottom lip began to quiver. And damn it all to hell, I didn't want to cry. Not now, not again. I was so sick of crying. I was so sick of feeling helpless and afraid and alone. But fighting it only made it harder, and tears began to stream down my face before I had the chance to stop them.

"Come here," he said, walking toward me and pulling me into his arms.

I didn't hug him back. Still as stone, I just stood there, holding my pill bottles and breast pump parts, while I cried against his chest. He smoothed his hands over my hair, kissing my head, until I found the strength to take a step back and collect my bearings.

"Sorry," I said, wiping beneath my nose with the back of my hand.

"Don't apologize to me."

I shook my head and walked to the fridge to grab a bottle of water. "This isn't how you wanted to spend your morning."

"Sure, it is. I'm spending it with you."

"Yeah," I snickered. "And what great company I am right now."

"What did they say on the phone?"

I popped three blood pressure pills into my mouth, along with a prenatal vitamin, and swallowed them all with a swig of water. As I plunked the bottle back onto the counter, I said, "He's back on the CPAP."

Goose nodded morosely. "Okay. But didn't you tell me just a couple weeks ago that sometimes that can happen? You can take two steps forward, then one step back?"

"Yes, but—"

"I get you're disappointed, but you and I both know that getting better isn't always a straight path to recovery."

Anger erased my sadness and disappointment, and as much as I hated to be mad at him, the day after we'd had such a perfect, romantic night, the control I had over my emotions was slipping. I slammed the pump parts onto the counter, and while Mrs. Potter scurried out of the room, Goose didn't even flinch.

"You cannot tell me how to feel, Eric. Do not even *pretend* to know what this is like for me."

"I'm not. I wouldn't. And you can be as pissed off as you want to be. Hell, I don't give a shit if you wanna smack me around, just to take it out on someone. But you cannot lose sight of what is important here, Kenny. Okay? You can't let that happen."

With my eyes on the bottle parts, I sniffled, as the anger dissipated as quickly as it came. "Sometimes I don't even know what's important anymore," I confessed meekly, spinning the bottle on the counter. "I feel like I'm torn into a thousand pieces every second of every single day."

"The good shit is what's important," he replied, leaning down against the counter and finding my eyes, that were once again full of tears. "Alex, the fact that you're both alive, and this really great thing we got goin' on. Those are your silver linings, Kenny. Don't lose sight of them, even when everything else gets really dark and ugly. That's what's important, and as long as you remember that, you're gonna be okay."

Chapter Thirty-Two

As desperately in love with Goose as I was, and as much as I knew I could tell him anything, there was so much I felt I couldn't say. On top of that, my relationship with my parents seemed to be stifled, as our phone calls became less frequent and I became more consumed by everything I needed to do for myself and Alex. And that type of isolation was, in a way, more suffocating than my grief and anger.

But at least I had the NICU.

My days spent there with my son and his nurses felt sacred and like we all belonged to a club that only we knew the password to. They understood the things I was going through, the things I saw and felt, and I knew I could be honest with them without facing the typical words of encouragement I received from my parents. And it's not that their sentiments weren't appreciated; they were just simply unwanted.

One night, after Alex had finally been successfully transitioned to being on oxygen, I got to hold him as he slept. I stroked his soft hair and hummed an endless number of lullabies. He had a pacifier that dwarfed his small head and he sucked earnestly in his sleep, the way you would expect any other baby to do. Then, seemingly out of nowhere, his monitors began to beep rapidly. Elle rushed over and took him from me without warning, rubbing his back and patting him repeatedly, until the monitors slowed in their alarming chorus.

When I looked to her with panic, she smiled and said, "He's okay. I just had to bring him back."

"What does that mean?"

"It means," she shrugged helplessly, hesitating before saying, "he just had a moment. But he's okay now."

She spoke of it like it was nothing, and like it was par for the course, but that moment had left me shaken. As I stared at him and his tiny nose and every one of his tiny fingers, tears filled my eyes, while I struggled to get the sound of his alarming monitors out of my head. All of that beeping. The monotonous, shrill drone. I couldn't listen to it without being transported back there, to the night he was born. To the week I spent hooked up to my own machines, not knowing what was going to happen to me or if I'd ever make it out of that room.

Panic had my blood racing through my veins, and I felt my heart repeatedly slam against the walls of its boney cage. Before I could cry, I made the split decision to leave. Alex didn't need to see me like this. He didn't need to wake up and find me crying, when I should just be happy to be there with him, and so, I called Elle over to help me get him back in his isolette.

As she fed his countless wires through the holes in the incubator, she took a glance at me and asked, "You okay, Mama?"

268

Wiping a hand over my sweaty brow, I nodded. "Yeah, I'm fine. I'm just hot, I guess."

"Are you sure?"

I lied and said I was fine and that I just needed some air. I told Alex I loved him and that I would see him again tomorrow, before I headed out into the hall to leave. But before I could make it to the elevator, Elle ran after me and told me to wait.

"Are you talking to anybody?" she asked, eyeing me with concern.

"What do you mean?"

"I mean, are you talking to a counselor or therapist?"

I shook my head. "No. But I'm okay, really."

She didn't look convinced. "It's okay to admit that you're not okay. So many parents who go through something like this suffer from post-traumatic stress disorder, did you know that?"

I shook my head in reply. I hadn't been aware of that, but after she said it, it made sense to me how it could happen. And then, it immediately made sense of what had been happening to *me*.

"You have been through a horrible ordeal," she said gently. "Pregnancy and having a baby are supposed to be these beautiful, natural experiences, but it almost killed you and your baby. And now, you are dealing with this, coming here every single day and never knowing what to expect. All of that is bound to take its toll on you. It *has* to. You're only human, Mama, and it's okay to admit when things are hard."

The tears fell faster than I could stop them and I broke down in the hallway, right outside the room I had stayed in just a couple of months ago. Elle wrapped me tightly in her arms but I didn't know what to say to her. I didn't know how to verbalize that she was right and that this was hard. So, she just hugged me quietly until the tears finally dwindled and I could breathe without sobbing.

"You okay?"

I shook my head and replied with a humorless laugh, "No."

"Well, listen," she said, taking out her phone. "I know it can be hard to find the balls to talk to a therapist. So, even if you just want to talk to me, you can text me whenever. I'm always here."

We exchanged numbers and I knew in that moment that I had made more than just a solid connection in the medical field. I had made a friend, one I would know forever, and I wished so badly I could think of a way to thank her for everything she had already done for me. But knowing I could never possess the power to do that, I simply said thank you, as I pocketed my phone.

"Of course, that's what I'm here for. Now, go home and get your mind off of everything here. Do R-rated things with your gorgeous boyfriend. Watch a movie, eat your weight in ice cream. We're with your little boy, so don't you dare worry about a thing. He's going to be fine, and I promise, one day, you will be, too."

***

"So, how did the hospital go today?" Goose asked, as I climbed onto a barstool, carrying a pint of Ben & Jerry's finest that I'd picked up at a convenience store down the block.

The Thirsty Goose was crowded for a Thursday night, and I wished he didn't have to work. He had a few staff members he could rely on to give him a day off every so often, but for the most part, he preferred to oversee things. It was his bar and he liked to be the boss, and as someone who also made the choice to be self-employed, I understood it entirely. But today, I wished he'd call it an early night, tell his cook to cover until closing, and come home with me, where I could talk to him without the crowd and "Sweet Home Alabama" vibrating in my ears.

"It was okay," I replied hesitantly, glancing behind me at a gaggle of singing, drunk girls.

"Oh, yeah, I'm convinced. What's up? Is Alex okay?"

Images of Elle rubbing and patting his back came rushing back, along with the shrill sound of his panicking monitors. After living through that experience, especially when it was still so fresh and vivid in my mind, it certainly didn't feel like he was okay. But Elle would have told me if he wasn't, so I nodded.

"He's fine," I said, before worrying my bottom lip. Then, I added, "But Elle talked to me and she thinks I might have PTSD."

Immediately I hated that I'd brought it up, knowing the horrible trauma he himself had experienced all those years ago overseas. Saying out loud that I could be suffering from the same condition as someone who had been to war felt like an insult to the veterans. It felt like an insult to *him*.

But Goose didn't seem at all shocked or taken aback. He just nodded and said, "It makes sense."

"Really?"

"Sure, it does. I mean, to be honest, I'm surprised you're handling things as well as you are, considering what you've gone through. Hell, just what you *continue* to go through. It's a lot for one person to handle."

"Yeah," I whispered, dropping my eyes to the ice cream and the plastic spoon in my hand. "It is."

Then, with a strong bout of curiosity, I asked, "Um, do you ... have it, too?"

His eyes narrowed to curious slits and he cocked his head. "PTSD?"

I faltered in my nod, and he pressed his lips together like he didn't know how to tell me to fuck right off. And if he had, I wouldn't have blamed him. I should never have asked such a personal, invasive question, regardless of who he was to me.

"I'm sorry," I said hurriedly. "I shouldn't have—"

But he wouldn't let me continue, as he held up a finger to me and called into the kitchen, "Hey, Marco! I'm headin' out, man. I'll see you tomorrow." Then, he grabbed his jacket from behind the bar and said, "Grab your ice cream, girlfriend. We're gettin' out of here."

***

"Okay," he said, sitting us down at the table with some tacos and a couple of water bottles. "So, first of all, I fuckin' hate it when people feel intimidated by my past. It's a big reason why I don't talk about it."

"But I'm not—"

"Yeah, but really, you are. You thought your problems right now don't hold a freakin' candle to what I went through back then, and so, you've chosen not to talk to me about them."

"I *do* talk to you about them," I said, which wasn't entirely a lie. I had previously mentioned things. But it was true that I'd rarely brushed the surface of what was going on, and it was also true that a big part of that was the fact that it all felt so trivial. This man had seen death. He'd witnessed the slaughter of his friends, had done unspeakable things in the name of war, and was now permanently branded with a reminder of the past. How could my experience with pregnancy and child birth even compare to that?

"Listen, I can't make you tell me everything, and if you really don't want to for whatever reason, that's your choice to make. I understand it. But I don't want it to be because you think it comes down to some sort of pissing contest. You can only imagine the shit I've seen, but that street goes both ways. I don't know what this is like for you, and I can't even pretend. So, when you tell me you're going through some really hard stuff, I'm gonna take it seriously. Because I understand better than most people how scary the ghosts of the past can be. Okay?"

I don't deserve him, was the first thought that came to mind as I nodded. "Okay."

"Cool." He sat back and grabbed his bottle of water. "So, you wanted to know if I have PTSD."

"Yes," I answered, nodding.

"I do," he replied.

It didn't surprise me. Anybody who had lived through that would have to suffer in some way mentally. But what did surprise me was, how well he seemingly carried himself now. It gave me hope that there could be a light at the end of this tunnel, and so, I asked, "What is it like for you? How do you ... how do you deal with it?"

He pursed his lips and looked toward the wall, like he was considering if he should answer or not, and I silently berated myself for even asking.

"If you don't want to tell me—"

He shook his head, as he uncapped the bottle and took a drink. "No, I want to. Really, I have to. Because that's kinda what being in a relationship with someone is about—knowing each other's demons and how to fight them together. Krystal and I didn't work out because I didn't know how to face it. And Tracey and I didn't work out because—" He cocked his head and laughed. "Well, we didn't work out because of you, actually, but we would've broken up eventually anyway because she ... she was too focused on herself."

It was funny to me, that a woman who spent her life channeling spirits to help others make peace, could be so self-centered. And while I didn't stop him to clarify, I wondered if maybe that was out of necessity. That perhaps she had to be selfish with her personal time because, otherwise, she would have none.

"Anyway," he went on, shifting in his chair and rubbing his thumbnail against his bottom lip, "I'm lucky in that it hasn't been completely detrimental to my life.

Some guys, they come back and they can't even function. It was like that for me at first, before I had the bar to focus on. And I think part of it was that I never really had the time to process things, you know? I went right from the hospital, to coming home to getting married, and then Krys got pregnant. It ... it was a lot to handle all at once, but I wasn't really handling any of it. I was just taking one big thing, then adding another and another, when really, I should've just taken time to focus on healing."

"Sometimes you don't have a choice though," I said quietly, staring at the untouched food and water in front of me. "Life just goes on, regardless of how you feel."

"No, that's true. You're right about that," he replied, before sighing and running his fingers through his hair. "Um, so ..."

He cleared his throat as he fidgeted in his seat, and I knew he was about to delve into the truth about his own mind. I braced myself, not sure I was ready to hear it, whatever it was, but I wanted to know. I wanted to know everything about him, and I realized, I wanted him to know everything about me.

"It comes and goes," he said. "During the day, at work, I can keep myself busy. I can focus on pourin' drinks and hating on Lynyrd Skynyrd. It's predictable and it's comfortable. Home is the same way, and I have Tony to keep me focused on something other than the shit in mind."

He reached down beside his chair and said, "Right, Tone? You and me, we're best buds, right?"

Then, as he continued to pet his dog, he looked back to me and said, "But when everything goes quiet, it's like

I never left that street. I can hear them screaming and feel the sun on my skin and taste the sand and sweat in my mouth. I relive those moments over and over and over again," he chanted, smacking the table with every word, "like it's fuckin' Groundhog Day. And it takes everything in me to remember that I'm not bleeding to death in the middle of the desert."

Exhaling and scraping my teeth over my bottom lip, I nodded and said, "I panicked earlier, when I heard Alex's machines beeping. I can't stand listening to them."

Goose blew out a breath and tapped the table with his pointer finger. He was nervous and hesitant, but still, he continued. "I was in the hospital for a month after the attack. I don't think there's any way you can go through some shit like that and not be triggered."

"Did it bother you when you came to see me?"

"Yeah," he answered honestly. "Only sometimes, though."

The moment felt strangely weighted and crucial. I knew that this conversation and the truths we were sharing were impactful to our relationship, and it only made our meeting feel that much more serendipitous.

Goose took in a deep breath and looked through the window as he said, "When I was really at the height of it, I wished I had someone who could really empathize with me. Like, I didn't need them to know exactly what I was going through, but just someone who could put themselves in my shoes and get it. And now, I feel like I could be that person for you, and I'm just really hoping that's enough."

Chapter Thirty-Three

I woke up by feeling my side of the bed being weighed down and I opened my eyes to a bouquet of flowers and a smile from the man I loved.

"Hey," I whispered, my throat raspy with sleep. "What time is it?"

"It's early, like eight o'clock," he answered. "But I woke up from some shit outside, and I couldn't get back to sleep, so I went out to grab these."

He held the flowers up and said, "Happy first Mother's Day, Kenny."

I sat up and accepted them, bringing their yellow and pink blooms to my nose and tried to smile as I admired their beauty. But a bouquet of pretty flowers couldn't take away the fact that I was still without my baby, the little person to give me reason to celebrate, and that left me wanting to spend the entire holiday in bed.

"We should go back to sleep," I told him, fighting away the emotions that seemed to constantly be at the ready.

"Aren't your parents coming?" Goose asked.

"Yeah, but not until later," I said, laying the bouquet on my nightstand. "And when they're here, we can just order takeout."

"What?" He laughed, kicking off his shoes and crawling back in, to lay beside me. "I mean, we can chill for now, but we gotta go out and celebrate."

"Or I can just stay here and pump my boobs until they fall off."

He nuzzled his chin against my shoulder. "Well, that doesn't sound like a good time at all," he muttered, before kissing beneath my ear. "It'll be good for you, to get dressed and do something."

I sighed, turning my head, to stare out the window. "It just feels wrong to not have Alex with me," I whispered, my voice quivering.

"I know," he said, wrapping his arm around me. "So, if you wanna spend the day with him at the hospital, that's fine, too. Nobody would blame you for that."

"I wanna see my mom, though," I complained, feeling conflicted. "I just want us all to be in one place at a time, and we can't be."

"Next year."

I nodded, cuddling the blanket to my chin. "Yeah. Next year," I muttered, while questioning against my will if there even would be a next year.

***

We went to lunch at a quaint restaurant on the water. It was a little windier than any of us would've liked, but other than that, the weather was beautiful. And I couldn't stop wishing that Alex was there, too.

"So, he's doing great," Dad confirmed with a grin.

I nodded, sipping slowly on a glass of Sprite. "Yeah, he's doing really well with his feedings. At this point, he's entirely bottle fed, which is crazy, considering just a few weeks ago he wasn't."

"They told you it would happen quickly," Mom reminded me gently, reaching out to touch my arm.

"It doesn't feel like it," I answered quietly, swirling my straw in the glass.

"He'll be home before you know it," Dad said, before digging into his lunch of shrimp and steak.

I hated the way he and my mother kept saying things like that. They were well meaning, and I knew it, but they always used this carefree tone, like it shouldn't be a big deal that I'd now been separated from my baby for two and a half months. I was living a double life, one that I spent inside a hospital and the other where I was socializing, having lunch, and developing a relationship with this really great guy I still couldn't believe was mine. And I was sick of them treating it so nonchalantly.

My mind disappeared inside my thoughts as I stared into the bubbles in my soda. Goose's fingers brushed my thigh, and I was yanked from the lonely abyss, to stare into his eyes.

"You okay?"

I hesitated before nodding. "Yeah, I'm fine."

Mom glanced at Dad and then asked, "So, we didn't want to say anything about this, but have you heard from Brendan at all?"

280

My fists clenched beneath the table at the mention of his name, angry that they would even bring him up on a day that should've been happy and without drama. "No. Why? Have you?" My voice was unraveled and shrill, like I was on the brink of losing it at any second.

Hell, maybe I would.

She shook her head rapidly. "Oh! No, no. It's just, we haven't talked much with you lately, and we were wondering if he had reached out to you since you, uh, saw him."

Since he ran out on us, is what I knew she wanted to say, as I replied, "No, he hasn't said a word to me."

"Good," Dad grumbled, and Goose raised his glass of water and grumbled back, "I'll drink to that."

But was it good? Was it good that the father of my child could so easily walk away and in the middle of a crisis? Sure, it was better than being dragged to court in a custody battle—God knows that's the last thing I needed—but how sad was it that he had no desire to know his own son?

No, I didn't think it was good. I actually thought it was heartbreaking. But it was a heartbreak I decided to keep to myself.

"Have they talked at all about when Alex can come home?" Mom asked. Yet another question I had grown to hate.

"Not really," I muttered, poking at my chicken parmesan.

"Well, they said sometime around his due date, right? That's in a couple weeks."

"Yeah, but there's so much involved, Mom. They don't know if they're gonna wean him off the oxygen yet, and he's just barely started taking his bottles. And we've seen how quickly things can backpedal, like with the CPAP. We just have to take it one day at a time."

"Well, in any case, hopefully, it'll be soon," Dad concluded, smiling across the table. "And then, you can come back home, too."

***

"So, you're moving back to your parents' place?" Goose asked, as we entered my apartment.

Lunch had been followed by a walk around The American Museum of Natural History, and while we took in the exhibits, Goose hadn't spoken a word about what my father had said earlier. I had hoped it would be swept under the rug to be dealt with another day, because truthfully, I still wasn't sure what I was doing and wasn't in any position to think about it. But now, there he was, getting ready to grill me as soon as the door was closed behind us.

"I don't know yet."

"Okay, that's fine, and I don't blame you for considering it. Hell, I wouldn't even blame you if you decided to. But I just would've thought that you'd mention something to me."

"I know, I'm sorry," I replied, as I got the breast pump set up. "I just didn't want to get into it when I wasn't sure what I was doing."

"There's nothing to get into, though. Just a heads up would've been nice."

Hooking myself up and turning the machine on, I looked at him incredulously and said, "So, you're telling me you'd have no issue with me moving back to my parents' place."

"Well, yeah. Why would I have a problem with that?"

I laughed. "You are so full of shit."

He chuckled, sitting in front of me on the coffee table. "Hey, I'm not saying I'd be *happy* about it. But you gotta do what's right for you and Alex, and if being with your parents is the best thing, then I'm gonna back you up."

"Would we ..." I didn't want to ask the question that weighed heavily on my tongue, but I didn't have a choice. So, I asked, "Would we be over?"

There wasn't a second of hesitation as he shook his head. "Hell no. I don't give up that easily. I mean, don't get me wrong. It would suck. But we'd work it out."

I kept that moment replaying in my mind as I finished pumping and got Alex's minuscule amount of milk together. I continued to think about it, as I headed to the hospital and went up to the Mom and Baby ward and down to the NICU. All because I couldn't stop from feeling so lucky, despite how unlucky I'd been.

After checking in and washing my hands, I approached Alex's side to find he had been moved from his isolette to an open crib. His big, brown eyes looked up at me and a flicker of recognition passed over his face as he stared, forcing my lips to spread in a tearful smile.

"Hey, baby boy," I whispered, scooping him up out of his crib, without any assistance from the nurses. "How are—"

"Happy Mother's Day, Mama!" Elle exclaimed, rushing over to wrap her arm around me in a hug. She outstretched her arm to a painting hanging above Alex's station, of of a flower and a sun, with two little footprints shaped in a heart. "Did you see what he made for you, to commemorate the day and his brand-new digs?"

"Oh, my God!" I smiled, tearing up just a little more. "You guys did arts and crafts!"

"We sure did," she replied, cupping Alex's little head. "You were a good boy, right? You had fun?" Alex only blinked at her and she laughed and said, "He's the strong, silent type, but trust me, we had a blast."

She sat down at one of the computers, as I sat with my baby, and we chatted about the weekend and the beautiful weather. She told me about her recent stint with retail therapy and how she was getting fed up with her husband's online gaming.

"Like, the guy is forty-five, you know?" She laughed, shaking her head. "Although, I mean, I guess there are worse things. One of my good friends is married to a guy who is a recovering cocaine addict. They got into drugs together, and … I just can't imagine."

Then, before I could stop myself, I blurted out, "Goose is a recovering alcoholic."

She turned to face me, surprise written on her features. "Really?"

It was almost comical to me, that someone in the medical field could be so surprised by such a common condition.

I nodded. "Yeah. He hasn't had a drink in something like, I dunno, thirteen years."

"Wow, that's amazing. Good for him." Then, she asked, "I mean, it's none of my business, but did he tell you why?"

"He was in the Army," I told her. "It was a coping mechanism after he got out."

Slowly, she nodded, a look of understanding crossing her features. "I think that's probably a really good thing for you, then. If he has a history of PTSD, then he'll understand what you're going through."

I smiled, staring down at the sleepy face of my little boy. "He's ridiculously supportive."

"That's great, for both of you. How are things going with you guys, otherwise? Things still going well?"

"Yeah," I said, unable to contain my smile. "I think I keep waiting for something to screw it up, since my last relationship was so crappy, but Goose is just such a good guy."

"Not every relationship needs drama," Elle pointed out.

"Well, I mean, you gotta understand, that's what I do. I write about relationships that *need* drama, because that's what's gonna keep the reader interested."

"Wait," she rolled her chair around to face me, "what?"

I felt my cheeks flush as I replied, "I, uh ... I write romance novels."

"Get. Out." Her mouth fell open in shock, and then she said, "I am totally looking you up. Do you have a pen name?"

"It's Kenny Wright," I laughed, blushing as she hurried to grab her phone and type it in.

"Oh, my gosh," she gushed, staring at the screen with an excited grin. "There you are. You have like, eleven books published!" She looked up at me, her eyes wide and her head shaking. "Girl! You were holding out on me!"

Then, she put her phone down and cleared her throat, before saying, "I'm totally buying those later and having you sign them. But anyway, fictional relationships might need drama sometimes to keep things interesting, but you know what? Life itself is full of enough drama. And you deserve something that makes you happy. Something that doesn't require work to make it happen. I think that's how you know it's right, and you guys really need that. Both you and Alexander the Great."

Those words hit hard and left me quiet for a few minutes, as I stared at Alex and his perfect little face. I actually wasn't sure what we needed, or what was best for us, and what kind of mother did that make me, to not know what was right for my son? It sat like a fifty-pound brick in my stomach, as I thought about leaving the city and moving back home. It seemed like it should be obvious and like the right answer should've come with an undoubtable sense of assurance. But when I weighed out the pros and cons, I realized there was no obvious choice. Both felt right, while also feeling wrong, and I wished someone could've just made the decision for me.

From the corner of my eye, I watched as a doctor approached me. I wasn't sure yet if he was there for me or one of the other babies, until he stopped at my side and smiled kindly.

"Hello, Ms. Wright," he greeted with a thick accent.

"Hi," I replied, as cheerfully as I could muster, while the anxiety of not knowing why he was there settled in, deep and uncomfortable.

"So, I don't know if any of the other doctors have talked to you, but the baby has a hernia. We want to go in and operate soon, okay?"

Time as I knew it seemed to warp, shifting so that I was crawling at a snail's pace while the rest of the world zipped by. I struggled to catch up to his abrupt announcement, not entirely sure of what he'd said.

"I'm sorry," I replied, giving my head a good shake. "Did you say you want to operate?"

He gave a firm nod. "Yes. The sooner, the better. The bigger he gets, the worse the hernia will get. So, we need to do this as soon as possible. Okay?"

"Is it ... is it serious?"

"Oh, no, no. It is very common and very minor."

"But it's still surgery."

"Yes," he answered robotically. "It *is* surgery. But I assure you, he will be fine."

"But it's *still* surgery," I repeated. But his bedside manner wasn't the greatest, and he only nodded before telling me to call the surgeon in the morning to schedule. Then, he was gone. Leaving me to marinate in the sudden news and the shock it brought with it.

I looked down at my sweet baby and thought about the trials he had already undergone in such a short period of time. After being born at twenty-seven weeks' gestation, being intubated for over a month, and being on a rollercoaster ride with his progression, I wondered, *hasn't he been through enough?* And I felt immediately guilty for even thinking such a thing, when I knew there were babies right there in the NICU who had it so much worse. But that knowledge didn't take away from the fact that he was still just a baby—*my* baby—and no baby, in my opinion, deserved to begin life like this.

The train of my thoughts brought tears to my eyes and I imagined him, a small, three-pound infant, put under anesthesia and cut open. I imagined him recovering. I imagined myself, helpless and waiting for the news to come, telling me whether or not the surgery was a success.

It was becoming too much and I needed air. I was suffocating in the sadness for my baby and my self-pity and anger that this was happening to me. That any of it had happened at all. I kissed Alex's head and laid him gently into his bed, promising to come back when I had calmed down, and I left.

Happy Mother's Day to me.

Chapter Thirty-Four

I arrived at Goose's apartment unannounced. It hadn't even crossed my mind that I should call or text first. I just got into a cab, gave the driver his address, and went. When I got there, I found the building's door unlocked, as it was held open by some guy taking out the trash, and I invited myself in.

After knocking on his apartment door, I waited, while hearing indiscernible voices on the other side. I began to question whether this was a good idea, and if I should have given him a heads up before showing up out of the blue, but there was no time to leave before the door was opened by Goose. Behind him was a blonde woman and a tall, tattooed man, and I was completely mortified to be standing there in my dirty leggings and spit-up-stained sweatshirt.

"Hey! This is crazy. I was just gonna call and tell you to come over," Goose said, reaching out to lay his hand on my shoulder and lead me into the apartment. He gestured toward his guests and said, "This is my buddy, Vinnie, and his wife, Andy. They were in the city and thought they'd drop by. Guys, this is my girlfriend, Kenny. She—"

"You live in the apartment above Famiglia Bella," Vinnie said, nodding slowly.

"Uh, yeah," I answered hesitantly.

"My family owns the restaurant," he replied. "I've seen you around. Nice to officially meet you finally."

I couldn't take the time to think about what a small world we live in or what the chances were that I would randomly fall in love with the man who was friends with the owner of the pizza place I lived above. All I could think about was my baby and what he had to go through and how unbelievably unfair it all was.

"Yeah," I replied, offering the kindest smile I could muster. "It's nice to meet you, too."

Goose steered me around to look into his eyes and asked, "Is everything okay? Did you go to the hospital?"

"Alex needs surgery," I told him without warning, trapping my bottom lip between my teeth to stop it from wriggling.

"What?" He sounded so instantly scared and alarmed, and I loved him for that. For caring and feeling so much compassion toward my little boy.

I nodded. "He has a hernia, and they need to operate on it as soon as possible. And I know it's minor and I know it's common, but oh God, I am so sick of everything. I am so tired of all this shit and I just want him to come home and be okay."

By the time I was finished, I was in tears and Goose had his arms around me. He gave Vinnie and his wife a brief rundown of the situation, and they both offered their sympathies, but God, I wished they hadn't. I wished they could have been the two people not to tell me they

290

were sorry. To not treat my situation and my son, like he was a sideshow when they heard how tiny he was when he was born.

I excused myself and went to Goose's bedroom, with Tony on my heels. I closed the door behind me and took off my dirty clothes, before pulling one of Goose's t-shirts over my head, and climbing into his bed. Tony jumped up, laid down beside me and nestled his back against my chest.

And then, I cried myself to sleep.

***

The door creaked open, and I awoke not knowing what time or day it was. Tony had moved from the bed to the floor, and I watched through bleary eyes as Goose kicked off his heavy boots and pulled off his shirt.

He spotted me, as I rolled over to lay on my back, and said, "Hey, I didn't mean to wake you up."

I shook my head as I rubbed the sleep from my eyes. "It's okay. I should get going, anyway. I have to feed Mrs. Potter, and … dammit, I have to pump, too. I haven't pumped in," I grabbed for my phone on the bed and squinted at the time, "four hours? Shit … I have to go. I have to go right—"

"Stay," he commanded gently, sitting at the foot of the bed and holding his hand to my leg.

"I really can't. I have to pump. I'm not supposed to go longer than two—"

"Kenny. It's okay. Just stay tonight."

The sadness, anger, and frustration from before all rushed back with a vile vengeance as I threw my phone to the mattress.

"It's not okay!" I shouted, as my hands reached for my hair and pulled. "Nothing is fucking okay!"

"I know," he replied quietly, beginning to stroke long lines from my knee to my ankle.

"You don't fucking know! You have no fucking idea! Nobody fucking knows what this is like for me! Not you, not my parents, not your goddamn friends or, or … whoever. Not a single one of you knows what it's like to have to see your baby attached to all those fucking machines. Not a single one of you knows what it's like to ask someone if it's okay to hold your own baby. He's *mine*! I shouldn't have to fucking ask but I do! Not a single one of you knows what it's like to walk away from him every single day, to go home to live your life like he doesn't even exist! God, not a single one of you fucking gets it and I am so tired. I'm so tired of it all. I just want to sleep for a fucking week and not have to worry about this shit, but I can't. Because Alex needs at least one parent who gives a fuck, and I'm all he fucking has."

By the time I was finished with my emotional tirade, I was breathing heavily and my face was covered in tears and snot. Goose sat there, watching and listening, and staying as still as the stone pillar that he was, with only the heartbreak in his eyes giving him away. His hand had stilled against my leg, and when he knew I was done, he squeezed my calf firmly.

"Can I hug you now?" he asked.

I sniffled and nodded, then went to him to cower in his embrace. His arms wrapped around me like a security blanket, and as he stroked my hair, he whispered, "You're right. Nobody knows what it's like to be you. Nobody can even begin to pretend to understand. And I know it's hard, I tell you all the time, but you're getting through it. You're doing it. And one day, hopefully soon, this part will all be a memory."

I knew he was right. I knew how quickly time was already passing. Hell, it had already been over two months since he had been born. His due date was rapidly approaching, and God willing, he would be coming home soon after. But the days were dragging by. I wasn't getting any work done and I missed him so much. I missed him and I hurt for him and I couldn't stand how much I hated it all.

I settled against Goose's body, taking comfort in his strength, and began to calm my breathing and tears. I listened to him talk gently to me, repeating the familiar reassurances that everything would be fine, and even though I still wasn't convinced of that, it was enough to hear him say it. It was enough to know I could rely on him and know he was there. That was something I had been missing for a long time and never really knew how much I needed it.

"God, I love you so much," I said, my voice muffled against his shoulder. "Do you even know how much I love you?"

"I know. I love you, too," he replied, before kissing the exposed skin of my neck.

It began softly, just a peck, but the abrasive scratch of his beard against my throat sent shivers down my throat and a groan from my lips. I hadn't intended on making a sound at all, but it happened, and he kissed me again in response. Longer, harder. So much more passionate than before. I soon found myself on my back, with his shirt thrown to the floor, and my thighs open to the width of his hips.

Then, as we made love, I felt my heart patching itself up, reinforcing its cracks and bruises with the foundation of his love for me. And even though I knew it would break over and over again, as this journey continued forward, I also knew that it would always mend. Just so long as I had this man in my life, to help me put it back together.

Chapter Thirty-Five

I did stay at Goose's apartment that night. I neglected my breast pump and fell asleep, after reminding myself that I always had a tendency to over-feed Mrs. Potter and that she'd be fine until the next morning.

When I woke up to the sun streaming through the window, Goose and I took a cab over to my place, where he fed the cat while I called the surgeon.

"Ms. Wright, how are you?"

I unintentionally scoffed. "Oh, just wonderful," I muttered sardonically, and the surgeon let out a little sympathetic chuckle.

"I know. Nobody likes these conversations. I do assure you though, this is for the best and it is a very simple surgery." Then, he chuckled again. "I suppose that doesn't help much."

I tried to unwind a little and forced a stiff laugh. "No, not really."

"Well, the sooner we can get it done, the better. So, I was hoping to schedule it in for this Thursday."

"That's only two days away," I said, before worrying my bottom lip between my teeth.

"Like I said, the sooner the better. You and the baby's father are welcome to see him before surgery, and then, you can wait in the lobby for him to come out. Okay?"

I nodded, staring blankly ahead and wishing I had more time to process this ordeal before sending my son under the knife. "Okay."

"Wonderful. I will see you Thursday. Have a wonderful day."

"Thank you. You too."

I hung up and dropped my phone to the counter as I muttered, "Have a wonderful day. Right."

"What's up?" Goose asked, sidling up next to me.

"They want to do the surgery on Thursday."

"Wow. That's soon."

"No shit. And the only people allowed are me and the baby's father. So, do you think I should call up Brendan and ask if he'd like to suddenly be a dad today?" I snickered bitterly, shaking my head and laying my face in my hands. "God, I was not cut out for this shit."

"Yes, you were. You wouldn't be going through it if you weren't," Goose said. "And I'll go with you."

"But they said—"

"They said the baby's dad, and how do they know I'm not?"

***

On Thursday morning, Goose came with me to the hospital bright and early at six o'clock in the morning, and got to meet Alex for the first time.

"Hey, buddy," he said, speaking quietly outside of the operating room. "You're gonna be fine, right? Yeah, you are, so tell your mom to stop worrying, okay? She won't listen to me."

"I can't stop," I muttered, as I felt the expansion of my heart invade my lungs.

"See?" Goose said to Alex. "You gotta get out of here, kid. I don't know how much longer I can put up with this by myself."

The surgeon and nurse came in to prepare him for his surgery and said it was time for us to leave. I made the decision to be strong, to hold my head high and allow my baby boy to feel my determination to make it through another day of this ordeal. As Goose stepped aside, I reached into Alex's crib, took his hand, and whispered, "You got this, baby boy. I'll be here when you get out."

As I exited the room, I left behind a piece of my heart. God, I was so sick and tired of walking away, of leaving him and putting my faith in the hands of strangers. Suddenly, my bones were too heavy for my skin to hold and I sagged, like the wispy branches of a willow tree, and let go of a ragged sigh.

Goose wrapped an arm around my shoulders, keeping me up, keeping me from collapsing on the hospital floor, and said, "So, I was a pretty weird kid. Like, when all of my friends were being *Spider-Man* for Halloween, I wanted to be Bob Ross. My parents called it eccentric, but that was just nice way of sayin' I was pretty freakin' weird."

He steered me into the waiting room and to a chair, as he continued, "Anyway, my mom was awesome. She always went all out for us when our birthdays rolled around. And when I turned six, I didn't want a *Ninja Turtles* party or any normal crap like that. No, of course not, 'cause my school's playground was always crawling with these freakin' Canada Geese and I was obsessed with them. So, naturally, I wanted a goose-themed birthday party.

"And the cool thing about my mom was that, even while my friends thought I was a freakin' whack-job, she never made me feel weird. She just said, okay, and threw me the most kickass goose party ever. The woman actually called a petting zoo and told them only geese were welcome."

His smile was one of melancholy and nostalgia, and he sighed heavily. "She started calling me Goose after that, and it just kinda took off."

I leaned against his side, too drained to hold myself up. "That's a way cuter story than I thought it would be."

"I never said what kind of story it was," he chuckled.

"Your mom sounds like a really great lady."

He nodded faintly and replied, "She really was. You would've liked her. The woman could cook like no other and she had this way of making everybody feel important. Like whatever you were saying to her was the best thing she had heard all day."

Stretching his legs out, he wrapped an arm back around my shoulders and said, "She would've liked you, too."

***

Hours had passed, and with all the worrying I was doing, I could have sworn I'd lost years from my life.

Goose had filled the time with stories about his mother, questions about what I was currently attempting to work on, and what my childhood had been like growing up as an only child. The persistent conversation hadn't stopped my nerves from running on overdrive, but I was grateful for the distraction.

I paced the length of the waiting room and back again, as I said, "God, they said it would only take about two hours. It's been three now. What the hell is taking so long?"

"I don't know," he muttered, shrugging and offering an apologetic look.

"Maybe I should call. Or I could ask one of the ladies in the NICU, right? They would know."

"I'm sure if something was wrong, they'd let you know," he replied softly, reassuringly, and I nodded, releasing a quivering breath.

"Yeah," I said, continuing to nod as I glanced at the wall clock for the thousandth time. "Yeah, you're probably right."

I paced again and again and again, until Goose groaned and shot a glare in my direction. "Kenny, you're gonna give me a coronary, okay? Come here, sit down and relax."

"I can't relax!"

"Well, then just come and sit down."

Like a child who had just been scolded, I slogged my way back to the seat beside him and dropped into it. I turned my gaze back to the clock, and with my legs jouncing and my nerves twitching with anxiety, I cursed the person who thought it'd be a good idea to put a clock in the waiting room of a hospital.

"I wasn't there when my daughter was born," he said abruptly, picking at the chipped paint on the arm of his chair. "I was in rehab when I had gotten that call."

I glanced at him, not quite knowing what to say. So, I only nodded, unsure if he'd continue or not, until he began to speak again.

"So, it kinda felt special to me, to be here when Alex was born. I mean, not that I don't feel close to Hannah or anything, but it's kinda cool that, maybe one day, I'll be able to tell him the story of where I was when he came into the world, you know? And that I was scared shitless for him and his mom, and that it was one of the best moments in my life, when I learned you were both alive."

There was a brief moment of calm as I smiled and tipped my head against his shoulder. "I'm glad you came," I said.

"Yeah, so am I," he replied, resting his head against mine.

A few minutes later, one of the nurses came to get us. She said that Alex was out of surgery and was doing great. Before I'd let her continue, I asked eagerly if we could see him and she nodded with a smile.

"But only for a few minutes. He really needs to rest," she mentioned, and that was okay with me. Because as much as he needed to sleep, so did I.

We were ushered into the NICU, where we found an isolette in his usual spot. The nurse explained to me that, during the healing process, he'd be in the isolette before moving back into his crib. Alex was sprawled out in nothing but a diaper, with the old familiar tubing of a ventilator fed through his lips. Surprised by this, I turned to the nurse and asked how long he'd have to be intubated again, and she assured me it should only be for a few days as he recovered. Relief washed over me like a gentle, cleansing rain, and I touched the plastic separating me from my son.

"I'll see you later, baby boy. I'm so proud of you," I whispered, before turning to Goose and saying, "Let's go to bed."

Chapter Thirty-Six

From the moment he was born, Alexander Wright was a warrior, and two days after his hernia surgery, he was off the ventilator and back to his oxygen cannula.

A week later, as I changed his diaper, I could hardly tell that he'd had surgery at all.

"His incisions look so good," I told Elle.

"I know, right? They did a good job."

The compliment sent me back, to right after my own surgery. The emergency cesarean I'd had done only a few months before. It was a moment I thought I had forgotten, but there it was, vivid and like it had just happened. I recalled Dr. Albrecht pulling my blanket down and my gown up, to inspect the fresh wound just above my groin. She had made mention that the surgeons had done a good job, while I laid in bed, wishing they had never needed to do it at all.

I inhaled sharply, bringing myself back to reality. I looked at Elle and agreed.

They had done a good job. Every single one of them.

***

Another couple of weeks went by, and I walked into the NICU one day wielding my freezer bag of tiny amounts of milk. Debbie spotted me and grinned, before running to Alex's bed and presenting him to me with a flourish of her arms.

"Something's different!" she exclaimed, and when I took a look at him, it was very obvious what that something was.

No more cannula.

No more oxygen.

I had been so worried about him being on the oxygen for an extended period of time, even beyond the NICU. I was so afraid I'd do something to screw things up, to hurt him, or hinder his progress and growth. But now, with his fresh face staring up at me, wearing the faintest of smiles and recognition in his eyes, I teared up and thanked Christ for giving me yet another reason to believe in miracles.

"Look at you, baby boy!" I exclaimed, reaching in to pick him up.

Debbie wrapped an arm around my shoulders. "One less tube to worry about," she said with a grin. "And soon, he won't have any."

I looked to her with widened eyes and asked, "Really? You think it'll be soon?"

She nodded. "Oh, yeah. The oxygen was the last thing we were really waiting on with him. Now, he just needs to pass his car seat test, and he's good to go."

I couldn't quite explain it but in that moment, a rush of panic swept over me and nearly set me off balance.

Our time in the hospital had felt so long and dragged out, that I'd foolishly thought of it as endless. It wasn't even that long ago that I had laid in a hospital bed, asking Elle if he was going to die, and feeling so certain that he would, even while she assured me that he would be fine. Now, the reality of him finally coming home was closing in on me, and while I knew I should've been excited, I found that I wasn't.

And it wasn't because I didn't want him to be with me, or that I didn't want to be his full-time caregiver—his mom. It was strictly because I couldn't imagine my days, my nights, my life without these women, my superheroes. I didn't want to imagine it. At the thought of going a day without seeing them, my eyes welled up and I held Alex close to me, assuring him it would be all right, while not certain I was sure myself.

***

I clawed at Goose's back at the very moment of penetration. With my head tipped back and my body arched to press my aching breasts to his bare chest, I chanted incoherent obscenities toward the ceiling, making him chuckle in my ear.

"I'm so glad it's gotten better for you," he muttered, his lips brushing the sensitive flesh of my neck.

Purring like the cat on the floor, I nodded. "You and me both."

He was always adamant on pleasing me first, and within minutes, I was groaning loudly, begging him breathlessly for more. I called his name, his real name, and that alone was enough to tip him over the edge.

"Holy shit," he murmured, slowly climbing down from his climax. "My name has never sounded hotter."

"You *do* have a hot name," I assured him. "And there's no way I could scream Goose during sex. Never gonna happen."

"You won't be screaming anything pretty soon," he jabbed playfully, pulling me to his side and nuzzling his chin against my shoulder. "Once Alex is home, we won't be having sex for a long, long time."

"Oh, stop," I grumbled, swatting his chest.

"No, seriously," he laughed. "My friends, Vinnie and Andy? Since their son was born, they hardly get two seconds to do anything without him, and if they do, they're too tired to get it on."

"I'm sure it won't be *that* bad," I said, pouting.

"You'll see. *Everything* is gonna change once he's outta there."

I knew that it was true and that my life was going to change so drastically, it would be nearly unrecognizable to my past self. Part of me was looking forward to it. I wanted Alex to invade my space and change everything forever. I wanted him to turn everything upside down and cry all night and smear poop on the walls. Because as much as I dreaded those endless, sleepless nights, I was more grateful just to be able to have them at all.

But another part of me was mourning.

I mourned the loss of my time with him in my belly. I mourned the coveted birth, the way things were supposed to be, the months I didn't have him with me all the time. And I mourned the loss of the NICU and the nurses that came with it.

"I'm going to miss them," I whispered to Goose, rubbing my cheek to his chest.

"Who?"

"The NICU nurses. I want him home so badly, but I hate that bringing him home means not seeing them."

"I'm sure you can still see them," he insisted.

"Maybe, but it won't be the same."

He nodded. "Nothing will be the same again. That doesn't make it bad or worse, it just makes it different. You'll settle into the new normal, just like you settled into this one, and it's gonna be fine."

"Yeah," I sighed, "I know. I just wish it didn't all have to be so damn hard."

"Everything is hard," he replied. "But you wouldn't appreciate the good shit if it wasn't."

Chapter Thirty-Seven

I hated being so far from the city, as Goose and I drove the hour and forty-five minutes to my parents' house on Long Island, with Tony wagging his tail in the backseat. Things can change so quickly in the neonatal unit, and all I could think about was, *what if something happens while I'm here? What if I didn't make back it in time to ...*

I didn't want to think about it or any of the horror stories I had read on Doctor Google or witnessed with my own eyes. I didn't want to think for even a second that any of those scenarios could happen to my baby.

So, instead I told Goose about my childhood, filling the time with memories and things I missed about the home of my youth. He had grown up in the city and couldn't imagine living in the suburbs, with a backyard and a dead-end street. It was just a different way of growing up, he said, and even though I agreed, deep down I kind of felt sorry for him.

When we arrived, he looked out the window with a wistful smile on his face. I asked what that look was for and he simply told me that it was nice and he could understand why I'd missed it so much.

"Hello, favorite daughter!" Mom bellowed, running out of the house and down the walkway to greet us.

"Hey, Mom," I said, rolling my eyes as I grinned.

She pulled me in for a big hug as she smiled at the Viking by my side and said, "How are you, Goose?"

"Doing pretty great, Mrs. Wright," he replied, opening the back door and taking Tony's leash, before pulling out a large aluminum tray. "Hope you guys love wings."

Dad chuckled. "Do I like *wings*?!"

I turned to Goose and said, "Dad's a bit of a wing connoisseur."

My boyfriend's jaw dropped. "And you didn't tell me this, why?"

I shrugged. "It never came up."

"You went through your entire pregnancy *living* on these wings and not once did you mention that your dad is a wing fan?"

I shrugged as I headed up the walk with my mom, our arms wrapped around each other. Goose walked with my dad, muttering, "Man, I can't believe she didn't say anything. I would've hooked you up."

Dad replied, "Don't worry about it, buddy. You'll have a lot of time to make up for it, I'm sure."

***

"I think your dad is trying to make you an honest woman," Goose whispered, as we headed down the upstairs hall to my room.

"Why do you say that?"

308

"Because the guy's been dropping all kinds of hints," he replied. "Like, just now, he was saying he's glad you're finally with someone he could see you spending a long time with."

Glancing over my shoulder, with my hand on the doorknob to my room, I asked," Well, I *have* told you how my parents hated Brendan, right?"

Narrowing his eyes, he shook his head. "No, you never mentioned that."

I opened the door, as I said, "I thought they made it pretty obvious in the hospital. Or on Mother's Day."

"Uh, well, yeah. But the guy ditched you after you had just had his baby. Of course, they would hate him. I didn't realize they had always felt that way, though."

"They always thought I could do better," I replied, suddenly realizing now how right they had always been.

Stepping inside, I swept my eyes over the bedroom I had missed so much since moving to the city. Big and spacious, with a bed I could've slept in for weeks, the room had never stopped feeling like mine, even after all this time. Goose let loose a long, impressed whistle.

"Damn, girlfriend. This place is as big as your apartment."

"Oh, my God," I laughed, shaking my head. "No, it's not."

It really wasn't. The room was a decent size for a child's bedroom, but it was nowhere near equivalent to a seven-hundred square foot apartment.

"Okay, maybe not, but this is just your bedroom. That's not counting the rest of the house that you'd have for both you and Alex."

I turned to face him, watching studiously as he wandered around the room, touching my comforter and the armchair I loved to read in by the picturesque bay window. I wondered what was on his mind and what was keeping his mouth in a firm, straight line. But before I could ask, he turned to me with a grin and a jump of his brows.

"So, tell me more about how they hated Brendan."

***

"So," Mom said, sitting at the edge of my bed, "we were thinking that, for now, you could put a crib or bassinet in here for Alex. Then, as he gets a little older and ready to have his own space, we could fix up the room next door for him."

"And you'd obviously have your own bathroom, too," Dad chimed in. "So, really, you'd only ever be sharing the living room and kitchen with us."

I laughed, dropping onto Goose's lap on the window seat overlooking the backyard. "You guys are acting like I hate living with you or something," I said, wrapping my arms around his neck. "I don't need separation."

"No, we know you don't," Mom insisted. "But you're also going to be raising your baby and I'm sure you'll eventually *want* some separation from us. Especially after you've had your own place."

"And," Dad interjected, pointing at Goose, "when this guy comes to stay, you don't want us on top of you, right?"

I took a peek over my shoulder, to watch as Goose's eyes widened, as if to say I told you so. Then, I laughed and said, "Goose doesn't mind. He loves you guys, too."

"It's true," he agreed with a lopsided smile.

"Anyway, we just wanted to talk about it a little," Mom said. "You know, throw around some ideas and whatever. And a few of your aunts and I were talking about throwing you that baby shower we were—"

"Wait, what?" I cut her off abruptly.

Mom's lips flapped a few times, startled by my abrupt interruption, before saying, "Well, you never had one, and I know it was something we had talked about, so I thought—"

"I really don't want one," I said, perhaps a little harsher than was necessary.

"But people just want to show they care. They want to—"

"Then, if they really want to, they can send me something. But I don't want a shower," I said, as my already tense emotions wound themselves just a little tighter.

Goose wrapped his arms around my waist and squeezed. "Hey, it's okay—"

"No, it's *not*," I said, raising my voice a little. "I don't want a party. I don't want to celebrate. I am still in the scariest time of my life right now and I have no idea what's going to happen *tomorrow*, let alone next weekend. Why the hell would I want to have a goddamn *party* in the middle of that?"

Mom's features softened, as she shook her head. "Kenny, you know it's just because people care. They

311

just want to do something nice for you. *I* want to do something nice for you."

Logic told me that was true, and the rational, "go with the flow" part of me wanted to just go along with it, just to avoid the confrontation. But then, there was the part of me who was always battling the silent enemy in my head, the one who was still working through the trauma and fear of having a special needs baby. I could see no rational reason to put myself in a situation that I knew would trigger my emotions.

And I hoped to God my mother, one of my best friends, would respect that.

"When I came home from Iraq," Goose said, speaking calmly, "my dad wanted to throw a welcome home party for me, because I mean, he was happy I was back and alive, and so was everyone else.

"But the thing was, I didn't *want* a party. I was all kinds of screwed up. My friends were dead, I was alive, I was in pain …" He blew out a loud breath and shook his head. "Between the guilt of surviving and the trauma of going through that … whole thing … The last thing I wanted to do was celebrate. There was nothing *to* celebrate, in my opinion. But my dad had insisted because I was, to him, some kind of hero for … I still don't know."

He cleared his throat and went on, as he reached down to lay a hand against Tony's head. "Anyway, he threw the party despite how much I insisted that I didn't want it. And I got pissed at him for disrespecting my wishes, not to mention ignoring the mental disorder I was struggling to cope with. So, I took a couple bottles of

Jack from the bar and didn't speak to him for the rest of the weekend."

The three of us—Mom, Dad, and me—all looked at him, taken by his story. His cheeks burned with the embarrassment of having all eyes on him and he lifted one side of his mouth in a smile.

"What I'm saying is, don't do what my dad did to me. His heart was in the right place, but his reasons for doing it were ultimately selfish. I hope you won't be like that, too."

Mom sucked her teeth, eyeing him studiously, and for a moment, I thought she might lash out on him for taking a stand against her. But God, I loved him so much for it, and when she finally smiled and relented with a gentle, "Okay," I loved him even more.

***

It was a gorgeous day in late spring, so my parents suggested we take a walk after lunch. With Tony leading the way and my fingers intertwined with Goose's, we took a stroll around the neighborhood. I tipped my head back to feel the sun, warm and fresh against my skin, and after what had felt like the longest, coldest winter of my life, I relished in the comfort of a more promising summer.

"It's nice around here," Goose commented, and I turned to find the smile missing from his rugged face.

"Yeah, I love it."

Mom pointed across the lake. "Right there is B. Davis's house."

Goose glanced behind him to ask, "Who?"

I gawked incredulously. "You don't know who B. Davis is?"

"Should I?"

Dad shrugged. "He's some author who moved here a while back."

"No, no, no," I chanted, shaking my head profusely and chopping my hands through the air. "He's not *some author*. He is one of the most prolific writers of my generation. Not to mention, he is living the actual dream. He landed a seven-figure book deal with his debut novel. That's pretty much unheard of, unless you get really, really lucky."

"Sounds like he got really, really lucky to me," Goose jabbed, smirking a little.

"Well, yeah," I muttered, rolling my eyes. "But his work speaks for itself. It's profound and meaningful and—"

"And you're totally fangirling over a guy who lives around the corner from your parents place," he laughed, not bothering to hide the envy deepening his blue eyes.

"And *you're* jealous," I teased, walking closer to poke him in the ribs.

"Nothing to be jealous of," Goose said with pride, shaking his head. "I don't need to be a millionaire to know my worth."

"Oh, yeah? And what is your worth?"

He waggled his brows, wearing a smug grin. "Girlfriend. I'm priceless."

***

The drive off Long Island was a slow one. Traffic from the weekend Montauk crowd was heavy and I tapped my fingers against the window ledge, as Goose took Tony out to find a tree to mark. The day had been nice, apart from my little upset over the prospect of a shower, and I already missed the distraction of the house and lake.

Part of me felt guilty that I hadn't thought about Alex much while I was there. It wasn't fair that my baby was in the hospital, while I got to enjoy the sun on my face. Especially when he had never even seen the sun yet. But I had to remind myself that I still needed to live my life and retain some semblance of happiness and joy. I had to in order to be the best version of me for him, ready for when he could finally come home.

After getting Tony back into the car, Goose returned to the passenger seat and buckled up. "You know, I told him to go before we left, but did he listen? Of course not …"

I laughed. "Kids."

"Seriously."

Pulling back onto the road, we began to crawl back into the city to a soundtrack of honking horns and Bastille, when Goose abruptly asked, "Have you decided what you're doing yet?"

I glanced across the car. "About what?"

"If you're going back home or not once Alex is out of the hospital."

My hands tightened on the wheel as I replied, "I don't really know—"

"You should," he interrupted without hesitation. "I know you weren't sure before, but now that I've seen it, I really think you should go back."

It wasn't what I would've expected from him, or any man in a relationship with the woman he loved. I would have expected him to beg me to stay, to keep me close to him. While I know he had once told me we would figure out how to make our relationship work, I never would've expected this eagerness for me to leave.

I unintentionally gawked at him, then said, "You really think so?"

He nodded. "I think you would be stupid not to."

I laughed, a sound with a harsh bite. "Wow, tell me how you really feel …"

"Kenny, come on. You don't like living in the city and your parents have two bedrooms and a bathroom for you and the baby. You'd live on a quiet street, in a quiet neighborhood, overlooking a goddamn lake. Why the hell would you *not* want your kid to grow up there?"

I knew he was right and that the alternative would be foolish, and if I was really looking out for the well-being of my son, I don't know that I could justify it.

So, I nodded and replied, "Okay," while wondering how I could leave this man I'd grown to depend on so much.

Chapter Thirty-Eight

My three-month lease was running out and I knew I wouldn't be renewing it. My landlord was already working on finding a new tenant, and when I stopped into the pizza place in my building, the man named Moe behind the register grinned in my direction.

"Girl, I heard you're movin'!"

I nodded and ordered two slices of pepperoni. "Yeah, I'm moving back home to Long Island as soon as my baby is out of the hospital."

He rang me up and replied, "I used to live out there."

"Oh, yeah?"

He nodded and handed me the change. "Yes, ma'am. I was out in Islip for a while. Then, I found myself here."

"I grew up in Brightwaters."

Moe whistled, shaking his head as his dreadlocks swayed. "That's one beautiful town right there. Can't say I can blame you for goin' back."

"My parents are there, so …" I shrugged, as a curly-haired woman handed me my pizza over the glass partition.

"Family is certainly a good reason to go home," he replied, nodding sagely. "But, sometimes, love is a good reason to stay."

I cocked my head with curiosity, and Moe laughed. "I read that one in a self-help book years ago. It stuck with me, you know? Just one of those things."

I smiled and nodded. "Well, thank you. Have a good day."

"You too, baby girl. I'll miss your face around here."

I didn't say it as I left and headed up the stairs to the apartment I felt wrong calling mine, but I would miss him, too.

***

It was just months ago that I had boxed up my things, with the plan to move in with Brendan, and thank God I hadn't. But now, everything was packed again, and while I knew it was for the better, the thought of leaving caused my heart to pulse with trepidation and sadness.

I had no attachment to this city. I had no attachment to this building or even this apartment. But there were now a few people and places here that I found it hard to imagine being without and I didn't know how to wrap my head around that.

I sat at my kitchen table, cluttered in things still needing to be packed, and opened my laptop to get in a few minutes of writing, when I heard the phone ring.

Glancing at it, I saw it was the NICU.

"Hello?"

"Ms. Wright?"

I nodded, as if they could see me, then said, "Yes. Is everything okay?"

"Well, yes, everything is fine right now. I just wanted to call and ask if anybody had told you about Alex's episode this morning."

"Episode?" My gut lurched toward my throat as I stood from the table and stuffed my feet into my shoes. "What do you mean, episode?"

"He bradied this morning," she said factually.

I knew what that meant—Bradycardia is when the heart rate drops to less than sixty beats per minute—and I paused in what I was doing to rest a hand over my own heart, just to make sure it hadn't stopped altogether.

"Is he … is he okay?"

"He should be just fine," she told me. "But we're going to need to keep him for another week or so, just to make sure it doesn't happen again."

"Another *week*?" There was too much defeat in my tone to disguise it, as I slumped back down into my chair.

"I know. He was getting ready for discharge soon, wasn't he?"

"They said it could be any day now."

I heard her sigh morosely. "Yeah, it's so hard. The last few weeks are always very touch and go. But he'll get there, Mama. I promise."

I thanked her and hung up. And although I knew she was right, and although I knew he was in the best place he could be, I couldn't help it as I laid my head on the table and cried.

***

319

"Hey, Mama," Elle said, a little less cheerfully than usual. "I heard our little buddy bradied today."

I nodded, watching as my son slept soundly in his crib. It was hard to believe that just hours earlier, his heart had slowed and given the nurses a scare. Not when he seemed so peaceful now.

"They told me he'd be here at least another week," I muttered, gripping the side of his plastic crib and wishing I was a stronger person. A stronger person wouldn't be on the verge of crying.

"It's hard," she sympathized, resting a hand on my shoulder. "I told you months ago, anything can happen here. One day, he's fine, and the next, his heart rate drops to fifty beats per minute. But I also told you he would go home, and he will. That's still happening. It's just going take a little longer, but he will get there."

She said it so casually, like it was just par for the course and not a big deal at all, and I guess for her it wasn't. For her, this was just another day at work. She had seen the worst cases, and my baby wasn't one of them. But for me, it felt like the end of the world, to have had his discharge day within my grasp, only to have it yanked out of reach without warning.

Again.

She walked off to tend to another baby and left me to sit alone with my sleeping son. He looked so quiet and peaceful, the thought of waking him up pained me, so I didn't. I just sat there, holding his little hand, as another mom walked in to stand beside the crib of a baby nearby.

She reminded me of myself, all those months ago, as she shuffled in, wearing her hospital gown and booties. She looked exhausted and scared, like she didn't quite know what to do. But I did. I'd been down that road before, so, I asked, "Hey, Mama. Do you need a chair?"

She turned to look at me, eyes sad but bewildered, and shook her head. "No, I'm … I'm okay," she replied quietly. "I just wanted to see her before I went to sleep."

I nodded, smiling. "Okay. Just let me know if you need anything."

"Thanks."

I turned my attention back to my baby, still sleeping soundly, as if nothing had happened that morning. I wished so badly that was the case, that I possessed the power to change it and to make him come home the next day.

Then, a voice spoke again from beside me. "Is that your baby?"

Looking back to the mother, I nodded. "Yeah."

"What's his name?"

"Alex," I replied with a smile. "What's your baby's name?"

"Janelle," she said, her eyes lighting up with pride. "She's jaundice, so she has to be here for a few days."

I nodded. "He was jaundice, too."

She squinted her eyes, looking at Alex with inquisition. "How long have you been here?"

"Three months," I replied without hesitation, and she blanched.

"Three *months*?!" she nearly shouted, clutching a hand to her gown-covered heart. "Oh, my God, I'm so sorry. And I'm here, feeling sorry for myself because my baby is only here for a few days."

I smiled reassuringly. "Whether you're here for three months or three days, it doesn't make it any easier."

She loosened her grip on her gown and nodded somberly, turning her attention back to her little girl. "They took her away before I could hold her, and I keep thinking it's not supposed to be like that, you know?"

"I do," I replied, remembering how I didn't get to hold Alex for a few weeks after he was born.

"Now, I feel like … like less of a mom. Or like I was cheated out of an experience I was supposed to have, and it's just not fair." Then, looking back to me again, she said, "And if that's how I feel, when I'm only here for a few days, I cannot even begin to imagine how you must feel."

I smiled again, a little more sorrowfully this time, and said, "I feel about the same as you."

The mom shook her head adamantly. "No way, absolutely not. You, you're so strong for doing this for so long. You've come so far and you're still going. That's incredible. I don't even know how you do it."

"I do it because I have to," I replied honestly, shrugging a little.

"Yeah, but that still makes you strong."

I held Alex's hand just a little tighter, and replied, "So are you."

Chapter Thirty-Nine

I could hardly believe it when, six days later, Alex was given the okay to go home.

It hit me as though I hadn't been expecting it, even though I knew it would be coming soon. I had just been to the hospital a couple of days before, learning the ins and outs of his medications, and he had just passed his car seat test. But even knowing it was coming, my insides were still on fire, as Goose and I took the cab ride to the hospital with the baby seat in tow. A psychotic menagerie of emotions were very much taking hold when the driver pulled up to the front entrance and asked if we wanted him to wait.

"Yeah, man," Goose said. "We'd really appreciate it."

I was grateful he had come with me and that I wasn't doing this part of the journey alone, but when we entered the hospital, I asked if he would wait in the lobby.

"You sure?"

I nodded, keeping my eyes on the ground. "I need to do this," I said, omitting the word *alone*.

He understood. Of course, he did, and he nodded and said, "Okay. I'll be right here if you need me."

That statement meant everything to me, as I carried the empty car seat to the elevator, knowing he was there and that I could count on him. Right now, Goose was all I had. Sure, my parents were always willing and able, but they were nearly two hours away by car. I had no other friends here, nobody else to help, and yet, somehow, just having Goose felt more than enough.

Stepping off of the elevator, I walked through the waiting room and down the hallway to the NICU. It hit me like a punch to the gut, to realize that this, God willing, would be the last time I would come through these doors. I was filled with so much hope mixed with sadness, as I washed my hands and headed straight toward his crib, where he waited with wide, brown eyes.

"Hey, baby boy," I whispered, my voice full of emotion. "You ready to get out of here?"

A throat cleared behind me, and when I turned my head, I saw Elle. My eyes instantly clouded with tears as she rushed toward me with her arms spread wide.

"What did I tell you?" she asked, hugging me tightly.

"I know," I sniffled.

"I wanna hear you say it."

The tears slipped down my cheeks as I nodded and said, "You said he would go home."

"That's right, and here we are."

My arms couldn't squeeze her any tighter. "We never could have done it without you," I said. "All of you, really."

"You did a lot of it," she said into my ear. "We only helped. Now, the rest of his healing will be done at home, and that's all you, Mama, and you got this."

I shook my head, holding onto her, too scared to let go. "I don't know what I'm going to do without you. I don't know how I'm going to do this. I'm going to miss you so much."

"I know," she said, her own voice wavering. "I know. But you know what? You have my number, and you can call or text me whenever you want. You have a friend for life now, and any time you need me, I'm here. But I'm telling you, you are going to be fine. You *both* are going to be just fine."

I took a deep breath and silently told myself that if I didn't let go now, I never would. So, I unraveled my arms and stepped away as I nodded. Elle was smiling, her eyes glistening with tears, as she held her hands to my shoulders.

"I remember when I rushed this little guy down here the night he was born. He was so tiny, but he was so strong, and I immediately knew he was going to be a fighter. Now, look at him."

And I did. I turned my head to look at my little boy and the faint smile on his lips. I couldn't help but smile back.

"He was meant to be here, on this earth, and I just have this feeling he's going to do amazing things. And so much of that is because he's got you as a mama. He's so unbelievably lucky to have you."

I nodded, staring into his eyes, and said, "I'm luckier to have him."

***

Elle ran me through the discharge papers, and then, unplugged all of Alex's monitors. It was a strange feeling, to see the wires hanging there, not attached to anything. I felt my heart skip toward a panic, wondering how the hell I was supposed to now know if his oxygen was at a good level or if his heart rate was where it should be, but Elle assured me that he was fine.

Alex watched me with confusion as I got his car seat set up to put him in, and then, I lifted the outfit I had brought and held it up.

"Ready to get dressed?" I asked him, and he blinked curiously in reply.

It was so surreal, to put him into his clothes and know that this was really it. We were moments away from walking out of the hospital together and officially entering the world as mother and son. He was going to see the sky, the setting sun, and the towering buildings, all for the first time, and as I struggled to get his arms and legs into the cute but cumbersome outfit, my eyes teared up for the thousandth time since entering the hospital that day.

Elle helped me get him into his car seat, and then, I signed the discharge papers.

"And there we go," Elle said, enunciating every word. Then, she looked at Alex, taking his hand in hers. "You're free, Alexander the Great, it's finally time to go home."

With a determination to be strong and free of tears in this moment I had waited so long for, I sucked in a deep breath and gave her one more hug, assuring myself that it wouldn't be the last. Then, with my throat clenching violently, I took the handle of his car seat and carried him out of the NICU.

It felt triumphant, sad, and so unbelievably bittersweet, as we walked together down the hall for the first and last time. We took the elevator down to the lobby, and there, we found Goose, wearing the biggest smile I had ever seen at the sight of us.

He went to take Alex from me and I shook my head. "I got this," I told him and myself, and he relented easily with an understanding nod.

With his arm around my shoulders, we walked through the doors together, and for the first time in his life, Alex was outside.

"What do you think, baby boy?" I asked, looking down at the bewildered eyes of my son. Cars honked in the near distance and he jumped. "I know, it's noisy. But you'll get used to it. It'll become normal, and then, it'll become home."

The cab driver had waited for us that entire time. Goose rode in the front, while I sat with the baby in the back, and with the driver uncharacteristically moving carefully through the streets of New York, we arrived at Goose's apartment.

When Goose took out his wallet to pay the fee, and the driver shook his head in protest. "Man, no," Goose protested, removing a credit card. "You gotta let me pay. That's gotta be close to two-hundred—"

"I'll make it up the rest of the day," the driver replied quietly. "I'm honored to have helped get your baby home."

Goose sighed with defeat. "Thank you so much."

"Seriously," I croaked from the backseat. "Thank you."

He nodded and replied, "Take care of each other."

Without another word, Goose helped me get Alex out of the car and we headed into his building. I had previously decided to spend the night, before getting my things from my old apartment and heading to Long Island with Alex and Mrs. Potter. When we got up to his place, I found my cat and his dog cuddled together on the couch. Hannah stood beside them as if she'd been waiting for us, her hands clutching her phone to her chest, as she smiled at the sight of the three of us.

"Can I hold him?" she asked immediately, and Goose looked at me to reply.

"Sure," I said with a gentle smile. "Just wash your hands first."

"Obviously," she replied, rolling her eyes as she headed toward the kitchen.

"Hey, be nice," Goose reprimanded, placing Alex and his seat on the kitchen table.

As I unfastened him from the carrier and held him for the very first time without the company of medical staff, I felt terrified and unsure, but yet, so free. For the first time, he truly felt like my baby, my son, and as clueless about it all as I was, I felt sure in knowing I'd be okay.

We both would.

Hannah hurried from the kitchen, her arms outstretched with eager, grabby fingers, and I told her to sit on the couch.

"Kenny, I know how to hold a baby," she grumbled, even as she did as she was told. I handed Alex to her and he snuggled right into her arms. "Oh, my God, he's so sweet! Dad, I want one!"

"Uh, sure," Goose muttered. "In thirty years."

"Stop it, Dad. You know what I mean," she grumbled, nuzzling her cheek against Alex's head. "I love him."

"Looks like the feeling is mutual," I laughed, smiling as I took out my phone to snap a few pictures of the two of them together.

Hannah looked up, spotting the phone in my hand, and demanded we all get a picture together. I imagined the way I looked, knowing it had been days since I had taken any time for self-care, and insisted we didn't need to. But Goose took the phone from me and demanded I sit, as he took a seat on the other side of his daughter. He held the phone out, got us all into the shot, and snapped the picture. When he handed the phone back to me, I looked at the image of us—Goose, his daughter, my son, and me—and it struck me with startling clarity that we looked so distinctly like a family.

And I was leaving.

Not wanting to walk away from Alex but also needing a moment to collect my feelings, I excused myself for a second and hurried into Goose's room. And there, beside his bed, was a bassinet.

"Hey, are you—" Goose's words were cut short as he entered the room and saw the spot my eyes had fixed upon. Then, he said, "I wanted him to have a place to sleep when you're here. If you wanted to bring him, I mean."

I didn't know what to say, as I stood and stared at the little bed, wooden with a small blue and white striped blanket draped over one side. Tears were frozen in my eyes, as I clenched my fingers together and struggled to string together the words I needed for this moment.

"Obviously, you probably won't be here any time soon," Goose went on, walking past me into the room to pick up the blanket and smoothed it out against his plaid button-down. "But I just figured, if you wanted to, he'd have his own bed."

I only swallowed in reply, and when he realized I wasn't going to speak, he continued. "Hannah picked this out with Krys. There's, uh," he laid the blanket back in the bassinet and hurried to his dresser, "there's some clothes and diapers in here, too. It's not much, and I know he'll have his own stuff at your parents' house, and I'm sure you'll be more comfortable there, anyway, but—"

"I don't want to go," I blurted out, cutting his words off and startling him.

"What?"

I shook my head, still wringing my hands. "I-I don't want to go to their house." Then, squeezing my eyes shut and shaking my head, I added, "I mean, I do. I want to see them. But I don't want to *live* there."

330

"Okay," he replied slowly, closing the dresser drawer. "So, then what do you want to do?"

I walked across the room to the bassinet and laid my hand against the solid wood railing. It was a beautiful, sturdy piece of furniture, and I knew I loved it more than anything I would have at my parents' house on Long Island. Because this, right here, was my son's first bed, and it was given to me by the man who was everything Alex's father never could be.

"Kenny?"

"I love this bed," I said, running my hand along its side.

Goose came to stand beside me and put a hand on my shoulder. "Uh … yeah, it was Hannah's. My dad had built it for her before she was born."

"Wow," I replied, realizing that this wasn't just a beautiful piece of furniture but a sentimental part of this family. "That's … that's so special."

"Yeah," Goose said, nodding. "Honestly, I thought the next babies to use it would be my grandkids, but …"

"Oh, I don't need to use it. I can—"

"No," he said hurriedly. "No, I want Alex to use it. This is better than waiting fifty years for my grandkids to come around, you know? This is … this is good. But, um …" He moving cautiously forward, eyeing me with question. "What do you mean, you don't want to go?"

Taking a deep breath and committing to the decision I was about to make, I said, "I wanted you the minute I walked into your bar. Have I ever told you that?"

He barely chuckled as he shook his head. "No. You never mentioned that."

"Well, I did. I liked you immediately, and I felt so guilty about that," I said, remembering how much better and comfortable he had made me feel that day, after just confirming that I was pregnant.

"I liked you, too," he confessed quietly.

"And the thing was, it was *wrong* to like you," I went on, keeping my hand on the bassinet. "It was wrong the way you laughed at my jokes and made me feel wanted and … all this shit that Brendan should've been doing all along but never did."

Goose took a deep breath and shifted uncomfortably on his feet. "Yeah, okay, but I don't understand what that has to do with right now."

Sighing in an irritated sort of way, I turned to face him. "What I'm saying is, even while it was kind of wrong then, it's always been *right*. You and I were with other people, but we were always right for each other. And lately, I've been thinking so much about doing what's best for my son and me, thinking that going back home to be with my parents was it, but that's wrong, too. Because I mean, really, what's right for us is to be here. With you and Hannah and his nurses and …" I shrugged, swallowing at the building emotion in my throat. "And I don't want to leave."

His smile was cautious, watching me through uncertain eyes, as he asked, "But don't you want to live on Long Island? I thought you don't like the city."

I nodded. "I don't love it here, no. And would I prefer to be on Long Island, getting buddy-buddy with B. Davis? Absolutely. But I'd prefer to be with you even more."

Goose turned, surveying the room and its furniture, then said, "Well, shit. I guess Alex is gonna need more than just one drawer, huh."

Unable to fight my grin, knowing I was now home in a city I never thought I would call mine, I replied, "We'll figure it out."

"And we should probably get you a desk, too," he muttered with a furrowed brow, smoothing a hand over his beard.

The thought of a desk was enough to make me want to jump around on the spot, but I refrained, as I stood on my toes, kissed his lips, and said, "I agree, but how about some wings first?"

"That, I can definitely manage," he replied with a grin.

We left his—*our*—room together, to find his daughter and my son asleep on the couch, beside his dog and my cat. We stood for a moment, watching over them, basking in the glow of our silver linings, laid out before us, as they shined brightly to conquer the shadows left by our scars.

"And just think," he said quietly, leaning down to bring his mouth closer to my ear, "all of this happened because a girl named Kenny walked into a bar and met a guy named Goose."

"It really would make a good book," I replied.

"Yeah," he agreed with a nod. "You should probably write that one."

"Hmm," I hummed softly, wrapping an arm around his waist and tucking myself into the comfort of his side. "I might just do that."

333

Epilogue

"Kenny Wright?"

Standing behind the table, I turned on my heel to face an older woman holding a stack of books. She smiled at me when she realized she had my attention, and I smiled back.

"Hi," I said, walking closer. "How are you?"

Blushing, her hands shook as she lowered the books to the table. "I'm g-good. Great, really. It … it's such an honor to meet you. I-I can't tell you how-how much I just love your books."

"Oh, thank you so much," I replied, honestly grateful as I took the first book from the pile. It was my first, one I had written so many years ago. "Wow. This is practically a relic."

"Yeah, I know," she laughed nervously. "But it's one of my favorites. Molly is probably your most relatable character, at least for me."

I nodded fondly, looking down at the cover. "I wrote her to be a lot like me at the time," I replied. "It's seriously crazy how quickly things can change."

Then, I asked, "Who am I making these out to?"

"O-Oh, uh, Judy. That's my first name. But I'm also a member on your message board, so you might recognize my full name. Judy Leanne House-Bowman?"

I was embarrassed, because my online community had exploded since the release of my most recent books and my online presence hadn't been what it used to be. Judy deflated a bit with the realization that her name wasn't ringing a bell, and I apologized for my inability to remember everybody.

"Oh, it's okay! Um, I'm always talking to my friends, Emma and Dana, so maybe you recognize them?"

I smiled apologetically again, and said, "I'm sure I'd know all of you if I was online and saw your profile pictures."

Judy grinned, nodding. "We are all such huge fans of your books. You are one of our absolute favorites."

I wished I could've sat there and chatted with Judy for hours. I also wished I could take compliments better, as she praised my work and everything I had ever done. Sadly I failed at both, because compliments were never going to come easily for me and there was a line of other readers, waiting to have their books signed. So, I gave her a hug and thanked her profusely for coming. Then, I moved on to the next reader, and then the next after that, until I reached the last person, and I could finally breathe.

That was when I saw him. The tall, reddish-blond Viking of a man approaching my table, wearing a plaid button-down and wielding a cup of coffee. And at his side was a little boy. A boy who looked like me on the outside but could've only gotten his sweet, loving heart from the man he called Daddy.

"God bless you," I gushed, reaching out with grabbing fingers for the cup of Seattle's finest. "And God bless the man who founded Starbucks."

"Long day?" Goose asked, rounding my table to inspect the boxes I had brought filled with books. "Wow. You've sold a lot of books."

"No kidding." I said, after taking a long sip. "It's been crazy. These last few books have done so well, I guess my name is making the rounds or something."

"It's a good thing," he replied, smiling. Then, he looked to Alex and said, "Hey, wasn't there something you wanted to tell Mommy?"

Alex looked up at Goose through his blue-rimmed glasses like he had just sprouted a second head. "I dunno," he answered with a shrug.

"Oh, come on, buddy. Remember? What did Daddy say before?"

Alex shrugged. "I dunno, Daddy. I no remember."

Goose sighed. "You wanted to tell Mommy to tell her weird friends that Daddy isn't gonna model for their book covers. Remember?"

I laughed as Alex, completely disinterested, found the toy car he had left beneath my table earlier.

"My friends aren't weird," I protested. "It's not their fault you'd be perfect for their mountain men books."

"What the hell are mountain men? Is that a *Hills Have Eyes*, *Deliverance* kind of thing?"

"Oh, my God," I laughed, nearly choking on my coffee, then shaking my head. "No, they're like—"

"You know what? I don't even want to know."

"Fine. Just feel complimented. They wouldn't ask if you weren't hot."

"Well, at least tell them to keep their hands off the merchandise," he grumbled, rubbing his bicep. "I'm not some piece of meat they can fondle whenever they want. I have feelings, too, you know."

I reached out to pat his bearded cheek. "I'll pass along the—"

"Sorry," a rich, deep voice said from across the table, drawing my attention. "I don't mean to interrupt, but—"

"You're B. Davis," I interjected in the most humiliating display of being star struck, as I stood abruptly from my chair and nearly knocked it over.

The infamous fantasy author stood on the other side of my table, wearing a leather jacket and an award-winning smile. He was almost something of a dream, had I not known for certain this was real. And what was even more startling was that, in his hands, was one of my books.

"So, you know who I am," he replied, still grinning.

"Oh, my God," I gushed. "*Of course*, I know who you are. You're … you're practically my hero. I have been reading your books since—"

"Babe," Goose cut me off gently. "Breathe."

B. Davis laughed coolly and replied, "Well, I'm honored that you would be a fan of my work, when *you* wrote *this*." He laid the book on the table, and I read the title of my most personal book, *Scars & Silver Linings*.

"I read this with my wife, and we were both blown away."

I blinked up at him—the man was huge—and said, "I … I don't know what to say."

"You don't have to say anything," he replied, smiling gently. "But can you write it out to Holly and Brandon? I'd really appreciate it."

I nodded in a broken, jittering sort of way and grabbed for my Sharpie with shaky fingers. "Sure, Mr. Dav—"

"Hey, we're peers," he said, cutting me off with a gentle tone. "I'll call you Kenny, and you call me Brandon. Okay?"

I nodded, hoping I never woke up from this dream. "O-okay, Brandon."

I signed his book and handed it back, wishing I knew what to say to keep him there longer. To keep him talking. To make him my best friend. But I wasn't that cool, and he tucked the book I wrote about a girl named Kenny who walked into a bar and met a guy named Goose under his arm.

Then, he said, "Thanks a lot. I'll see you around."

"S-Sure," I replied, nodding awkwardly.

"Knock on my door the next time you're in town visiting your parents. I'd love to chat craft with you."

Stunned, I asked, "How did you know my parents live by you?" And with blushing cheeks, he replied, "I might've gotten wind from my agent that Kenny Wright grew up in the area, and I might've gotten a little excited about it."

With that, he wished me a successful signing and walked away, clutching my book beneath his arm. When he was no longer in my sights, I turned to my husband and with mouth gaping, asked him what the hell had just happened.

"Well, girlfriend," he said, wrapping an arm around my shoulders, as we listened to our son play beneath the table, "I think that's what we in the biz call, making it."

***

One night, shortly after Alex had come home from the hospital, Goose had proposed to me with a replica of the ring that Eric gave to Shelly in *The Crow*. A few months later, we were married on Long Island in my parents' backyard. Even at the time, it had struck me as funny, how quickly I wanted to move things along, just for us to feel that much more like a family. Even though, in our hearts, we already were.

The first year or so was a little rocky. We had to distance ourselves so much from friends and family, to ensure Alex stayed healthy and out of the hospital with his weakened lungs. It was scary and stressful, and I feared we would never mend these broken ties with people we cared for. Then, when Alex had reached his first birthday and our restrictions were loosened just a little, I started to wonder if we'd ever have more children. My body had begun to crave the feeling of new life and movement, something I never thought I'd one day miss, and I brought it up to Goose over dinner.

"You want more kids?" he had asked, and when I nodded and asked how he felt, he'd replied, "Hell yes. I just didn't know if you wanted more, or if … you know … you even could."

That moment made me pause with a harsh hit of reality, because I had never really thought about it before. I had known it was possible, but I hadn't really taken the time to wonder if my body could even carry another baby. And when I went to the OB/GYN for an exam, I found that his question was indeed our reality.

I was strongly advised to never carry another baby. And just as I had cried and mourned my old life when I found myself pregnant with Alex, I cried and mourned the thought of never being pregnant again.

But even despite the heavy blow to our hearts, we weren't unhappy. Because we had a girl who was our world, and a boy who was our universe, and between the two of them, we realized we already had everything.

***

"Hannah got him to sleep," Goose said, as he entered the kitchen. "He just laid down, cuddled up to her, and was out," he snapped his fingers, "just like that."

"He's just happy she's here. Tomorrow night, he'll be refusing to go to bed again," I laughed.

"Yeah, you're probably right about that, but that doesn't mean we can't enjoy this right now."

"Oh, yeah?" I asked, smirking as I put the dishes away. "And what do you suggest we do?"

"Well …" He invaded my space with the scent of his skin and heat of his body, before wrapping his arms around my waist. "It *has* been a while since I did this …" His mouth dipped to my neck and he kissed me gently behind the ear. "Or this …" His kisses trailed further down and to my shoulder, where he opened his mouth and kissed me with a passion that had nearly been lost in sleepless nights of toddlers and writing.

"Oh, yeah, it *has* been a while," I agreed, leaning back against his chest, to tip my head and grant him better access.

"It has," he muttered, his lips moving against my neck as he spoke. "You think we still remember how to do this?"

Laughing, I shook my head. "Nope, definitely not. I think I might need to take a couple of classes before we try. Do you think the library offers any?"

Goose chuckled in the way I had always found contagious. "You know, they might. Maybe you should ask that old dude Alex likes."

"Oh, God. The one who does the kids' crafts?"

"Yeah, that's the one!"

"*Chip*?!" I squealed, giggling wildly.

"Oh, right! Yes! You know that guy's gotta be freaky as fuck."

I turned around in his arms, swinging my arms around his neck. "I do not want to be responsible for his heart attack, thank you very much."

"Well, then, if you won't let me ask, we should definitely do our own research," he said, speaking in a low, sensual growl, before leaning down to kiss me hard on the mouth.

With his arms wrapped tight around my waist, Goose effortlessly lifted me onto the kitchen counter. As his hands moved to the waistband of my sweatpants, mine worked at the drawstring on his plaid pajamas. We made out feverishly, kissing as if we were in a race against time. With a needy groan, he pulled at my pants as I yanked his down, revealing his boxers.

"Oh, God, stop!" Hannah exclaimed, as she wandered into the kitchen and shielded her eyes with her hand. "You do have your own freakin' room, you know."

Goose sighed, keeping his eyes on me. "Should I mention that we *own* this kitchen?"

"Should I mention that we all *eat* in this kitchen?" Hannah fired back, opening the fridge.

"I guess we shouldn't tell her what we've done against that fridge," he whispered loudly, waggling his brows as he pulled his pants back up.

"Stop it, Dad!" she groaned, grabbing a bottle of water. "God … I can't wait to leave for college."

The comment hit his heart. He wouldn't let it show, but I saw it in the way his gaze hardened. He filled his chest with a heavy breath before exhaling, and turned to his daughter, who looked so much older than she did when I first met her three years ago.

"You're gonna miss the hell out of me and you know it," he said, grinning to hide the ache I knew he was undoubtedly feeling.

Hannah was as sweet as she was sardonic, and she smiled at her father. "Yeah, I will," she said, as she uncapped the bottle. "But I am *not* gonna miss walking in on you two making out. You're scarring me for life."

After she left the room, Goose turned back to me with an adoring smile spread across his face. He wrapped his arms around my waist and stepped between my spread knees.

"I'm gonna miss her attitude most of all, I think," he said, finally revealing the sadness that he felt.

"She'll only be a few hours away," I reminded him, cupping his bearded cheeks in my hands.

"Yeah," he replied, putting on a smile. "But the last time we were that far apart, she was a baby, and I was fucked up. I deserved it then, and for some reason, it didn't hurt nearly as much as it does now."

I nodded, forcing myself to stay strong for him, just as he had always been strong for me. "It was easier then because you didn't know her. But now, you do. You're buddies. And I know it's hard letting go, but you should also be so proud of yourself, Eric. Because you are a *huge* reason why she was accepted to a ridiculously good school. She's going to go so far in life, and that's all because you survived and fought your demons. She might actually be your greatest success story."

For a moment, he lost himself in my eyes, with his arms still around my waist and his lips set in a soft, straight line. The longer he stared, the more I felt unsettled against the counter, and I laughed, shaking my head.

"What?" I laughed, pressing my hands to his chest.

He broke free from his stupor with an easy smile. "Nothin'. I just love you."

"Well, I love you, too."

"I know," he replied, and pulled me from the counter. "Come on. Let's go hide in our room and have crazy good sex without scarring the kids for life."

***

"You know," he said, tracing my scar with the tip of his pointer finger, "I could say the same thing about you."

"What do you mean?"

"I mean, look at you and everything you've accomplished over these last few years. You're a bestselling author, you're a kickass mother, you're a better wife than I ever thought I'd deserve ..." He kissed the softness of my belly and flattened his hand over the place I once carried Alex years ago. "You did all of that because you survived."

Looking down at him over breasts that were no longer perky and a belly that was no longer flat, I laughed. "I didn't have a choice," I replied, but he didn't laugh back.

"Yeah, you did. You could've given up. You could've rolled over and let life get the best of you. But you didn't. You built a whole freakin' life from the shit that could've destroyed you," he said. "And I think what makes you so fucking beautiful to me is that you really have no idea how incredible you are."

"I just did what I had to do," I replied quietly, shrugging gently.

"I know," he whispered, kissing me again, before moving his way up my body. He kissed my stomach, breast, shoulder, and neck, until he laid over me, his scar touching mine. Then he said, "I'm just glad I got to be part of it."

We made love the way married people do. A comfortable sort of way that might not have been exciting to someone looking in from the outside, but to me, to us, it was perfect. It was gentle, it was quiet, and it was romantic. It made the time we'd gone without seem worth it, just as life with him had made all of those years without seem worth it. All to end up here, in a bedroom that was adjacent to our son, my little warrior, and the brightest silver lining in my life.

Acknowledgments

There are so many people to thank. I'm afraid I'll forget someone, but I'm going to try.

To Danny—for being my rock, for being the best daddy and husband I could ever ask for, and for helping me pee when I was in the hospital. I don't know what I would've done if you ended up being a Brendan. Thank you for being more of a Goose.

To Mommy & Daddy—for being there, for helping whenever and wherever you could, for the endless amounts of formula, and for giving up so much to keep Jude safe. There is no way for us to ever repay you for what you have done for us, and we will always be forever grateful.

To Karen & Kelly—for helping me shower, for taking care of Ethel, for supporting me wherever you could, and for being amazing aunts to Jude. You are my best friends, and I don't know where I would be without you.

To Mike—for always being there even when you weren't, for insisting on keeping Jude safe, and for always understanding. I wish things had been different, just to be able to make some more memories before you were taken away from us. I love ya, bro, and I will never stop missing you.

To Kerry—for that first night I remember meeting you (even though you insisted I met you the night before), for your encouragement, for your endless support, and for your friendship. You will never fully understand how much you helped me, or how much I relied on you and needed you, but I will always be grateful.

To Melissa, Donna, Ancella, Tracey, Elisabeth, Bermingham, Jackie, Caitlyn, Megan, and every other nurse and doctor in the Good Sam NICU—for the laughs, kinship, support, and every single thing you ever did to help Jude, Danny, and me during our 96-day stay. Our time with you would not have been the same without the friendship we forged. I will never forget the late night chats and the countless laughs. I will never forget you.

To the pediatric specialists—for being good ones. Thank you for all you do for Jude and babies and children like him. You are all superheroes.

To my in-laws, all of them—for your understanding, love, and support. I have heard some horror stories about family during situations like ours, and I will forever be grateful to not be living one of them. You are all amazing, and I am fully aware of how lucky I am.

To Neil—for being there for Danny when nobody else could be. You know what I mean. You are a good brother, and a great brother-in-law. We love you.

To the Indie AFers—for every ounce of support and love you gave to us during our time of need. You showed me then just how amazing the author world can be, and I will never forget all you did for us.

To Judy, Kerry, Dana, Melanie, Emma, and Leanne—for being there, for keeping the group running, and for being amazing friends. You guys keep me going. Thank you for everything. One day, I'll figure out how to repay you, but until then, just … thank you.

Finally, to you, Dear Reader—for sticking by me, for reading my words, for hanging with me online, and for your never-ending support. You are ultimately why I am where I am, and for that, I am eternally grateful. Thank you.

(Dear God, I hope I'm not forgetting someone.)

About the Author

Kelsey Kingsley is a legally blind gal living in New York with her family and a black-and-white cat named Ethel. She really loves doughnuts, tea, and Edgar Allan Poe.

She believes there is a song for every situation. She has a potty mouth and doesn't eat cheese.

Books by Kelsey Kingsley

Holly Freakin' Hughes

Daisies & Devin

The Life We Wanted

Tell Me Goodnight

Forget the Stars

Warrior Blue

The Life We Have

Where We Went Wrong

Scars & Silver Linings

The Kinney Brothers Series
One Night to Fall (Kinney Brothers #1)

To Fall for Winter (Kinney Brothers #2)

Last Chance to Fall (Kinney Brothers #3)

Hope to Fall (Kinney Brothers #4)

Printed in Great Britain
by Amazon

58335912R00203